BARE

WOLFES OF MANHATTAN FOUR

HELEN HARDT

RAKE

WOLFES OF MANHATTAN FOUR

Helen Hardt

HARDT & SONS ❤

For those who beat the odds

Reid Wolfe is a master of seducing women.

This time, his life may depend on it.

He's known as the Wolfe of Manhattan. Reid Wolfe sees women as playthings, and most are happy to be arm candy and bed warmers for the handsome billionaire rake. He knows the art of seduction like no other, so surely he can get a Las Vegas showgirl into his bed in record time. He must, because she has information he and his family need to prove their innocence in their father's murder. And Reid is at his most persuasive between the sheets.

Zinnia Rehnquist, now known as Zara Jones or simply Zee, lives her life under the radar. Chorus line girls are supposed to be invisible. The audience sees the big picture, not a single dancer, and that suits Zee just fine...until Reid Wolfe shows up and turns her life upside down. He needs her to talk—to tell the story of what his father did to her— but she's finally put that part of her life to bed.

Reid is ready to pull out all the stops to get Zee under the covers and talking, but when new evidence comes to light, the game changes for everyone...and Reid finds he may feel more for the beautiful Zee than he ever meant to.

PRAISE FOR HELEN HARDT

STEEL BROTHERS SAGA

"*Craving* is the jaw-dropping book you *need* to read!"
~*New York Times* bestselling author Lisa Renee Jones

"Completely raw and addictive."
~#1 *New York Times* bestselling author Meredith Wild

"Talon has hit my top five list...up there next to Jamie Fraser and Gideon Cross."
~*USA Today* bestselling author Angel Payne

"Talon and Jade's instant chemistry heats up the pages..."
~RT Book Reviews

"Sorry Christian and Gideon, there's a new heartthrob for you to contend with. Meet Talon. Talon Steel."
~Booktopia

"Such a beautiful torment—the waiting, the anticipation, the relief that only comes briefly before more questions arise, and the wait begins again... Check. Mate. Ms. Hardt..."
~**Bare Naked Words**

"Made my heart stop in my chest. Helen has given us such a heartbreakingly beautiful series."
~**Tina, Bookalicious Babes**

WOLFES OF MANHATTAN

"It's hot, it's intense, and the plot starts off thick and had me completely spellbound from page one."
~**The Sassy Nerd Blog**

"Helen Hardt...is a master at her craft."
~**K. Ogburn, Amazon**

"Move over Steel brothers... Rock is *everything!*"
~**Barbara Conklin-Jaros, Amazon**

"Helen has done it again. She winds you up and weaves a web of intrigue."
~**Vicki Smith, Amazon**

FOLLOW ME SERIES

"Hardt spins erotic gold..."
~*Publishers Weekly*

"22 Best Erotic Novels to Read"
~*Marie Claire* **Magazine**

"Intensely erotic and wildly emotional..."
    ~*New York Times* **bestselling author Lisa Renee Jones**

"With an edgy, enigmatic hero and loads of sexual tension, Helen Hardt's fast-paced Follow Me Darkly had me turning pages late into the night!"
    ~*New York Times* **bestselling author J. Kenner**

"Christian, Gideon, and now...Braden Black."
    ~**Books, Wine, and Besties**

"A tour de force where the reader will be pulled in as if they're being seduced by Braden Black, taken for a wild ride, and left wanting more."
    ~*USA Today* **Bestselling Author Julie Morgan**

"Hot. Sexy. Intriguing. Page-Turner. Helen Hardt checks all the boxes with *Follow Me Darkly!*"
    ~**International Bestselling Author Victoria Blue**

BLOOD BOND SAGA

"An enthralling and rousing vampire tale that will leave readers waiting for the sequel."
    ~**Kirkus Reviews**

"Dangerous and sexy. A new favorite!"
    ~*New York Times* **bestselling author Alyssa Day**

"A dark, intoxicating tale."
    ~**Library Journal**

"Helen dives into the paranormal world of vampires and makes it her own."

~Tina, Bookalicious Babes

"Throw out everything you know about vampires—except for that blood thirst we all love and lust after in these stunning heroes—and expect to be swept up in a sensual story that twists and turns in so many wonderfully jaw-dropping ways."

~Angel Payne, *USA Today* bestselling author

WARNING

The Wolfes of Manhattan series contains adult language and scenes, including flashbacks of child physical and sexual abuse. Please take note.

PROLOGUE
REID

The Lone Wolfe.

Ha! Great pun, huh?

Within less than a month, my three siblings had all met their life mates and gotten married.

Not in the cards for me. I was the Wolfe of Manhattan, always with a new lady on my arm. Now, though, since all my siblings were off the market, I was indeed the Lone Wolfe.

The phone call I got after the wedding was from the NYPD detective on our case, Hank Morgan. Consequently, Rock and the rest of them headed back this morning on the jet.

Again, not in the cards for me.

Someone had to stay here in Las Vegas and deal with our damned luxury hotel and casino. *Money is money.* Words of wisdom from the bastard who'd fathered me.

Sure, all of us were being investigated for the fucker's murder, but someone had to take care of business.

That someone was me.

Always me.

I wasn't CEO of the company, but only I could deal with the

contract mess here in Las Vegas. Story of my life. Under-appreciated to the max.

The rest of them were called back to New York for more questioning.

I wasn't going down for his murder, and neither was anyone else in my family. Not on my watch.

Zinnia—or Zee—seemed to be the key.

I just had to get her to talk.

The Wolfe of Manhattan.

I'd never met a woman I couldn't seduce.

So I'd seduce her.

And oh, she'd talk.

1

ZEE

My mother was the typical Long Island "stage mom." She'd decided as soon as I crawled out of her womb that I was going to be in show business. I spent my formative years being dragged to audition after audition. What little time left was devoted to ballet, tap, and acting classes.

I was good at the dance part. I always got top roles in all the recitals. The acting part? Not so much. I got a commercial here and there, probably based solely on the fact that I was a really cute kid. The big break my mother hoped for never came.

Then puberty hit. I grew to five feet ten inches seemingly overnight, which ended any dance aspirations as well. My mother's answer?

Modeling, of course. I was thin, well-built, a natural blonde, and free of an awkward stage, so she enrolled me in classes. Yeah, we really did walk with books on our heads. I also learned how to create the perfect smoky eye.

You know, things you need in life.

Despite my mother's persistence, no agent ever signed me, and by the time I turned eighteen, my modeling career—if it ever truly existed—was effectively over.

My mother was more disappointed than I was.

I wasn't disappointed at all. I was free! Free to pursue what I wanted. I'd been homeschooled by a tutor because of my grueling schedule, so when I was a high school graduate—or the equivalent thereof—I accepted admission to Smith College in Massachusetts. I drove my car—the one luxury my mother allowed me—to college via a stop in the city to do all the touristy things my mom never took the time to show me—sights I'd been promised by my mother after I made it in modeling. Which of course never happened.

I made it to New York.

But I never made it to Smith.

I was taken. I was hunted.

Then saved by a man whose name I never knew.

REID WOLFE WAS AN ATTENTIVE DATE. He didn't know me from Eve, but he never left my side as we celebrated the weddings of his brother and sister. I'd seen my share of Las Vegas chapel weddings, but very few included a toast with Dom Perignon.

I wasn't a champagne connoisseur by any means, but Dom Perignon was in a class by itself.

It tickled my tongue and tasted like crisp apples and— believe it or not—toasted bread. Sounded terrible, I knew, but it worked. It glided down my throat effortlessly, so when Reid brought me another flute, I took it.

I didn't drink, normally. I never did anything that might take away my faculties. I was on high alert at all times.

All times.

This would be my last glass of bubbles. Riley and her brothers all wanted me to tell my story. To go public. Although I understood why they needed me to, I couldn't. Which was why this would be my last glass of champagne. I couldn't risk getting too talkative.

Not that getting talkative was really a risk with me. I didn't talk. To anyone. Especially not about my past. I could fly under the radar in Las Vegas. No one in the dressing room questioned me about my scars, because most of them had their own. Beatrice always had new bruises on her thighs and back from her abusive boyfriend. Marie had special pancake makeup for her nearly omnipresent black eyes. And Frannie? She had the worst of all. She danced almost every night in constant pain from the five pins holding her right tibia together. Her ex shattered it five years ago, and though you'd never know watching her dance with that toothy smile pasted on her face, she was in agony.

But bills had to be paid, so you do what you must. Frannie danced. Beatrice and Marie danced.

And I danced.

I was the only one with scars like mine. Two perfectly straight cuts above each breast. Over the years they'd faded, but still they stood out like bright red lines to me.

I didn't let myself think about them much anymore.

Until recently, when two private investigators accosted me in the dressing area after one of last week's shows.

"Hanging in there?"

I jerked out of my thoughts. Reid Wolfe stood next to me.

He was crazy handsome. Tall and muscular and gorgeous with dark brown—nearly black—hair. But even so...

He looked too much like *him*.

Like his father. Derek Wolfe. Reid's eyes were different, though. They were a blue so bright and sparkling it almost seemed too beautiful to be real.

All the Wolfes were gorgeous, and the three significant others weren't anything to sneeze at either. I felt so out of place.

Sure, I had the body of a Vegas dancer, but the rest of me was a huge mess.

"Why do you color your hair?" Reid asked.

I wrinkled my forehead. "What?"

"I'm just wondering."

"I like it." I took a sip of champagne.

The answer wasn't a lie. When I arrived in Las Vegas six years ago, I needed to reinvent myself. Zinnia "Zee" Rehnquist was a blonde. Zara Jones? She had dark hair. Not just dark hair. Jet black. The kind of jet black that said, *don't fuck with me or I'll kill you with a butcher knife.*

It worked fine with my own blue eyes—slightly lighter than Reid's, and the black hair made them seem even lighter—and my dark brown eyebrows and lashes, colored black with makeup. I was a dark blonde, not platinum by any means.

"You're beautiful no matter what," Reid said. "I'd just love to see what you look like with your natural color."

My stomach clenched. I never let men get close to me. The few times I'd tried had ended in disaster.

"Black hair is who I am now." I handed him my empty champagne flute. "I should be going."

"Sure. I'll take you home."

"I'm fine. I'll just hail a cab."

"Zee," he said, "I have three limos on call. Already paid for. There's no reason for you to take a cab."

Three limos. Already paid for.

Wolfe money.

The Wolfes had so much money that their patriarch could afford to build his own human hunting ground. Unreal.

"He's dead," Reid said.

Had I spoken aloud? I hadn't drunk *that* much champagne. "What?"

"You had a look on your face."

"What kind of look?"

He sighed. "It's the same look I've seen on my sister's face forever. I just didn't know what it meant until now. You were thinking about my father. About what he put you through. I know the look."

"Actually, I was thinking about his money. About how you can have three limos on standby for no reason at all."

"There's a reason. My family is here in town. We need to go places, so we have cars available."

"No, you have *limos* available."

He smiled. God, he was truly gorgeous.

"Semantics," he said in a teasing tone.

I shook my head. "Don't play that card. The Wolfe money was enough to put me through hell. Hell that you people want me to revisit."

Reid's smile faded. "I'm not my father. Neither are my brothers or my sister."

"I know that."

Now I felt like crap. But wait. Why should *I* feel like crap? I went through what I went through, and I shouldn't have to apologize for it. I *won't* apologize for it. Someone should be apologizing to *me*.

Of course, that wasn't fair. They'd all apologized profusely, even though none of them was at fault.

Reid took a sip of champagne. "My brother saved you that day."

"I've never forgotten that," I said. So true.

"Then don't equate the rest of us with our father. We're not anything like him."

He was right. Still, I couldn't help, "Except you're pretty much a dead ringer for him."

Reid's jawline tensed. It went rigid, to the point where his lips trembled slightly.

That wasn't fair. Not even a little. "I'm sorry. That was out of line."

"Slightly," he agreed.

"I owe your brother everything. I've never forgotten that."

And I never would.

2

REID

The black hair goth look was too harsh for Zee. She was a beautiful woman—with a rocking showgirl body—but the black hair wasn't working.

I understood well why she wore her hair black. It gave her a hard look. A "don't fuck with me" look.

She'd been fucked with more than enough for one lifetime.

But I'd deal with the hair, because I had to seduce this woman. I had to, not just for myself and my family, to help clear our names, but also because...

Well...because I fucking wanted to.

Zee was a challenge, and I never backed down from a challenge.

My father might have been a raging psychopathic rapist, but he did teach me a few things. Oh, I hated the bastard, but I learned some excellent lessons from him.

First, he taught me about hard work. There was simply no substitute for it.

Second, he taught me the value of the dollar. Sure, we Wolfes had thrown money around for decades, but only because we could. We kept a lot of our money in non-liquid assets where it was safe.

Third, he taught me about challenges. Nothing came easy, and challenges were to be embraced.

Not until his death did I realize just *how* he embraced every challenge. Criminal activity? Just another challenge. He figured out how to get away with it, and he succeeded.

Another thing I never knew, until after he died, was how much he truly hated his children.

How else would we all be suspects in his murder?

Derek Wolfe was the ultimate egomaniac. A megalomanic, even.

More and more, I wondered if he'd orchestrated his own death. My siblings disagreed with me, but they hadn't worked with him. I had, and I knew him better than anyone.

In his warped mind, he'd see it as a challenge. Going out on his own terms.

Whatever Derek Wolfe had or hadn't done, I was going to prove my siblings and I were innocent of his murder.

But I needed to get the cops off our tails to do it.

That was where Zee came in.

I cleared my throat. "You don't owe Roy anything," I said to Zee. A little reverse psychology never hurt anyone.

"You can't actually believe that."

Right, I don't. "Of course I believe that. We're all so happy he was able to rescue you. He didn't even remember most of it until recently."

"I'm sure it was horrible for him to realize what his father was."

"Horrible for all of us. That's why it's so important to us—to me—that you know we're nothing like him."

"I never thought you were."

This was where I'd normally try to touch her, but I held

back. Zee required a different approach. I'd be in Vegas for another several days, so I had all the time I needed.

The Reid Wolfe seduction was usually a twelve-hour-or-less thing. I was willing to go slowly with Zee. Accept that she'd suffered terribly at my father's hands.

But in the end, I'd get what I wanted.

I had to.

For my family.

My phone buzzed, and I pulled it out of my pocket. "The limo's here for you. I'll walk you down."

She gave me a smile. Sort of. "You don't have to."

"Don't be silly. It's no trouble."

Nope, no trouble at all, because I'll be sliding into the limo beside you.

"I want to say goodbye to Riley," she said.

"Of course." I followed her across the room to where my sister stood with her new husband, Matt Rossi, a Montana man with long blond hair and light blue eyes in sharp contrast to my sister with dark hair and eyes.

"Thank you for inviting me," Zee said.

Riley smiled, and I swore I'd never seen her look so happy. Funny. All those years, and I never realized how unhappy my little sister was.

I felt bad about that. Really bad, like I kind of wanted to puke right now. All those years I thought she was the favored one who got to go on special trips. My brothers and I had no idea what actually went on during those trips.

We knew well what our father was capable of. He was a monster, but we never knew just how much of a monster he truly was. Beyond monster. He was Satan.

My sister knew this well, and so did Zee.

Zee, who I was planning to use to get the information we needed.

I didn't like the idea. Not the whole idea, anyway. The part about seducing her? I was good with that. Even with her gothic black hair. The rest of her was to die for.

"I hope you know you can call any of us anytime if you need to," Riley said to Zee. "We're all here for you."

"Absolutely," I agreed. "Anytime, day or night."

"How long will you be in town?" Zee asked.

"Matt and I are leaving tomorrow. So are Rock and Lacey and Roy and Charlie."

"But I'm staying." I smiled. "We're having issues with one of the contractors for our new hotel, and someone has to handle it."

"Why doesn't Rock stay?" Zee asked. "I heard he was the CEO."

Yeah, in name only. My father's little dig still stuck firmly in my craw. But it wasn't Rock's fault. I kept telling myself that, though it didn't take the sting out. At all.

"He is," I said. "But I'm the COO. I'm in charge of operations." *And my big brother doesn't have a clue how to handle contractors and lawyers.*

I kept the last part to myself.

"Yeah," Riley said. "The rest of us have to get back, as we're all persons of interest in our father's murder investigation."

"And you're not?" Zee said to me.

"Oh, I am, but someone has to see to business. I'm only a plane ride away if I'm needed in New York."

"So Reid will be here for you." Riley pulled out a card. "Did I already give you my card? If not, here it is. My cell's on it. Call me if you need anything. I mean *anything.*"

Nice touch, Sis. However, Zee will be coming to me with all her needs.

And I intend to fulfill them.

3

ZEE

R eid took my hand—it felt good in his—and led me out of the chapel to the waiting limo. And man, was it ever a limo! I'd lived in Vegas for the past six years, so I'd seen my share of limos. This one was longer than most, and maybe my imagination was working overtime, but it seemed shinier and blacker as well.

The chauffeur held the door for me. I opened my mouth to thank Reid, when he slid in beside me on the lush white leather seat.

"Thank you for everything," I said. "I'll... I guess I'll be in touch."

He didn't move.

"I should give the driver my address," I said.

"Already taken care of."

"Then...goodbye. Thank you again."

Again, he didn't move.

But the limo did.

"I don't need a chaperone."

"I'm not your chaperone." He smiled.

And oh my, his smile dazzled. Perfectly straight teeth surrounded by those full Wolfe lips.

So handsome.

And so... So...*familiar.*

I scooted away from him, just enough so that no part of him was touching me. Then, for the first time, I looked at my surroundings. This limo had a full bar. Seriously. A full bar. Another leather bench seat sat on the other side of the bar, and then two large bucket seats sat adjacent to it. All white leather with black accents.

I'd never seen anything like it.

I'd had two limo rides during my time here. The first was a few months after I started in the show. One of the producers took a few of us out after our New Year's Eve performance. He wanted plenty in return. I escaped when we stopped to fuel up.

The second time was with a casino owner who took a liking to me. We dated a few times, but then, in the limo, he wanted to consummate our relationship. I wasn't ready. Truth be told, I wasn't ready now either.

Luckily, he didn't press the point. He was quite persuasive, but he stopped before raping me. Then he never called me again.

Just as well.

"I'm your date," Reid continued, "and I always see my dates safely home."

I didn't know what to say, so I chose to say nothing.

"Would you like a drink?" Reid asked.

"No, thank you." After two flutes of champagne, I wasn't feeling much pain, but I still had my right frame of mind. I didn't want that to change anytime soon.

"Do you mind if I do?"

"Not at all."

He scooted toward the bar and poured himself something

dark. Bourbon or scotch, I'd guess. He took a drink and then set the glass in a holder, turning to me. "Tell me a little about yourself, Zee."

I cleared my throat. "You know more about me than most."

His cheeks turned a little ruddy. Had I embarrassed him?

"I know *one* thing that most probably don't. There's a whole lot I don't know."

"Well, the one thing you know isn't something I've told anyone."

"You told your lawyer."

"Correction. I told your father's lawyer. I didn't have a lawyer."

He nodded, taking another sip. "I see. Is that anything you'd like to talk about ?"

"I think I made it clear that it's the one thing I *never* talk about," I said.

"You did, but sometimes it helps to tell a friend."

"I'd hardly call you a friend, Mr. Wolfe."

"Please. Reid. I don't like to think of myself as Mr. Wolfe."

"Why?"

"My father was Mr. Wolfe."

"Oh." I nodded. I got it. Reid didn't want to be associated with his father. Who could blame him? Certainly not I.

"So I'm Reid, just like Riley is Riley."

I nodded again.

"I'd like to see your show."

My show? Why would he want to see my show? "I'm sure with your resources you'll have no problem getting tickets." Did that sound snotty? I didn't mean it that way.

"Of course. I'll be here for a few days, at least."

"I'm just part of the line," I said. "I'm not a star or anything." Which suited me just fine. I liked being invisible.

"I know that. I still want to see your work."

"But you won't see me. That's the idea behind being a show-girl. The audience isn't supposed to see us, really. We're back-ground. They're focused on the star."

He swallowed another sip. "Yes, yes. I've seen Las Vegas shows before. I'd just like to come. Perhaps I could take you to dinner afterward?"

"I'm usually beat afterward. Two shows a night and all."

"You're not making this easy," he said under his breath.

"Making what easy?"

"Nothing. Just talking to myself." He polished off his bourbon just as the limo pulled up at my building.

I touched the door handle. "Well...thank you again."

"I'll walk you up."

"You don't have to." *Please don't.*

"You're my date," he said again.

Right. He had to see me home. Except my home was a tiny apartment with three roommates.

So...best way to keep him from seeing my place?

"I'm not feeling very good," I said. "Please, just let me go up."

"If you're sick, all the more reason to have someone make sure you get up there safely."

I was fighting a losing battle. I wasn't embarrassed about my living situation, I was just... This was Reid Wolfe. A freaking billionaire.

The driver opened the car door, and Reid slid out. He offered me his hand.

A slight shiver slid through me as our hands touched.

Odd. I didn't normally react that way to men. Not since...

Well, since the incident in the Wolfe building.

I stepped out of the cab, and—

"Oh!" One of my heels caught in a grate, and I stumbled.

Reid caught me, and in an instant our bodies were melted together.

I looked up into his blue eyes.

His gaze was so intense, I almost felt I should close my eyes against it. At the same time, I couldn't look away. As the lights from the strip flickered in the background, his blue eyes outshone even the brightest neon.

"Easy," he said. "I got you."

He held onto me as I broke free from the grate. Except—

"Crap. Really?"

"What?" he asked.

Warmth spread over my cheeks. The heel to my shoe had broken off and was still stuck in the grate.

I let out a harried sigh. "Nothing. Just my best pair of shoes." I pointed.

"I'm sorry. You okay on your feet?"

"Yeah."

He steadied me, and then he knelt down and pulled my broken stiletto out of the grate. "I know a good cobbler who can fix this."

"Please. Don't worry about it."

"I'm not worried."

Then I gasped as he hoisted me into his arms. "What are you doing?"

"I can't let you stumble up to your apartment." He laughed. "You're light as a feather!"

That was a lie. A big one. I was five nine and muscled from dancing. I weighed one fifty-five. He was probably used to scrawny models. I said nothing, though, as he carried me along the walkway up the steps into the building.

"Which floor?" He approached the elevator.

"Fourth, and that elevator hasn't worked in years."

"Oh? We'll see about that."

"What's that supposed to mean?"

"Nothing. Which way to the stairs?"

I gestured toward a door, and he carried me through. Then up one flight. Two. Three. Four. My God, the man wasn't even winded. Somehow, he turned the knob on the door and carried me into the hallway.

"Apartment 404," I said, "on the left."

A few more steps and then we stood in front of my place.

"Got a key?" he asked.

"Just knock. Mo is home, I think."

"Mo?"

"Short for Maureen. One of my roommates. She's in the show, and we're dark tonight, as you know."

"Ah. Okay." Reid knocked.

A few seconds later, Mo opened the door, clad in her Lucy and Linus pajamas. "Zee! What happened?"

"Nothing. Just broke the heel off my shoe."

Mo smiled. "And who's this?"

"Reid. Reid Wolfe," he said as he walked into our tiny place.

"You can put me down now," I said.

"You sure? You didn't twist your ankle or anything?"

"I'm fine. Seriously."

He let me down gently, and I stood, placing weight on both legs. The left ankle was slightly weak, but once I kicked off my other shoe and was level, I felt better. A little sore but nothing I couldn't live with. I'd danced with worse. A little ice tonight and tomorrow, and I'd be ready for rehearsal at three and showtime at seven.

Reid gathered my shoes. "I'll have these fixed for you."

"Please. It's not necessary. They weren't expensive." I'd gotten them secondhand on Posh, but I kept that to myself.

"It's no problem. They'll be messengered back to you tomorrow."

"I'm working tomorrow."

"Right. About that dinner after the show?"

"Shows are at seven and ten. There's no time between for dinner, and I said—"

"Then I'll make reservations for midnight. I'll see you after the show."

"Wait, I—"

"Great meeting you," Reid said to Mo. "I'll see you tomorrow."

Then he was gone. Like a flash. Totally forgetting how I'd said I was always beat after two shows...

"Those are some crazy gorgeous eyes," Mo said, "and the rest of him... Wow."

I said nothing. What could I say? She was spot on.

"Where'd you find him?"

"Just a...get-together."

"And you didn't invite me? Are there any more like him?"

"First of all, we're not together. I broke my shoe."

"And he carried you up here."

"Yes," I said matter-of-factly.

"Lucky girl." Mo flashed me a smile and then walked to our tiny kitchen.

Funny.

I didn't feel so lucky.

4

REID

O h, yes. This was going to be a challenge.
Any other woman would be in bed with me right about now, screaming my name.

Of course any other woman—at least any other *living* woman—hadn't been so viciously victimized by my psycho father.

No problem. I had a few days at my disposal. I'd be working my ass off with the legal team, of course, but I never had trouble finding playtime.

I'd sleep on it.

I texted my assistant, Terrence, quickly and told him I needed tickets to Zee's ten o'clock show tomorrow, pronto, and then I turned to emails.

I'd gotten through a few when my phone dinged with a text.

Terrence was damned good. He'd been my assistant for a couple years now, and I swore the dude had connections even the Wolfes didn't have.

Except...the text wasn't from Terrence.

I hear you're in Las Vegas, gorgeous. So am I, as it happens. Want to meet for a drink?

Nieves Romero. My brother's old flame who I just happened to fuck a couple weeks ago when she showed up in New York.

Not my finest moment.

But damn, she was hot. Rock had given her the brush-off, so she'd been ripe for the picking.

What the hell did she want? Then again, what did it matter? I could use a good fuck.

Sure. I'm staying at Wolfe Premiere. Meet me in the bar in a half hour.

You got it, hot stuff.

How did she know I was here? Maybe I could also get some information out of her. She and her sister, Leta, seemed to be involved in this mystery somehow, but how? And why? They had no connection to my father.

Not that we knew of, anyway.

The limo dropped me back at the hotel. I checked my phone for the time. I had fifteen minutes before Nieves showed up in the bar. Time for a few games of blackjack. I was a whiz at the game.

The high-stakes tables called to me. I found a spot and laid a thousand dollars on the table for some chips. Then I laid all the chips out for the next deal.

The rush of gambling had been my downfall when I was younger, until my father taught me how to control the urge. He taught me never to leave too much to chance and to stay in control of every situation. If the table wasn't cooperating, leave.

Lose two games in a row, get up and walk away, was his motto.

It hadn't failed me yet. Sure, I lost sometimes, but more often than not, I left richer than I started.

Funny. My father was an asshole extraordinaire, but he taught me the ins and outs of business and pleasure.

I was fucking lucky he hadn't drawn me into his hunting games. Had that been his plan?

I'd never know, thank God.

What would I have done?

Didn't matter. I washed the thought away as the dealer dealt me a jack and then an ace.

Fucking blackjack!

I gathered my two and a half thousand dollars' worth of chips, tipped the dealer a couple hundred, and then cashed out.

After a drink and quick fuck with Nieves, I'd be back at this table.

I didn't need more than four hours of sleep a night. Another weird trait I'd inherited from Derek Wolfe. He'd slept even less, and his brain was always at a hundred and ten percent.

Fuck. I'd always known he was a master of manipulation, but even *I* never imagined *everything* he was capable of.

Nieves was sitting at the bar, dressed in a green mini dress and black stilettos. Her long, dark hair and fair skin were an intoxicating combination, as was the tat on her shoulder. A scarlet rose and a skull. Like light meeting dark. I loved my sister-in-law, and she was certainly beautiful in a white picket fence kind of way. Nieves, though? Hot. As. Fuck.

"I took the liberty of ordering you a Macallan," Nieves said in her smoky voice. "Neat, with a touch of water to release the bouquet."

Macallan. My favorite Scotch, and what I'd drunk the last time we were together. She remembered my order in its entirety. Since then, I'd grown accustomed to Pappy Van Winkle's fifteen-year bourbon, but Nieves had no way of knowing that.

I smiled. "On my tab, of course."

She laughed. "Of course."

I took a sip of the scotch. Smooth and peaty. Nice. Again, it was Derek Wolfe who taught me that just a touch of water released the fragrances and flavors tenfold.

Damn.

I owed so much to that man. That man I hated to the marrow in my bones.

"How did you know I was here?" I asked Nieves.

"A little bird told me."

Another sip of scotch. "Oh?"

She batted her eyes. Yes, she seriously did. I wasn't going to get an answer out of her, and I didn't care, anyway. She had information I needed, and if I could get laid in the process? Even better.

"Did you know Rock is still here?" I asked her.

"He's an old married man now," she said.

"True."

"What's he see in that uptight attorney?" she asked.

He sees someone who isn't you. Yeah, Nieves was hot as fuck, but she was also a manipulative little cunt. Great in the sack, though.

"Lacey's a great woman," I said. "Smart, too."

"Yeah, but how is she in bed?"

I tool another sip of my scotch. "He hasn't divulged those details to me."

"Rock is a fucking master in bed." Nieves sipped her dirty martini. "But even he doesn't equal your talent."

Nice touch. I doubted my brother had been celibate all those years in Montana, but already I knew I'd had more women. Hell, I'd had more women than most billionaire playboys in Manhattan. They didn't call me the Wolfe of Manhattan for nothing.

"Thank you for the compliment," I said.

"Tell me," she said. "What's your whole family doing here in Sin City?"

"Business."

"Not pleasure?"

"Business. But I always find time for pleasure."

"I was hoping you'd say that."

"First, though"—I cleared my throat—"what are *you* doing here in Sin City?"

She took another sip of her drink and smirked. "I just love sin."

Oh, she was good. And I was happy to bed her. But first, I needed some intel.

"What's going on with you?" I asked. "Have you talked to your sister lately?"

"Leta or Ciara?"

She had another sister? News to me. "Leta, I guess."

She shook her head. "Not since she talked to your brother in Helena." She polished off her drink.

"Let me get you another." I signaled the bartender. "Another dirty martini for the lady."

"Sapphire, remember?" Nieves added with a wink. "And make that *extra* dirty."

The young bartender blushed at the double entendre.

"Where are you staying?" I asked Nieves.

She touched her bottom lip coyly. "With you."

Oh, she was good. Too good, really.

But not as good as I was.

"We'll see about that," I said.

The barkeep slid a fresh martini in front of her.

She gave him another wink. "Yes, we certainly will."

I sipped my scotch slowly. Not that I was a lightweight or anything, but tonight was about getting information. It was also about a good fuck, but that was the less important part. Better to keep my faculties while I assisted Nieves in losing hers.

My phone buzzed in my pocket. I pulled it out.

Rock.

"Excuse me," I said to Nieves. "I have to take this. I'll only be a minute."

"Of course." She puckered her red lips around an olive.

My groin tightened as I walked far enough away for privacy. "Hey," I said into the phone.

"So Nieves is here."

"I know."

"Oh?"

"Yeah, she and I are having a drink at the bar as we speak." Rock laughed uproariously.

"And that's funny because…"

"Because she's so predictable. I'm taken, and you're not. So she's after a new Wolfe."

I couldn't fault his observation, but— "Are you sure? I mean, you were involved with her in Montana when you didn't have a pot to piss in."

"True enough, but she's seen the green now. Trust me. She wants a piece of whatever pie she can get."

"And you think I'm going to give her a piece."

"Nah. I think you're going to take a piece, if you haven't already." Rock laughed again.

"I'd say you know me too well, but you really don't," I said. "Since we really only just met a few weeks ago."

"I read the tabloids. I know all about you, Reid. The Wolfe of Wall Street."

I cleared my throat. "Actually, it's the Wolfe of Manhattan."

"My bad." Rock chuckled again. "So what's the plan with Nieves?"

"I'm going to pump her for info."

"You sure that's all you're going to pump?"

"For God's sake, Rock."

"Am I wrong?" He laughed again.

"You know, most guys wouldn't want their little brothers poking their castoffs."

He guffawed. Literally. It even sounded like *guffaw*.

"Nieves Romero is a hot little number and a fucking lioness

between the sheets. She's nothing compared to what I have with Lace, but bro, if she's offering—and I'd bet your father's fortune she is—go for it."

"What if I've already poked that?"

Another guffaw. "Wouldn't surprise me."

"Is there anything else you wanted to tell me?" I asked. "I've got a hot number waiting for me in the bar, and yeah, she's been innuendoing all evening."

"Lacey wanted me to ask you to go easy on Zee," he said.

"What's that got to do with anything?"

"We're all leaving tomorrow, but you'll still be here. We want her cooperation, but not at the cost of her mental health."

"You seriously think I'd do something untoward to her? To one of our father's victims?"

"No, no. Of course not. It's just... Your way of getting your way is usually...you know. Sexual."

He wasn't wrong. "I believe I can seduce her," I said.

"I believe you can too. That's not the point. The question is whether you *should*."

"Look," I said. "I feel just as bad for Zee as the rest of you do. She had the shitty luck to come into contact with Derek Wolfe, and she paid the price. But if we look at it another way, she was actually really lucky. She lived through the ordeal, and as far as we know, no one else did."

"Doesn't mean she owes us anything."

"Did I say that? But all of our lives are on the line here, including your wife's. We're all implicated, and if Zee has information that would clear us, we need it."

"She doesn't have that kind of info, Reid," Rock said. "All she has is her own story."

"Which will prove what kind of guy Dad was, and that there were many more out there who wanted him dead."

"But there *aren't*. Not with Zee's story, anyway. They're all dead. Hunted and killed. The only thing Zee's story will do is make *her* a suspect instead of us."

Again, Rock was not wrong. We could easily prove Zee wasn't in New York the night of the murder, but what good would her story do other than to fuck with Dad's character? It still wouldn't absolve any of us of the crime. In fact, it would only give us more of a motive to off the psycho.

Something niggled at the back of my neck. That something called a conscience, which right now I wished I didn't have.

"Why?" I asked Rock. "Why didn't any one of us inherit Dad's lack of conscience?"

"It'd make this a lot easier if we had."

Truth be told, I was probably the closest to Dad's lack of conscience. On more than one occasion, I'd ignored the angel on my shoulder in favor of the devil. Usually for business, though, not for personal gain. And never for sexual gain. I'd never bedded a woman without her explicit consent.

But wasn't this business? I couldn't run this business from a prison cell. And I sure as hell wasn't going to prison for killing the bastard when my hands were sparkling clean.

Okay, maybe not sparkling, but still clean. I hated the mofo, but I didn't kill him. Neither did Rock, Roy, Riley, or Lacey. I believed all of them. Hell, Lacey didn't even have any motive.

"So about Zee," Rock was saying.

"What about her?"

"We can sure use her story, but please don't push her."

"Is this you or the wife talking?"

"Both, to be honest, but Riley most of all."

Riley. My kid sister, who had suffered more at our father's hands than the three of us guys combined.

Riley, who I used to envy because of our father's attention.

Boy, had I been dead-ass wrong.

For Riley, I'd do anything.

Even this.

"All right, brother. For Riley. Tell her I'll treat Zee with kid gloves."

It was a promise I knew I'd keep.

Didn't mean I wouldn't sleep with her, though.

5

ZEE

That innocent eighteen-year-old girl had a plan.

Acceptance to Smith. Yeah, it was an all-girls school, but she didn't worry about that. She looked at it as a gift. She'd be forced to spend more time on her studies. Her beauty wouldn't be a hindrance in a group of all women. No one would envy her for the physical characteristics she couldn't control.

The girl had aced the SAT and ACT, hitting a perfect score on the latter. She wanted to break free from the acting and modeling career her mother had forced on her and expand her horizons.

Turned out, though, that the acting and modeling stuff had helped her in the long run. She'd been homeschooled by a qualified teacher, and she was way ahead of her public school educated colleagues. Hence the amazing scores on the standardized college admission tests.

She was always bright. But even her intelligence couldn't make an actress out of her. She didn't have that kind of talent, and she just wasn't interested. She wanted more. She wanted to help others. What better way than to become a physician? A healer? She dreamed of bringing new lives into the world, so she'd already decided that when —not if—she made it to medical school, she'd specialize in obstetrics.

Her mother was against Smith.

Her mother was against a career in medicine.

But the girl was eighteen. She could make her own decisions. Her own choices.

Her first choice was to leave acting and modeling behind.

No more auditions.

No more dieting.

No more dance classes.

Though she'd actually enjoyed the dance classes. She was a capable dancer, and she'd reaped the benefit of the hard work for the last ten years. Her body was toned and muscled.

But she just wouldn't have time for dancing as she embarked on her new life.

Her brief foray into modeling had given her a lovely wardrobe, and she packed all of her clothes into her car for the road trip to Smith.

Her mother refused to go with her. Refused even to co-sign on her student loans.

No problem. She'd get deferments until she was done with school altogether, and as a physician, she'd be able to pay off the loans in a reasonable amount of time.

She and her mother said their goodbyes. There was no hug. No handshake, even.

Just a goodbye.

They both seemed okay with that.

The girl drove herself into the city. She'd been there many times before, to meet with agents, but she'd never done the tourist thing.

She wanted to visit the Statue of Liberty, the Metropolitan Museum of Art, Ground Zero, the MOMA—so she allotted herself three days in Queens in the only hotel she could afford, and she learned the subway system to see her heart's desire.

She ate the best bagel she'd ever tasted at a deli. Okay, maybe it was the best because at least five years had passed since she last ate a bagel. Still, it was delicious with the smear of cream cheese and the zing of poppy seeds.

She ate a hot dog from a street vendor. Then a slice of New York-style pizza.

She laughed, knowing what any agent—or her mother—would say about these treats.

Didn't matter. That was her old life.

This was the new.

She was exhausted after her first day of tourism. She'd walked miles and miles and breathed in all she could of the beautiful culture of New York.

She perused her guidebook and made plans for the next day, and then she snuggled into the lumpy bed in the cheap room filled with cheap seventies furnishings, and fell into a deep sleep.

When she woke up, she was in the fight of her life.

6

REID

Nieves sipped her third martini. I'd ordered another scotch, but each time I brought it to my lips I feigned drinking. Age-old game of getting your adversary drunk so he'd talk. I was good at it.

I'd learned from the best.

Not that I considered Nieves an adversary. Not yet, at least. I still didn't know how her sister was involved in all this, but tonight I'd find out.

If I had to fuck her to get the intel, I would.

No sweat off my back.

"Tell me about your sister's doctor," I said. "Dr. Manfred."

She rolled her eyes. "Manny? That slimy guy? I wouldn't let him near my pussy."

I smiled, holding back a chuckle. "Why?"

"Have you met the man?"

"I have, actually. I've checked him out. He's in good standing with the Montana Medical Board. He was at the top of his class in med school."

"Where'd he go to med school? Guatemala?"

"University of Virginia, actually. Quite a good school."

"He couldn't get into Harvard, huh?"

I laughed this time. "Without connections, it's almost impossible to get into Harvard Med School. But his undergrad record was excellent. He was a great candidate for any med school."

"So?"

"So he's a capable doctor, which doesn't jibe with your dislike of him."

"He's just...slimy."

"Meaning..." I knew exactly what she meant. He wasn't tall and good-looking. I wanted her to say it. Why? I wasn't sure.

"Meaning, my body, my choice. I don't want him near my pussy."

Okay, she wasn't biting. Fair enough. Time to try another tactic. "Apparently your sister only went to him once."

"Did she?" Nieves stared down at her nearly empty third drink.

"Her previous physician was a Dr. Isabel Caleb."

"She's good. I've gone to her."

"If she's good, why would Leta switch to Dr. Manfred?"

"I don't know. I'm not my sister's keeper." Again, staring into her now-empty martini glass.

"It's puzzling, don't you think?" I took another fake drink of my scotch.

Nieves met my gaze. "The only thing puzzling is why we're not hitting the sheets yet."

I smiled—that devilish grin that no lady could resist. "Oh, we will. But I find anticipation makes it even better." I signaled the barkeep. "Another for the lady."

The still-blushing bartender slid another dirty martini in front of Nieves. She daintily took a sip.

"How did Leta know that Rock had left Montana?" I asked.

Nieves kicked off one of her stilettos and slid her bare foot underneath my pants, rubbing her toes against my ankle. "I don't know."

Oddly, I wasn't getting turned on. I still enjoyed a woman who was a challenge, and Nieves Romero clearly didn't fall into that category. Partially my fault. I'd gotten her drunk. Alcohol, the great social lubricant. Not that Nieves needed any lubricant. Of *any* kind.

But Nieves hadn't been a challenge back in Manhattan either, and I'd been sloppy seconds after she couldn't seduce Rock away from Lacey.

That night, I hadn't cared. I'd been horny, and she'd been available.

Tonight, though? She wasn't appealing to me.

Damn Rock and his ill-timed phone call. If I hadn't answered, I'd be doing the horizontal tango with Ms. Romero right now.

Instead, I'd gotten her too drunk too quickly, and now she wasn't going to be any good to me.

"Nieves," I said.

"What?" Then she burst into giggles. "You have four eyes."

Her remark puzzled me. I wasn't wearing my glasses.

Her next gesture removed any puzzlement. She poked at my forehead. "One, two, three, four." Then she blinked incessantly for a few seconds and then widened her eyes. "Nope. Still four."

Was she too drunk now to give me any helpful information?

What a lightweight. Four drinks? Really?

Except she probably weighed half of what I did.

I signaled the barkeep again, rising to speak to him privately. "How much booze did you put in her drinks?"

"They were doubles," he said.

"Doubles? Are you freaking kidding me?"

"That's what she ordered when she got here."

Shit. He was right. Nieves had arrived at the bar before I did, and she'd ordered my first scotch.

Nieves had drunk the equivalent of eight drinks while I was fake drinking my second. Four drinks would have put her right where I wanted her.

Eight? She was a hair away from passing out.

I returned to my stool and sat down.

"I don't feel so good, Rock," Nieves said.

"Reid," I said, taking a good look at her. "You look a little green."

She laughed hysterically. "I think I'm going to puke on you later!"

Great. Just great. I threw some bills on the wooden bar. "That's your tip. Put the drinks on my tab. Reid Wolfe."

The bartender's eyebrows flew up. "Reid Wolfe? Who owns this place?"

"That's the one." Then I lifted Nieves off her stool, carried her out of the bar toward the elevators.

She closed her eyes and let out a soft snore.

So much for my quick fuck.

I'd never taken an incapacitated woman to bed, and I wasn't going to start now. Still, she'd said she was staying with me. Did she have a room somewhere? A small purse dangled from her wrist. Once I got her to my suite, I'd take a look through it for a hotel key.

The elevator dinged and the double doors parted.

And there stood my brother Roy with his new wife, Charlie.

Fuck it all.

7

ZEE

My eyes darted open.

Where was I?

Right. My hotel in Queens.

Except...

My bed was a full-sized, and this bed...

This bed was narrow. Like a cot. The mattress was thin, and—

I jerked upward.

Darkness surrounded me. There was a window in my room. Where was it? It must still be nighttime.

I waited for my eyes to adjust.

And my whole body turned prickly.

This wasn't my room.

And then the hammering in my head began.

Or became more pronounced, because it had been there since I woke up.

A nauseating headache. Was this what a migraine felt like? I'd never had one. But this pounding was on both sides of my head, not just one. In fact, it was all over my head, behind my eyes, on the crown, at the back of my neck.

A jackhammer.

Pounding so quickly I couldn't get a grasp on the speed. Like a hummingbird's heartbeat, only loud and obnoxious and pulsating through my body, landing in my gut.

Crap.

Literally.

I had to go to the bathroom. I stood. The bathroom was...

I stumbled, trying to orient myself. The bathroom was to the right.

Except all I saw to the right was a wall. This room was small.

Really small.

Where was the door?

I walked the small room blindly, feeling at the walls to support myself. I could pass out at any moment. My stomach was gurgling, my head hammering.

My heart stampeding.

Finally, something hit me in the belly.

"Ouch!" I reached down and touched my bare skin.

Then my fright increased a hundredfold.

I was naked.

I'd gone to bed in a T-shirt and panties. Hadn't I? My mind was so muddled I didn't trust my thoughts.

My hand brushed against the object that had hit my belly.

A door knob!

I twisted at it frantically, to no avail.

I'd found the door, but I couldn't open it. I fumbled along the door-jamb for a deadbolt or something to unlock.

Nothing.

I was locked in.

Locked in a strange room.

Naked and ill and my head throbbing in time with my heart.

I slid down, scratching my unclothed back on the wall.

I sat on the floor, shivering.

Naked, afraid, and shivering.

~

"IF YOU DON'T WANT HIM," Mo said, handing me a glass of wine, "mind if I take a stab?"

I didn't want the wine. Two flutes of champagne was enough for one evening. Plus, it was my night off, and I really just wanted to go to bed. But Mo was in one of her chatty moods, and we did have the place to ourselves since our other two roomies were out.

I took the goblet from her. "Help yourself."

"Can you arrange an introduction?"

"I just met him."

Then her eyes went wide. "Oh. My. God."

"What?"

"He's Reid Wolfe!"

"Well...yeah. I believe he introduced himself to you."

"Reid Wolfe the billionaire!"

"Oh. Yeah."

"Oh. Yeah." She mocked me. "Seriously? That's what you have to say? Spill it, girl. How the hell did you end up getting Reid Wolfe to bring you home tonight?"

Long story. One I didn't want to rehash now. So I said simply, "Right place at the right time, I guess."

"What place would that be?" she demanded. "Because I plan to be there tomorrow."

"I was over at the Wolfe Premiere."

"What for? You hate gambling."

"I had a...spa appointment." A little white lie never hurt anyone.

"Whoa. Expensive stuff when you can hit Massage Avenue for fifty bucks."

"I won a gift certificate in a contest." Yeah, the white lies kept coming.

"Oh, that makes more sense. How was it?"

"Good. But no better than Massage Avenue. Definitely not worth the extra expense."

"Really? I've heard their relaxation room is phenomenal. Aromatherapy, hydrotherapy, the works."

Like I'd know. "Yeah, but not worth the extra, at least not on our income."

She nodded, finally. Good. I wanted to get off this subject. I hated lying, but I couldn't tell Mo why I was really at the Wolfe. No one knew my story here in Las Vegas. No one but the Wolfes.

I took a sip of wine and then feigned a yawn. "I'm exhausted. Think I'll hit the sack."

She giggled. "Nice try. Drink your wine, and tell me how I can get a stab at Reid Wolfe."

"I hardly know the man."

"Didn't look that way to me. He carried you in here."

"Because the heel on my shoe broke."

"And that means you can't walk, of course."

"Well, my ankle's slightly sore."

"I've seen you do a show with an ankle twice the size of what you've got now." Mo shook her head. "Not buying."

I sighed. "Fine. He's taking me to dinner tomorrow night after the late show. Why don't you come along?"

"Dinner? Damn, you're lucky."

"I'm trying to help *you* get lucky."

"Three's a crowd, Zee."

"It's not a date. I just met the guy."

"You just met Reid Wolfe, and now you've got a date with him. Damn." She took a big drink of her wine. "You have all the luck!"

All the luck.

Did Mo have any idea how ridiculous her words sounded to me?

All the luck.

I'd been *hunted*. Then I spent the next several years on drugs, trying to deal with what had happened to me. Finally, I got off the drugs and found the strength to confront Derek Wolfe about what he'd done. That led to the settlement. He paid me off, and I let him.

Then I came to Las Vegas and changed my name. I wasn't qualified to do anything, so I put those years of dancing classes to good use. Turned out I fit the bill for a showgirl. I was tall, well-built, and strong. The head pieces we wore often weighed twenty pounds or more. The modeling classes helped as well. My posture was outstanding. After two months, I got a job in a revue.

I supposed I was lucky in that respect. I found work. I'd used most of my settlement money then to finance my move to a new city. In retrospect, I should have demanded more. I had a ton of debt from rehab, and a big chunk of that settlement went to pay it off.

And lucky...

In one big respect I *was* lucky.

Lucky to be alive.

Those other girls...

They weren't so lucky. I never saw any of them again.

"Earth to Zee." Mo waved her hands in front of my face.

"Yeah, what?"

"You went catatonic there for a minute. You okay?"

"Yeah, just thinking. You're right, Mo. I am lucky, in some ways."

"Try *all* ways, girl. You've got a face and body to die for, and you're dating a Wolfe."

"I'm not dating a Wolfe. And not in all ways."

She scoffed. "I suppose no one is lucky in all ways."

"True story," I agreed. If she only knew.

"So...about dinner tomorrow. You sure I won't be a third wheel?"

"Absolutely not. I want you to come."

No truer words. Reid Wolfe scared me senseless.

I was scared of what he wanted from me.

And even more scared that I kind of wanted it as well.

8

REID

Charlie's eyes went wide. Roy's didn't.

My brother knew me pretty well.

"Who's the lucky lady?" he asked.

"The lady's passed out," I retorted. "I'm taking her to bed."

"Clearly." My brother smirked.

I let out a huff. Did my brother seriously think I'd take an unconscious woman to bed? What the fuck?

"Isn't this supposed to be your wedding night?" I asked.

"It is. We're sharing a late dinner at Massey's, and then—"

"Please," I said, "spare me the details." Especially since, at this point, I clearly wasn't getting any tonight.

"Looks like you'll be busy as well." Roy nodded to Nieves.

"This is Nieves Romero, Roy. She passed out in the bar, and I'm taking her to bed. Not *my* bed. Is that really what you think of me?"

"Of course not," Charlie said.

"You *are* the Wolfe of Manhattan." This from Roy.

"I can be the Wolfe of Manhattan without preying on the defenseless. Damn." I walked into the still-open elevator.

"Hey, bro, I didn't mean—"

"Yeah, you did," I said as the elevator doors closed, erasing Roy and Charlie from my view. No, I didn't actually believe my brother thought so little of me. I was just pissed at this situation.

I arrived at my suite and laid Nieves on the bed in the second bedroom. Thank goodness Jarrod or Charlie or whoever had made these reservations had booked us all in two bedroom suites. I did *not* want to sleep on a couch tonight.

First things first. I removed the wristlet bag hanging from Nieves's hand and unzipped it. A credit card, a couple bucks, and her ID. No hotel room key. All right. No problem. I reassessed my decision to let her sleep in my extra bedroom, made a quick call to the front desk, and booked her a room. Then I carried her to it, met a concierge there, and put her to bed.

Nicely done, I said to myself. This way she'd wake up somewhere other than my suite. As much as I'd enjoy a good fuck, I wanted to deprive myself for now.

So I'd be hungrier for Zee tomorrow night.

I needed to be in full Wolfe mode to get her into my bed, and I planned to do it.

Oh, I'd stay loyal to Riley. I wouldn't push. No. I'd seduce Zee *slowly*. In fact, I'd wait. It didn't have to happen tomorrow. It could happen the next day. The hungrier I got, the better I'd seduce her.

I'd *make* her want me.

When she wanted me, she'd want to please me.

And I'd convince her that the way to please me would be to tell her story.

Simple enough.

Back in my suite, I stripped off my clothes and went to bed in my boxer briefs. To my surprise, I fell asleep to visions of a black-haired beauty with immensely sad light-blue eyes.

≈

I JERKED UPWARD IN BED.

Someone was pounding on my door. My phone lay on the nightstand, flashing the time. Six a.m.

Certainly not Rock. He wasn't an early riser. Riley and Matt were still on their wedding night. Ditto Roy and Charlie.

Had I ordered breakfast? Yeah, I had, but room service wouldn't be pounding. I grabbed a robe from the bathroom, headed to the door, and looked through the peephole.

"Nieves," I said under my breath.

Against my better judgment, I opened the door.

She blew past me and into my suite. "Nice try."

"You were passed out," I said.

"I could've slept it off here, and we'd be fucking right about now."

Oddly, her words had no effect on me. She was hot, no doubt, but my dreams had been filled with another woman.

A woman I planned to seduce, but who I didn't realize I actually wanted...until now.

Yeah, I'd have seduced her anyway, but now, I actually craved her.

"I'm afraid our ship has sailed, Nieves."

"Has it?" she said. "Because I might be willing to part with some interesting information. For the right price."

"If the right price is a romp in my bed, I'm afraid I'll have to pass."

She smiled. "You do drive a hard bargain, but I'm willing to settle for cash."

Cash I had, and plenty of it. "What do you know?"

"Uh-uh. I need to see the cash first."

"Nieves, you know cash isn't an issue for me. Give me what you've got, and I'll decide if it's worth anything."

Nieves *did* have information. Somehow, she'd known about my father's death before it actually happened, according to her sister and to forensics on the scene.

She'd also known before Rock had.

None of us were exactly sure how she and Leta were involved, but I had a suspicion it had to do with money.

Not so much a suspicion. More like I knew damned well it had to do with money. I just didn't know how.

"This isn't how it words, Reid," she said. "I'm not a fool."

"No, just a mercenary. I can respect that." No lie there. Money was money.

She looked great, especially for someone who was most likely twelve shades of hungover. Which meant either she had a great hangover remedy or she just looked that good all the time.

Probably the latter. The Romero sisters were hotness personified. I'd been into it last night. What was wrong with me this morning?

"Then we understand each other," she said.

"Do we? Because if you think I'm handing you any money before you tell me anything, you can think again."

"Fine." She smiled seductively. "I'll give you a hint."

"I'm listening."

"When Rock and I dated, I came across something at his place. Something I never told him about."

"And...?"

"That's it. You want to know the rest? You pay."

"For all I know you could have found a dead mouse and disposed of it without telling him. That would fit your current narrative."

"You really think I'd fuck with you like that?"

"Already I know you weren't above keeping something from my brother. So yeah, I think you'd fuck with anyone for a buck."

She let out a short laugh. "You're the one who called me mercenary."

"I did, and obviously I'll stand by it. Thing is, though, my brother didn't have any money when you were with him. But you knew who he was, didn't you?"

She twisted a strand of her long dark hair. "Maybe I did. Maybe I didn't."

"Cut the crap, sweetheart, and don't insult my intelligence. You knew damned well whose son he was."

She raised her eyebrows. "It's not like he changed his name or anything."

"He didn't, but the Wolfes are hardly a household name in a small Montana town."

"That's true."

"So how did you find out who he was?"

"I do my research."

"On small-town bikers?"

"On everyone, Reid. *Everyone.*" She met my gaze, her eyes serious.

There was meaning behind those words, but I didn't for the life of me know what it was. I had to make her think I did, though.

"Do you?" I asked. "Because the Wolfes do their research as well, Nieves, and I'm pretty sure our resources are far superior to yours."

She looked away.

Good. That got her.

"What makes you think," I continued, "that you know anything we don't know already?"

"If you knew, why did you question Leta?"

Good for her. She was smarter than I gave her credit for. "We question *everyone*," I said simply.

She stayed quiet for a few seconds. *Nicely done, Reid.*

Finally, "Show me the money."

I laughed. I couldn't help myself. "A grand. That's what I'll offer. It'll get you home to Montana."

"I could get a grand from any high roller here."

"Yeah, but you'd have to work for it."

Her cheeks reddened. I'd struck a nerve. Yeah, I was being an asshole, but she was being a first-class bitch.

"A grand," I said again. "And you don't have to get on your back."

She huffed. "Fine. But if you find the information helpful, I get another nine grand."

"Fair enough. I don't have any cash on me. I have to hit the ATM. Let's meet for a late lunch at one, and I'll give you the cash then."

"Fine. Then you'll wait for the info."

I nodded. I actually did have a grand on me. Two and some change, actually, from last night's blackjack winnings. But I wanted to check in with Rock first. He knew Nieves a lot better than I did, and he might have an idea of what she had found at his place. If he did, I could save myself a grand. Not that a grand meant more than a penny to me, but I didn't particularly want to enrich Nieves Romero.

"Good enough," she said. "Text me with the deets."

"I will. Now, if you'll excuse me, I have business to attend to."

She advanced toward me, gesturing to the door that led to the master bedroom. "Sure you don't want to...?"

"Thanks," I said, "but no. I've got a meeting."

No lie there. I did have a meeting, but not for an hour. In the meantime, though, I had other things that needed my attention.

"Your loss." She walked toward the door. "See you at lunch."

9

ZEE

The nice thing about working nights was that I could sleep in. I'd learned to ignore the sunlight streaming in through my window. Mo, who shared my bedroom, got up earlier, but she didn't make a lot of noise, so she never woke me.

Until this morning, when she pounced on my bed and shook me.

I jerked out of dreamland with a scream.

"Easy, Zee," she said. "Where the hell were you?"

Not an easy question to answer. I could have been anywhere. My dreams were nightmares more often than not, but I never remembered the details. Probably a blessing. I gathered myself quickly. I'd learned to in the past decade.

"I'm fine," I said. "What is it? You know I like to sleep in."

"I know, but a huge delivery just came for you."

"Huh? I'm not expecting anything."

"All I know is that it's here, and your name's on it."

Curiosity won out over sleeping in. I scrambled out of bed and slid my bare feet into slippers. "It's probably a mistake."

Sure enough, two boxes—one large, one small—sat on our tiny table, and both were addressed to me.

I grabbed a steak knife out of the flatware drawer and cut the small one open first. Inside was a shoebox. "Oh!" I opened it and found my shoes from last night, the heel now repaired.

"What is it?" Mo asked.

I lifted out the shoes. "The heel I broke. Reid said he'd have it repaired."

"That's some quick service."

"Sure is. I guess money talks."

Mo giggled. "If that's your shoes, what can possibly be in the big one?"

"Wait," I said, picking up a note. "It's handwritten."

Good as new. Looking forward to our dinner tonight.

Reid

"What's it say?"

I handed the note to Mo.

She scanned it. "Hmm. I'm getting more of those third-wheel vibes."

"How?"

"He says he's looking forward to his dinner with you."

"Yes. It'd be impolite to say he wasn't looking forward to it. This is a basic note."

"I think I shouldn't join you."

"Yes, you should," I said. "I want you there."

The thought of dining alone with Reid Wolfe scared the hell out of me.

Mo giggled. "If you say so. Now open the big one!"

I slid the steak knife under the packing tape and flipped the cardboard box open. Inside were packing peanuts, which I hated. They got everywhere!

They didn't stop Mo, though. She pawed through the

peanuts until our floor looked like snow had fallen and pulled out another shoebox. "Louboutins!"

"What?"

She shoved the red box in my face. "Louboutins! In your size! Oh my God." She pulled out another box. "Prada! And Jimmy Choo!" She waved her hands in front of her face. "This is total shoe porn!"

I wrinkled my forehead. "What?"

"Look at these!" She opened the Louboutin box and picked up a cotton bag. "May I?"

"Yeah. Sure." My mind had turned numb. What was going on?

She pulled out a pair of black stiletto pumps. "Gorgeous! And that red sole is to die for!" She threw one to me.

Oddly, I caught it instinctively.

"Try these on. They'll be amazing on you."

I regarded the four-inch heel. "They'll make me six feet tall."

"So? They're spectacular."

I slid my feet out of my slippers and into the Louboutins. They were a little tight, but no more so than any new shoe. I wobbled a little, but I'd get used to the skinny heel. I could walk in anything, thanks to my years as a showgirl.

"Wow," Mo said. "You already have great legs, but those shoes make them even more amazing!" She continued pawing through the boxes. "There's at least five grand in shoes here."

My eyes shot wide. "Five grand?" I gulped.

"At least. Probably closer to ten."

"Is there a note?" I asked numbly.

"Looks like... Yeah, here it is." She handed me an envelope.

My fingers trembled as I broke the seal and pulled out a note card.

A few more things for your pretty feet. Enjoy.
Reid

I handed the note to Mo.

"He's not really a poet, is he?" she said. "Not that it matters with his looks and bucks."

My jaw dropped to the floor. I couldn't accept these. Repairing my second-hand shoes was one thing, but this? The man spent ten grand on my feet, which weren't even pretty, by the way. They were too big, and my little toes were crooked.

"I so wish we wore the same size," Mo was saying, "so I could borrow all of these."

I didn't reply.

"Hello? Earth to Zee?"

I shook my head to clear it and picked up my jaw from the floor. "I'm sending them back. I can't keep them."

"Why not?"

"Because...I don't even know the guy. And he..."

He wants me to tell my story.

That was the truth. Reid Wolfe wanted something from me, and he was trying to buy me.

Problem was? I wasn't for sale. At any price.

Plus, unlike Mo, I didn't care much about shoes and clothes. Sure, these shoes were beautiful and I'd love to have them, but even if I could afford them, I wouldn't buy them for myself. One pair, maybe. But five? No way.

Mo was drooling over the Jimmy Choos when I walked—still in the Louboutins—to the small kitchenette and shoved a K-cup into the Keurig. Coffee. Coffee would help me see clearly. Right now, my mind was a screwed-up mess.

The machine whirred as it squeezed out coffee into my favorite mug. I took a cautious sip, making sure I didn't burn my tongue. Then I walked the few steps back to where Mo was trying on the Jimmy Choos.

"Too big." She sighed.

"Bet you never thought you'd wish for bigger feet." I couldn't help a chuckle.

"I'm only a size smaller than you are," she said, "and at the moment, you're right."

"You're a size and a half smaller," I reminded her.

"I could stuff the toes."

I laughed. "You would. But no deal. They're going back."

She shielded the boxes with her body. "Shh! They'll hear you!"

I rolled my eyes as I removed the Louboutins. Oddly, I felt a little sad to take them off and see them go. These shoes probably represented three months of my income, and my feet seemed to feel the loss. I placed them back in their bag and nestled them into the box once more. Then I checked the delivery carton. The return address was Golden Personal Shopping.

Of course. Reid Wolfe used a personal shopper. Not that I thought for a minute that he'd gone in search of women's shoes. Still, though, to see the evidence of a personal shopper bummed me out a bit.

I wasn't sure why.

"Sorry, Mo." I handed her the Jimmy Choo box. "Back they go."

"Goodbye, my pretties." Mo removed the pumps and placed them back in their box. "You're a meanie," she said to me.

"If you want a box of shoes, you can snuggle up to Reid tonight at dinner. I'm sure he'll be happy to oblige you."

"Ha! He's clearly already smitten with you, if this"—she gestured to what she called shoe porn—"is any indication."

Smitten with me? I held back a slight smile at the thought. He wasn't smitten. He only wanted something.

Which was why I hated the fact that a small part of me wanted Mo to be right.

10

REID

A hundred million.

That was what Wolfe Enterprises would have to pay to get this contract back on track.

Some meeting.

I was pissed.

Really pissed.

Rock had already flown back to New York, and though he was the CEO, he had given me authority to do whatever was necessary to get things moving as we were already losing millions per day because of contractor issues.

I could sue.

Indeed, I wanted to sue, because this contractor had screwed up. Why should we pay the price? But as a businessman, I knew a lawsuit would ultimately cost us more money. Some system, huh?

My father taught me one thing very early in the game. When you had money, people would constantly try to take advantage of you. The trick was to pay them off if it would ultimately cost you more money in the long term. Then never do business with them again.

Las Vegas Ace Construction was now on my short list.

Wolfe Enterprises had a lot of business in Nevada, and after this current project was over? LVA would never get another penny of it.

Rock had been holding out. He'd been a loner too long. A rebel too long. He didn't understand that sometimes, it made more sense to pay than to fight.

He wouldn't be happy, but I had the authority, and in the end, Wolfe Enterprises would come out on top, and Las Vegas Ace would pay.

Yeah, the Wolfes had a lot of power.

I'd watched my old man destroy one business after the other once he'd gotten what he wanted out of them.

LVA was next on that list.

"Fuck it all," Rock said, when I told him the news. The jet was an hour outside New York, and Rock and the others were in flight when I called.

"You gave me the power."

"I did," he admitted. "It's a fucking shitload of cash, though, man."

"Cash we can well afford, and LVA will get what's coming to them."

Silence for a few seconds, until, "I still can't quite wrap my head around how much we're all worth."

"I get it. One day, you will, and you'll see I made the right decision here. There are still some kinks to work out of the deal. I'll be here for a few more days to make sure it all goes as planned."

"Thanks, Reid. This should be your show. Don't think I ever forget that."

"I know."

Our father's snub still stuck in my gut, but he'd taught me

another valuable lesson when I was starting out. *Don't ruminate on things you can't change.*

Good advice, coming from a psycho bastard.

"So Rock..."

"Yeah?"

"Nieves says she has information for us."

He scoffed right into my ear through his phone. I could see his face in my mind, green eyes rolling and all.

"She says she found something at your place that she never told you about."

"She's lying."

"Is she? Did you have anything that might indicate your relationship with Dad?"

"Are you kidding? I tried to never think about the asshole."

"Think," I said. "Did you notice anything missing from your place recently?"

"Nieves and I broke—" He stopped abruptly.

"What?" I demanded.

"She and I broke up a while back, but my gun—the same model that killed Dad—was stolen."

Bingo. "You think Nieves might have taken it?"

"I'm trying to remember. We broke up, but she showed up from time to time. I didn't think anything of it. We ran in the same circles."

"Was she ever alone at your place?"

"No. Not that I know of, anyway."

"What does that mean?"

"Fuck."

His tone reeked of defeat. I wasn't going to like what was coming.

"She had a key. She gave it back to me after we parted ways, but..."

"But...she could have had a copy made."

"Yeah."

What were you thinking? I wanted to demand of my brother. But the fact was, he hadn't been thinking about Dad at all. He all but admitted he tried never to think of the bastard. Most ex-girlfriends weren't mercenaries, so he didn't bother changing his locks.

Made perfect sense.

Except we were all fucked now because of his little faux pas.

"She never had the combination to my gun safe, though," Rock said.

"Okay, that's good. But think. Did you put the gun back in the safe the last time you went to the shooting range?"

Silence.

He wasn't sure.

Fuck.

"I'll take that as a no."

"Fuck, man. It's not a no. But the thing is, I just don't remember."

"Shouldn't you always replace a gun in the safe?"

"Of course, if you have small children around. Or you fear someone living with you might be suicidal. But I lived alone, Reid. I wasn't going to blow my own head off, so I didn't worry about shit like that."

My mind raced. "So she could have taken your gun. But we already know your gun wasn't used to blow Dad's head off. It was just the same model."

"Right, so who cares if she took it?"

"Well, *you* should."

"I do. She's a conniving little shrew. But the fact that my gun is missing doesn't implicate me any further, because it's not the murder weapon."

"No, you're the only one with a seemingly ironclad alibi."

"What do you mean seemingly?"

"The cops still think you could have had it done."

"Why would I do something so stupid as to have it done with a gun that's a duplicate of mine?"

"Good point. Honestly, I'm not sure why they haven't ruled you out. Something's fishy about all of this."

"It has been from the get-go, bro."

"I know."

"Honestly, Nieves could have taken my gun. Or she could have taken something else that I have no clue about."

"I'll find out at lunch." I glanced down at my watch. "In fact, I have to go. I'll check in with you later."

"Sounds good."

I ended the call and shoved my phone in my pocket.

Time to turn on the charm once more to get what I wanted.

11

ZEE

After I got the shoes all packed up and lugged the damned package to the post office—and paid twenty-plus bucks in postage, thank you very much, Reid Wolfe—I headed into work early to have some repair work done on my costume. Several of the opulent beads had come loose during the last show, and that was a recipe for disaster.

Beads falling off and rolling on the floor while we're all dancing in stilettos...

Not good.

Tonight was a topless night for me. We took turns baring ourselves. That way, we all knew all the dance moves for all the parts and could substitute for anyone with no notice. Revue shows like the one I was in were a dying breed in Las Vegas. Sure, topless shows were available in smaller venues in the city, but our show, *Best of Sin City*, was one of the last large revues that featured nearly a hundred showgirls. Celebrities like Donny and Marie Osmond and Celine Dion, among others, were taking over the biggest venues and drawing huge crowds, making traditional Vegas shows a thing of the past.

Consequently, I was lucky to have this gig. Many showgirls

weren't so lucky and had resorted to stripping and lap dancing at local clubs. Each night, I thanked the stars that I had this job. I didn't know how to do anything else. My childhood foray into acting had proved I was no actress, and my modeling days were long over. My medical career had gone up in dust years ago. I was just too old. Too old, too tired, and too scarred.

Topless nights no longer bothered me. My scars were well hidden with creative makeup and costuming. Plus, the bright lights on stage made the leering men invisible to me, if they even existed.

I was, simply, grateful to be alive, even as the wreck I'd become.

"Good thing you came in," one of the seamstresses said to me. "This needs to be taken in anyway. You've lost an inch around the waist."

"I have?"

"Yeah. Have you been eating?"

Hmm. Had I? No, I hadn't. Not really. Only the barest sustenance since that PI for the Wolfe family had found me.

"Well," I said, instead of answering her question, "I don't think any woman alive worries about taking *off* a few pounds."

"You should," she said. "You dancers are all muscle. If you lose weight, you lose muscle."

Not in the mood for a lecture, thanks. I didn't reply.

I sat at my dressing table—not mine, actually, the dressing table I shared with several others, though none of them were in yet—while the tailor finished working on my costume, checking my phone, when the star of our show, Candice Hall, whisked by, cigarette in hand, leaving a mixture of smoke and Chanel hovering in the air.

"I need a seamstress, stat!" she yelled in her raspy voice.

Candice was known as a diva, but she was always nice to us

dancers. She'd started as a showgirl on the line herself. But she talked terribly to the tailors and makeup artists.

"Be with you in a minute, Ms. Hall," the woman working on my outfit said.

"That can wait," Candice said. "This ribbon on my sash is nearly threadbare. I want it replaced before the seven o'clock show." Then she turned to me. "Hello..."

"Zee," I said. "Zara Jones."

"Yes, of course. How are you doing today?"

Loaded question, for sure, but she didn't know it. "Fine. How are you?"

"Ugh. I'm so sick of these costumes. They may as well be second-hand. Have you ever seen anything so ridiculous?" She nodded to the garment she'd thrown at the seamstress.

What was I supposed to say? My costume was fine. But then, I wasn't the star of the show, either. Candice was gorgeous—auburn-haired and tall with amazing hazel eyes—and talented to boot. And though I'd never been sexually attracted to women, I wouldn't kick her out of bed. She had the most gorgeous pair of breasts in the show. More importantly, she was an amazingly talented dancer and singer. She deserved her stardom, and I respected her, especially since she'd worked her way up from the chorus line.

"I need a bottle of Evian, please!" she called to anyone listening.

"I have some water." I offered her my bottle.

"Thank you, but I only drink Evian." She smiled. Then her lips curved slightly downward. "Are you all right? You seem a little...distracted."

"I'm fine." I forced a smile.

Like I said, Candice was always nice to us, but we knew she really didn't want to hear our life stories. Not like I'd tell her mine, anyway. No one knew. Except, of course, the Wolfes.

"Ready for you, Miss Hall," another tailor finally said.

She huffed. "It's about time. Nice seeing you, Sara."

"Zara," I said, "but everyone calls me Zee."

"Zee. That's cute!" She waved and was on her way.

Back to my phone. Except I didn't have any messages or emails. Not overly surprising, since I basically had no friends other than Mo and my other roommates, and we were more friends by circumstance.

Except I'd been hoping...

In the back of my mind...

That I'd have a message from Reid Wolfe.

12

REID

Nieves ordered the Dover sole Beaujolais, the most expensive item on the menu.

Not surprising. I didn't really care, as long as she gave me something useful. I feared, though, that the "thing she found" at Rock's place was his gun, which wasn't going to help me at all.

Still, it was worth a grand and an order of Dover sole to find out.

I slid an envelope containing ten crisp Benjamins toward her. She opened it and pulled out the bills.

"Really?" I said. "You're going to count the money at the table?"

"You gotta know when to hold 'em and when to fold 'em." She winked.

"That makes no sense at all." I shook my head. "This isn't a game."

"Everything's a game." She quickly counted out the bills and stuffed them back in the envelope. Then she stuffed the envelope into her bra.

Nice touch, though I no longer found her as attractive as I

had when I'd fucked her in New York. Sure, I was going to bed her last night, but now? I was just as glad I hadn't. She was hot, no doubt, but I had someone else on my mind.

I took a drink of my water to soothe the dryness in my mouth. Too much drinking last night. Then I lifted my eyebrows, saying nothing.

"You have to ask," she said.

"I don't *have* to do anything."

"If you want to know what I know, you have to ask."

"I just paid you."

"Pretty please?"

"Fuck it all." I raked my hand through my hair. "Tell me, Nieves. What did you find at Rock's place that you never told him about?"

She smiled. "You think I'm going to say his gun, don't you?"

"I think I don't have a clue what you're going to say, and I wish you'd end the suspense."

"I did see his gun," she said, "but I didn't take it."

"Fine. What *did* you take, then?"

"So, it wasn't so much that I took something as much as it was that I erased something."

"What's that supposed to mean?"

"Rock was kind of old-school," she said. "He still had an answering machine and insisted on using it instead of the voicemail on his phone."

Somehow, that didn't surprise me. My oldest brother had done everything he could to escape his upbringing. Going old-school fit right into that mold. "So you heard a message and erased it."

"Yes."

"What did the message say?"

"You should already know."

I let out a heavy sigh and rubbed my forehead. "You're giving me a migraine, Nieves. What the fuck is that supposed to mean?"

"It means," she said, "that the message I intercepted was from you."

"And...?"

"And what?"

"What the hell did the message say?"

"You can probably tell *me*."

"No, I can't. I hardly ever called my brother, and when I did, it was usually just to check in. I was the only one who communicated with him with any kind of regularity."

"Except for that one time."

I seriously thought about pulling my hair out, strand by strand. She was making me that crazy. "*What* one time?" I said through gritted teeth.

"It was a few weeks before your father died. Sure you don't remember?"

Seriously, I wanted to tear my hair out chunk by chunk. Scratch that. I wanted to tear *her* hair out.

"At the risk of repeating myself"—clenched teeth again—"I do not remember, Nieves."

She smiled sweetly. "Good thing I transcribed it, then." She fished a small piece of paper out of her purse. "Here you go."

I snatched the paper from her with more force than necessary and unfolded it.

Hey, Rock, it's Reid. A hit's been put out on Dad. We're looking into it. Thought you might want to know. Call me.

My eyes popped into circles. The hell?

"You fucking made this up, didn't you?" I darted knives at Nieves with my eyes.

"No, I didn't. I swear to God. Look." She pointed to the paper. "I even wrote down the date and time."

She had. It was a little over three weeks before the murder.

"Interesting. Except I swear to God I never said any of this, and I'll be able to prove it easily."

"Oh? How do you think you'll do that?"

"Ever heard of phone records? I'll be able to prove I didn't call Rock's landline on that date and time."

Her lips curved downward slightly, but I wasn't buying. Nieves Romero wasn't stupid. Any good mercenary was never stupid. She knew about phone records, so she didn't invent this little scenario. She actually intercepted the message, which meant someone had impersonated me.

"Too bad you didn't save the message," I said. "Then we could easily prove it wasn't me with voice identification."

"I've heard your voice. It sure sounded like you."

"You hadn't heard my voice three weeks ago," I said. "It's doubtful you'd recognize the difference between a recorded message that you heard three weeks ago and talking to me in person now."

She didn't reply. I was right, and she knew it.

"Why didn't you tell Rock?" I demanded. "Don't you think he had the right to know about the message?"

"I was going to tell him," she said, "but then…"

"Then what?"

"I talked to Leta. And we decided that…"

"For fuck's sake. You decided to try to make some money off the deal. Am I right?"

She looked down at her place setting. Yeah, I was right.

One thing about a mercenary, you always knew where to find him.

Just follow the money.

"Time to 'fess up," I said to her. "We know you received a phone call about the murder an hour before it actually happened, so there's something you're not telling me."

She sighed. "How much more is this information worth to

you?"

I stood and pulled out my wallet. "You're seriously trying to get more than the extra nine grand? This meeting is over."

She gasped and darted her gaze around the room. "Reid, sit. Please."

Good. I sat. "Get to the point, Ms. Romero. You've admitted to breaking into and entering my brother's home. You've admitted to stealing."

"I didn't steal anything!"

"You stole a message from his answering machine. Trust me. My lawyers will make it stick."

She looked down again.

"I can have you and your sister arrested and thrown in jail, and I *will* do it if you don't start leveling with me."

"All right. All right." She sighed. "Leta and I developed a plan. I know about phone records, of course. I'm not an idiot."

I rolled my eyes. I agreed she wasn't an idiot, but I couldn't help myself. I was *that* pissed off.

She opened her mouth, but her phone chose that second to vibrate against the white table covering. She looked down. "Sorry."

"Go ahead." Heck, I'd waited this long. I could wait a little longer.

She picked up her phone and answered it. "Hello."

Pause.

She widened her eyes and gasped. "Oh my God! What hap— I mean— Oh my God!"

Pause.

Tears formed in her eyes. "I'll be there as soon as I can. Thank you. Oh my God..." She ended the call and stood. "I have to go."

"What's going on now?" I didn't even try to disguise the impatience in my voice.

"It's Leta. She's in the hospital in Helena."

"Why? What happened?"

"She was beaten to within an inch of her life." Nieves closed her eyes and two tears squeezed down her cheeks. "This is... It's all my fault."

"What the hell is going on, Nieves?"

"I can't. I can't do this. Look what it's already cost my sister!"

"Wait, wait, wait... You think Leta was beaten up because you're talking to *me*?"

"Of course I do! And because *she* talked to you. We had a whole plan. We did. We thought every detail out. We..." She crumpled back into her chair and laid her head on the table, tears falling slowly onto the covering.

I wasn't an unfeeling person. Not at my core. But this? I had no sympathy for her. I didn't wish pain on Nieves or her sister, but they'd fucked with dangerous people, and this was the result.

"Nieves," I said, "there's only one way out of this mess."

She lifted her head far enough to meet my gaze. "What's that?"

"You need to level with me."

13

ZEE

My costume, now sized correctly and with no loose beads, hugged my body. My tits stuck out like two cereal bowls thanks to invisible strapping tape. Unlike some of the other girls, I hadn't done any enhancements. First, I couldn't afford any, and second, I had a pretty good pair of breasts thanks to nature. But as any woman would tell you, with nature's bounty comes nature's gravity. Breasts aged, and they weren't as perky as they were when I was eighteen. Enter tape.

I'd gotten used to it. My skin no longer reddened from the adhesive. No more tape rash. Just another day's work.

An hour until showtime.

This was my least favorite time of the day. We had to be fully costumed and ready to go so the tailors and makeup people could tend to Candice and her understudies. So here we stood, decked out and uncomfortable with nothing to do. We didn't dare sit down. Our costumes might tear. We didn't dare eat, as even the slightest amount of food could cause our waistlines to expand...and our costumes might tear. We couldn't even take off our uncomfortable stilettos, because we'd have to bend down to put them back on and—you guessed it—our costumes might tear.

Like I said, my least favorite time. The hour ticked along like a month. Once we got on stage, things got better.

Between the seven o'clock show and the ten, we were in the same situation. No sitting, no food, no taking our shoes off, but at least Candice and the understudies weren't hogging the dressing area and staff. They had to be available for everyone, because costume problems happened during every show. Some girls pulled a ribbon off just to be able to sit down during this time. I'd done it more than once. The trick was not to do it too often. Just enough so they thought it was a true issue that had occurred during our numbers.

At the moment, though, Mo and I stood together, not talking much. She was topless tonight too, and she looked great. Unlike me, Mo'd had an augmentation a few years ago, and it was one of the best jobs I'd seen. Not all the girls were so lucky.

"Zee..." Mo finally said.

"Hmm?"

She sighed. "You sure it's okay if I come to your dinner date tonight?"

"I've told you. It's not a date. And yes, I really want you to come." *Really, really.* Because if she didn't come, I wasn't sure I'd be able to resist Reid Wolfe's charms.

And I needed to resist them. I couldn't tell my story to the police. I just couldn't.

She smiled. "If you're sure."

"I wouldn't have invited you otherwise."

"Ten minutes to showtime, girls!" the director's assistant yelled.

We heard him easily, as we weren't allowed to talk above a whisper during this time.

Mo smiled and walked swiftly toward her place. I followed. I was in the back line because of my height, and that was fine with me. We weren't supposed to stand out, and we didn't, but being in back meant I didn't stand out even more.

Good, good, good.

I never wanted to stand out again.

I was pretty sure my modeling days had led to...

Yeah, and never would that happen again.

I took my place and listened as the band tuned up.

Then I pasted a smile on my face as the curtain rose.

How many shows had I done? I'd counted once, but that was over a year ago. I didn't even have to think. My feet knew exactly what to do, my legs how high to kick. Our line was so in sync that we'd been compared to the Rockettes on more than one occasion. In fact, the famed chorus line had stolen one of our girls within the last two months.

I had no Rockette aspirations myself. They were too well known. I didn't want anyone looking that closely at me.

Kick! Then shuffle ball change. Kick again, other leg this time.

I was on autopilot, and I never missed.

The show went off without a hitch, and when intermission came, I was allowed a few sips of water. Just enough to stave off dehydration. Too much, and we'd bloat, which wasn't good for the costume. Wasn't good for how it made us feel either, but the director was only concerned with how we looked, of course. Not how we felt.

My ankle was still a little sore from my ordeal with the grate last night, but I'd danced on much worse. This was nothing.

Our twenty-minute intermission always flew by quickly, unlike the hour pre-show and the hour and a half between shows.

In a seeming instant, I was back on stage, smile pasted on, executing high kicks once more.

≈

SECOND SHOW OF THE NIGHT. For some strange reason, I always had more energy for the ten o'clock show. Adrenaline, the director said. The adrenaline stayed with me until about two a.m. on show nights. Just as well, since I had dinner plans afterward tonight.

Thank goodness Mo was coming along.

Right now, Reid Wolfe was somewhere in the audience. Once more I was thankful for the bright lighting that kept us from seeing anything other than shadows in the theater. I had no doubt that if I could see faces, Reid's would stand out.

His image was seared into my mind.

He was easily the best looking of his brothers. Rock was rugged and sexy, and Roy had that boho look you'd expect from an artist. Plus, he was almost too pretty to be real.

But Reid...

Suave and debonair to the max. He looked like he'd walked straight off the pages of *GQ*. Always dressed to the nines, hair perfectly swept across his forehead, full lips and perfect white teeth.

And those blue eyes.

He reminded me of the model David Gandy, only better. I'd never known anyone who could surpass David Gandy.

Until now.

Funny. I hadn't memorized any man's looks in ages. Well before...that horrible time. Sure, I noticed good-looking men, but I wasn't moved by them.

Until now.

Reid Wolfe scared me.

He made me want to bare my soul. Indeed, he asked me to tell my story publicly.

It wasn't so much that *that* scared me.

It was that he made me want to.

14

REID

"Nieves," I said, "*there's only one way out of this mess.*"
She lifted her head far enough to meet my gaze.
"*What's that?*"
"*You need to level with me.*"

She hadn't. She'd run off in tears to tend to her sister in Helena, promising to call me as soon as she knew Leta was all right.

What could I do? Tell her not to go? I'd run to my own sister in a second if she needed me. Especially now, since I hadn't been there for Riley when she *had* needed me. All those years... Roy and I never knew. In fact, we'd been envious.

Reality had a way of kicking you in the nuts. Big time.

The ten o'clock show of *Best of Sin City* was about to begin. Terrence had gotten me the best seats in the house. God himself only knew what he'd paid for them, but that didn't matter. I was a fucking billionaire.

Jazzy music from the pit, and then...

Up went the curtain.

I found Zee instantly. She was in the back, but still she stood out. And wowza. What a body! And those high kicks!

And...

Fuck me.

Those *tits*.

Big and luscious and her nipples were bright red. Yeah, it was probably makeup, but damn... Already I was hard.

Seducing her wasn't going to be an issue at all. So I wasn't a huge fan of the black hair. The rest of her was fucking perfect.

My gaze never left her for the entirety of the show.

I'D TEXTED Zee earlier to meet me at the theater entrance after the show was over. I expected to wait a while, as she needed to change out of her costume and all.

She was earlier than I expected...and she had a friend in tow.

Zee wore black skinny jeans and a royal blue silk camisole. I never noticed clothes on a woman, but this ensemble was perfect with that black hair. Her lips were painted red, and all I could think about was her red nipples during the show.

Damn. I wanted to bite them. Really badly.

"Good evening, Zee," I said.

Her cheeks pinked. "Hello, Mr. Wolfe."

"Reid."

She nodded and then cleared her throat. "Reid, you remember my friend Maureen. Mo."

"Nice to see you." I took the hand Maureen held out.

She blushed and smiled with mega wattage. "My pleasure, Mr. Wolfe."

This time I cleared my throat. "Reid. Mr. Wolfe is that bastard who died."

Maureen's eyes widened a bit. Had my words been too crass? Probably. Within seconds, though, she was back to smiling.

Zee looked down at her feet. "I invited Mo to come to dinner with us."

Fuck. Really? How was I supposed to seduce the woman when she had a friend tag along? I could tell her our reservation was for two—truth—but as a Wolfe, I could change that easily with no problem at all.

I forced myself to smile. "How nice. I'm sure she'll be a lovely addition."

Mo's smile dazzled at my words, and her cheeks blushed further. "I'm so glad you feel that way. I didn't want to be a third wheel."

"Of course not." *Except that you are, but no matter. I've seduced women in the middle of crowds before.* This wasn't anything I couldn't handle.

"Where are we dining?" Mo asked.

"Here," I said, "at the Mosaic."

Four eyes widened at me. Yeah, the Mosaic was posh and expensive.

"I've never been there," Mo gushed.

"Have you, Zee?" I asked.

"No." She didn't meet my gaze.

"Then you ladies are in for a treat. Please..." I held out both of my arms.

Mo linked her arm through mine right away. Zee was little more timid, but soon her hand rested on the inside of my elbow.

"It's not often I get to escort the two most beautiful ladies in the show to dinner," I said in my best Wolfe of Manhattan voice.

Mo giggled. Zee stayed silent.

The maitre d' greeted us when we entered the restaurant. "Mr. Wolfe! So wonderful to have you with us tonight."

I disentangled my arm from Mo's and went for my wallet. I pulled out a hundred and handed it to the man. "We're going to need a table for three instead of two."

"Not a problem at all, Mr. Wolfe." He slid the bill discreetly into his jacket pocket. "Right this way, sir."

We followed him to the back of the restaurant where a private curved bench booth had been set for two. "Only a moment, and we'll have another place setting for you."

"Thank you," I said. Then, "Ladies?"

Mo and Zee slid onto the curved bench. Nicely done. Now I could choose which one to sit next to, which, of course, was no choice at all.

I slid in adjacent to Zee.

The additional place setting appeared within about ten seconds, and then the sommelier arrived.

"Do you have any questions about our wine list, Mr. Wolfe?" she asked.

"I'm afraid I haven't had the chance to peruse it yet. We just got here."

"Excellent," she said. "If you do have questions, my name is Eleanor, and I'm at your service." She bowed slightly and then left us alone.

I was used to obsequiousness in restaurants. The servers were all out for Wolfe tips. The thing was, they didn't have to kiss my ass. I always tipped well for good service. That was all I ever expected.

My old man used to like having his ass kissed.

All this time, I'd known he was a bastard. Never in a million years, though, had I considered that he might be a psychopathic criminal as well.

What he'd done to this woman next to me...

She was so strong. She didn't even know how strong she was.

She turned to me, still with red cheeks. "Thank you for...for having my shoes repaired."

"You're very welcome. It's the least I could do."

"But the other stuff," she continued. "The other five pairs. I'm afraid I couldn't accept them."

"Of course you can. I want you to have them."

"I'm sorry. I've already shipped them back to the return address."

My stomach dropped. Why did I care so much? I'd sent out a personal shopper with Zee's shoe size on a whim. This shouldn't bother me.

But it did.

"I told her she was nuts," Mo said.

"You'll have to excuse Mo," Zee said. "She's a shoe whore."

Zee's description shocked me a little, but Mo brushed it off.

"I admit it," she said. "I love shoes, and those were some beauties."

"It was very generous of you," Zee said, "but it was just too much."

"I'm sorry you feel that way." I picked up my menu. "What are you ladies in the mood for tonight?"

Nice save, Reid. Why was this bothering me? I'd sent the shoes as a way to woo Zee, but now I realized I truly wanted her to have them. Why?

Was it because...?

Guilt? Guilt for what my father had done to her?

Maybe, though what he did wasn't my fault in any way. If Roy and I had known what he was doing all those years, we would have stopped it. Tried our damned best, anyway.

But as Riley told us, he most likely wouldn't have let us.

Derek Wolfe held all the power.

No longer. The bastard was dead and cremated. but his partner in crime—Father Jim—was still very much alive.

And Zee could identify him.

This dinner wasn't going to get me into Zee's head or into Zee's bed. She'd seen to that by inviting Mo along.

I couldn't blame her, honestly. She was scared. It was written all over her face.

"I'm in the mood for a giant hunk of lasagna," Mo said and then sighed. "But I'll probably have the braised cod with lemon."

I glanced over the menu. "I don't see that option."

"It's not on there," she said. "It doesn't have to be cod. Tilapia is fine. Or sole."

"Sole?" Nieves had ordered the Dover sole at lunch, though I'd had to cancel her order when she left abruptly after getting the call about Leta.

"Any kind of white fish," Mo said. "Zee and I are on strict diets."

"Not tonight," I said. "The sky's the limit. You ladies order whatever you'd like."

"And then we'll have to deal with Tiger tomorrow," Mo said.

"Who's Tiger?"

"She's the choreographer. I swear the woman can see one extra ounce on our bodies."

"Do you agree, Zee?" I asked.

"I agree about Tiger," she said, "but Mo knows I don't stick to her diet as strictly as most of the girls do."

"Zee is lucky. Nothing ever changes on her gorgeous bod."

"You both look amazing to me," I said.

Mo giggled and blushed. Zee stayed silent and blushed.

"Seriously," I said. "I want you both to order what you want. Even if you only take a few bites. Take the rest home in a doggie bag and have few bites each day until it's gone. You've got to live a little sometimes."

"Actually," Zee said, finally meeting my gaze, "I couldn't agree more."

R eid's eyebrows nearly shot off his forehead, which didn't surprise me. Of course my words shocked him. They shocked me as well.

I wasn't sure where they'd come from.

Mo was a stickler for our strict diet, but she was right. I was not. I'd been starved during my modeling years. I knew hunger, and it wasn't pretty.

So never again. Not that I overindulged much, but I never starved myself.

"I'm glad to hear you say that, Zee," Reid said. "What looks good to you tonight? Or do you want to wait to hear the chef's specials?"

I picked up the menu and scanned it quickly. "Cedar plank salmon. Salmon is my favorite fish."

"Salmon is wonderful," Reid agreed, "but it seems like a red meat kind of night."

"I don't eat a lot of red meat."

"Why not?"

"Never had the taste for it." True story. It just wasn't my thing.

"Fair enough. Salmon it is. And you, Mo?" Reid asked.

"I'm afraid I'll be going with the cod with lemon."

"As you wish. I'll see that the chef prepares it to your specifications."

Eleanor appeared tableside. "Just checking in, Mr. Wolfe."

"I'm afraid I haven't glanced at the wine list yet, but I'm in the mood for a red Burgundy tonight. Just bring me your best bottle. How does that sound, ladies?"

"Lovely," Mo gushed.

"I know very little about wine," I said.

"It'll go nicely with your salmon," Reid replied.

"Red wine? With fish?"

"Oh, yeah. That old only-white-with-fish thing is a myth."

"I agree," Eleanor said. "I have a lovely aged Burgundy that will enhance anything on our menu. Thank you, Mr. Wolfe." Again, she bowed slightly.

Finally our server came by for our cocktail order. Reid declined for all of us, saying we'd already ordered a bottle of wine. The server—Jason—left red-faced and embarrassed.

"I feel bad for him," I said.

"He should have come around before the sommelier," Reid said. "He's late, and he feels guilty. Rightfully so."

"Rightfully so?"

"Yes. The server should take the cocktail order before the sommelier offers wine. Wine is more traditionally drunk with dinner." He perused the menu again. "Do you ladies want an appetizer tonight?"

"Goodness, no," Mo said.

"Zee?"

"You know what?" I said. "I do. I'd like to try the Maryland crab cakes."

"Your wish is my command."

~

DINNER WENT SMOOTHLY, mostly because Mo dominated the conversation, which was, of course, why I'd invited her in the first place. I wasn't a good conversationalist.

But that was far from the only reason I'd invited her.

I was scared to death of being alone with Reid Wolfe.

He looked so much like his father. Yes, I knew in my head that he *wasn't* his father. But somewhere deep inside me I couldn't escape the fact that this man's father had abducted me, hunted me.

And now I was attracted to his son.

So unreal. What the heck was wrong with me?

Jason—who'd been extremely attentive since his earlier faux pas—appeared tableside with dessert menus.

Mo waved him away. "I couldn't possibly."

Yeah. She'd eaten about a third of her plain fish with lemon and half of her broccolini.

"I'll take a look," Reid said. "Zee?"

"I'll always look." I took the menu Jason handed me.

"The pastry chef has prepared a special dessert tonight as well," Jason offered. "Chocolate crème brulée with raspberry coulis."

My stomach growled, despite being full. I was a sucker for anything chocolate and creamy.

"Sounds amazing," Reid said. "Zee, see anything you like?"

I'd already thrown caution to the wind, so an eight-hundred-calorie dessert was definitely off the table. "I guess I'll pass."

"You sure?" Reid asked.

"No. It sounds wonderful, but I do have to fit into my costume tomorrow."

Reid smiled. "Bring me the special," he said to Jason, "with two spoons."

"Of course. Coffee?"

Mo and I declined.

"Yes, black please," Reid said.

Mo stood. "If you'll excuse me, I'm going to use the ladies room."

No. You are so not leaving me here alone with Reid. I stood as well. "I'll come along."

"I'm totally envious," Mo said in the ladies room as she freshened her lipstick. "He can't take his eyes off you."

"You're imagining things."

"Are you kidding me? I may as well be invisible."

I regarded my reflection in the mirror. I'd always been attractive. I wouldn't have been able to try making it as a model otherwise, but I had scars, both visible and invisible.

The invisible ones were worse, to be honest.

When I saw myself in the mirror, I didn't see beauty.

I saw pain.

I saw brokenness.

I saw scars.

I saw someone trying to hide under garish black hair and darkened eyebrows and lashes. My natural hair color was dark blond, and my eyebrows and lashes were dark brown.

How long had I been hiding?

So very long.

Maybe it was time to pull my head out of the sand.

Maybe...

Maybe, in the morning, I'd make an appointment with my stylist.

Maybe I'd have her bleach the black out of my hair and then give me something close to my natural blond.

Maybe I'd throw away my black eyebrow pencil and mascara.

Maybe...

Or maybe not.

"I think I'll make a quick getaway." Mo pressed her lips together to distribute her gloss.

She shocked me out of my thoughts. "No. Please. Stay."

"He's obviously into you. I'm just in the way."

"You're selling yourself short, Mo."

She sighed. "I wish I could agree, Zee, but I'm not. His gaze hasn't left you all night. Whatever he wants, you've got it."

I had it, all right, but it wasn't my looks. It was a story. A story that could shed light onto who his father truly was. A story that could take the focus off Reid and his siblings...

...and onto me.

I hadn't killed Derek Wolfe. I'd been here, in Las Vegas. Though I didn't have an ironclad alibi, because the show was dark that night. But I could easily prove I hadn't made any trips to New York. I didn't own a gun. In fact, guns scared the hell out of me.

This wouldn't fall on me, no matter what I did.

Still, I didn't want to be dragged into the middle of the Wolfe family dysfunction. Hadn't I been through enough at the hands of a Wolfe?

"...so attracted to you."

Again, I jerked out of my thoughts.

"Sorry, what?"

"I've never seen a guy so smitten," Mo said.

"Smitten?" Smitten meant...well, smitten. Reid Wolfe might find me attractive, might even like me as a person, but smitten? No. He simply wanted something from me.

Not that I didn't want to help him and his siblings, especially Riley. I'd watched her modeling career since she came on the scene. Though modeling never interested me as much as it did my mother, I admired those who did well. Riley Wolfe was the best.

She seemed the most real to me of all of them, almost as if she understood. But how could she? Surely Derek Wolfe never hunted his own daughter.

"Please don't go," I said to Mo again.

She nodded.

We left the ladies room and headed back to the table, where Jason was setting down the chocolate crème brulée Reid had ordered. I slid into the booth, and—

"Thank you so much for including me tonight, Reid," Mo gushed, "but I just got a phone call and I have to go."

My jaw dropped. *Seriously, Mo? You just lied to me?*

Reid stood and gave her a chaste kiss on the cheek. "You're most welcome. I enjoyed meeting you."

Mo whisked away, fingers pressed to the spot Reid had kissed, and was gone in a flash before I could even stand.

Reid sat back down quickly and smiled. "Alone at last."

My stomach fluttered.

I was in big trouble now.

16

REID

Finally.

Finally, I could begin to work my magic on the lovely Zee. I tapped my spoon on the burnt sugar topping of the crème brulée and spooned a modest portion. Then I held it to her lips. "You first."

Her cheeks reddened, but she parted her lips and licked the cream off my spoon.

My groin tightened.

Damn.

She was so sexy, and she had no fucking clue.

I wanted her badly.

"So?" I asked.

"It's delicious."

A smudge of chocolate lay on her upper lip. I leaned in closer, closer...almost...

She backed away abruptly.

"You just have a little..." I brushed the chocolate off with a finger, wishing I were licking it off instead.

"Oh." Embarrassed again, she dabbed at her lips with her napkin.

I stared at her for a few timeless moments. She was really quite lovely. Her face was a perfect oval and her chin was slightly prominent, giving her an aristocratic profile. Her eyes were big and blue and long-lashed, her nose perfectly aquiline. And those lips. Full and pink and luscious.

"Zee..." I began.

She lifted her eyebrows.

"I'm dying to kiss you right now."

Her eyes widened, which of course didn't surprise me.

What *did* surprise me were the words that had just come out of my mouth. I never asked a woman if I could kiss her. I never even mentioned it. I was a doer. When I wanted to kiss a woman, I did it.

Zee was different, though. I got some signals from her, but I also knew what she'd been through. Even though my original intention had been to seduce her, I was having second thoughts.

And third thoughts and fourth thoughts.

I had faith in my ability to seduce any woman, but for the first time, I wondered if it was really the right thing to do.

It was an odd feeling—considering someone else's needs.

It disturbed me a little, though I supposed it shouldn't.

Was I more like my father than I wanted to admit? Not the rape, incest, and murder part, of course, but the "I'll have what I want at all costs" attitude.

For the first time, I wanted to go slowly with a woman.

Unfortunately, time was not in my favor at the moment. Slowly really wasn't an option. My family needed Zee. *I* needed Zee.

But she had needs as well, and they might not align with ours.

She didn't reply to my statement. Just stared down at our dessert.

"I'm sorry," I said. "I tend to say what's on my mind."

She paused a moment. Then, "I'd be lying if that thought hadn't occurred to me as well."

My heart jumped. Funny. Normally I'd be all over this, but now? "You seem like you're not ready to go there, and I want you to know that's okay. I'll never push you into anything."

Damn it all. I meant every word I said.

If she was never ready to go to the police with her story, I'd live with that. I'd find some other way to exonerate my siblings and myself.

"I believe you," she said.

She was right to. I wasn't lying.

Then, "About the shoes."

"That was presumptuous on my part," I said. "I don't blame you for returning them."

Man, I was being so unlike Reid Wolfe. And it felt... Good?

Yeah, it felt good. Considering someone else's needs felt damned good, especially someone I cared about.

I liked Zee. I really did. And though I knew I wasn't responsible for my father's actions, I felt guilt for what he'd put her through. I wanted to make up for it.

"Listen," I said, "if you need anything—I mean *anything*—I'm here for you. I know you've been through hell at my father's hands, and if I could erase it all, I would. I wish I could."

"I'm the lucky one," she said softly. "I never forget that. There were other women there. Other women who didn't escape."

Wow.

Like literally, the word "wow" was audible in my head. All she'd suffered, and her thoughts were with the others who hadn't made it out of my father's twisted maze.

Wow.

Without thinking, I covered her hand with mine. "I know. I'm going to make sure they all get justice."

"How can you? Your father's dead."

"But the other guy isn't. I'm going to see that he pays for what he did to you and those countless others."

"The other..." She gasped softly. "He's still..."

"Yes. And there may have been others as well. Do you remember anyone other than those two that you signed the non-disclosure agreement with?"

"It's hard to say. Those two were always together, but I think... I think there might have been others."

"If you can remember what they looked like, or whether anyone called them by a name..."

She shook her head. "I'd help you if I could. I'd love to see all of them go down."

"Does this mean you'll tell your story?"

She paused another instant. "I didn't know the priest was still around."

"He is."

"Then, I... I really should, shouldn't I?"

I squeezed her hand slightly—only slightly, so as not to frighten her. Yes, I wanted her to tell her story. But I ultimately wanted what was best for her, even if it didn't align with what was best for me. Surprising, but no less true.

"It's up to you, Zee. As I told you, I won't push."

17

ZEE

He seemed so sincere.

And God, he was so gorgeous!

Sitting here next to him stirred up emotion in me that I'd thought was gone forever.

Then...about my story... I hadn't thought of the priest. Derek Wolfe was always the leader of the hunt, but the other one... Father James, who'd given me my first communion. Did he remember me? When he looked at me, did he see that eight-year-old girl in a white lace dress? He signed the document I signed. The settlement covered both of them.

He was still around, according to Reid.

He could be caught. Tried. Convicted.

If—*and only if*—I told my story.

How easy it would be to tell Reid I'd cooperate. Then to let him kiss me if it was what he truly wanted. It certainly was what *I* wanted.

I hadn't wanted to kiss a man since long before...

His hand on mine felt good. Like the comfort of a warm blanket on a cold afternoon. As if it were a barrier to the stormy weather.

As if he would protect me.

Part of me wanted to look into his beautiful eyes and tell him I was there for him. That I'd tell my story.

And part of me—that part between my legs—wanted to tell him to kiss me. *Yes, please kiss me, and then take me home with you.*

I wasn't ready for the second part, no matter how much my body pleaded with me.

But the first part?

Could I?

Finally, I said simply, "Thank you. For not pushing me."

"You're welcome." He scribbled his signature on the check and shoved his credit card back into his wallet. "Shall we?"

"We didn't finish dessert," I said.

He smiled—and oh, it was a dazzling thing to behold. "Please, then." He nodded toward the dessert.

I kind of wanted him to feed me again, but it dawned on me that he hadn't yet tasted the chocolate deliciousness. I gathered my courage and dug my spoon into the cream. Then I held it to his lips.

He closed them around the crème brulée, swallowed, and then licked his full lips.

And yes, I imagined that tongue on my flesh.

On intimate parts of my flesh.

He then took another spoonful of the dessert and held it to my mouth.

We spoon-fed each other until the crème brulée was gone.

I'd never experienced anything so intimate in my life.

Feeding each other. Silly, right? Maybe it was the dessert that was so ridiculously decadent. Or maybe it was the fact that a handsome man was feeding me.

But honestly?

The intimacy came from the bond I didn't realize I'd formed with Reid Wolfe.

I wasn't ready for it. Maybe never would be.

But it was there, and it was as real as anything in my life.

His gaze burned me with hot blue flames. I couldn't be imagining this intimacy.

Could I?

I patted my napkin to my lips. "Thank you for dinner. I haven't eaten a meal so good in a long time."

"You're welcome, Zee." He smiled that dazzling smile once more. "I enjoyed myself."

"I'm sorry about..."

"About what?"

"About dragging Mo along. The truth is she wanted to meet you. And I didn't think this was a date or anything. I mean, I know it wasn't a date, and I—"

He touched his fingers to my lips to stop my babbling. For that was what I was doing. Nervous babbling.

"I enjoyed meeting your friend"—he dragged his finger over my jawline, making me shiver—"but this *was* a date."

My cheeks grew hot. Really hot. I didn't want to think about how red they undoubtedly were.

"I'd like to see you again while I'm in town," Reid continued.

"I'll... I'll be working."

"I know." He continued his path with his finger, letting it meander onto my neck. "My loss."

"I'm... You know... Free in the morning." Already I wanted to smack myself. I slept in each morning. Much needed sleep.

"What about breakfast tomorrow, then?" he said.

"Maybe brunch would be better."

"Brunch would be great. The Wolfe has a wonderful brunch buffet. I'll send a car for you at, say, ten?"

"All right." I grabbed my phone. "That should work well. I want to try to get in with my stylist sometime before my call."

"Your call?"

"Not a phone call," I explained. "A call means what time a person has to be at the theater for a show."

"Got it," he said. "Ten it is, then. Expect a car at your place, and when you arrive we'll enjoy the Wolfe's famous brunch."

"I... That sounds...nice." At least I didn't stutter.

"Are you ready, then?"

I nodded. He slid out of the booth and then offered his hand. When I took it, warmth slid through me. Warmth coupled with sparks of energy.

This had been a date in his eyes. A date.

I'd just had a date with a billionaire. A billionaire who wanted something from me, yes, but a billionaire who also said he wouldn't push me.

I liked him, so I chose to take him at his word.

I hoped very much I wouldn't regret it.

18

REID

The limo pulled in front of Zee's building, and I walked her to the elevator.

"I told you, that thing hasn't worked in—"

I pressed the button, and the elevator whizzed to life.

Her eyebrows popped upward. "What's going on?"

"I made a phone call earlier today. No more climbing all those stairs, though for a dancer I'm sure four flights aren't anything."

We rode up to her floor and then walked to her apartment. She fumbled in her purse, and when she found her key, I took it from her.

"I don't think I'm ready to say goodnight yet," I said.

She reddened, the rosiness so lovely in her cheeks.

I slid the key into the keyhole and unlocked the deadbolt. "But I think you *are* ready to say goodnight, so goodnight, Zee." I handed the key back to her.

She shoved it in her purse, and then she met my gaze. "Maybe I'm not ready to say goodnight either."

This time I lifted my brows. "Oh?"

"You said..."

"Yes?"

"I'm... I'm not inviting you in. I mean, I share a bedroom with Mo. And I'm not—"

I touched her lips softly to stop her. "I'm not asking for anything like that."

She slid her tongue between her lips, inadvertently touching my finger.

And damn, I got harder than ever. I moved my hand away quickly.

"What *are* you asking for, then?"

"Just this." I leaned in and brushed my lips lightly over hers.

She stumbled slightly, and I steadied her, gripping her shoulders. Had I gone too far?

Funny, this tiny kiss had me turned on all the way down to my toes. I was hard as a fucking rock for her. Just being near her. Just kissing her lightly. Man, what would happen when she let me slide my tongue between her lips?

Between her legs?

Just the thought had my dick pulsing inside my pants.

"I... I have to go in."

I nodded and turned the doorknob. "Goodnight. The limo will be by for you at ten."

"Thank you. And...goodnight." She leaned toward me and brushed her lips over my cheek. "Goodnight," she said again and then disappeared through her doorway like a flash.

The spot where she'd kissed my cheek stayed warm as I rode back to my hotel.

AFTER DEALING with the boner Zee had left me with, I sat down at my computer. It was nearly two a.m., but we had people working around the clock, and I wanted to see what Rock's phone records showed.

First things first, though. I reserved a spot for brunch at ten thirty.

Then, onto business.

Sure enough, a phone call had gone into Rock's Montana landline at the exact date and time Nieves had recorded.

And—

I gulped.

It had come from *my* business landline at the office.

I had *not* made that fucking call.

Which meant...

Someone who had access to my office had.

The call had come in during the day. Okay, easy enough. Where had I been that day? I traveled frequently, so there was a good chance I hadn't even been in New York, in which case I could easily prove I hadn't made the call.

I wrote a quick email to Terrence for him to check my whereabouts on the date and then rattled off another email to my siblings about the findings.

We hadn't had any idea our father was about to be murdered. If we had? I don't know what we would have done, but we hadn't known, so the question wasn't of any consequence.

Unfortunately, I still needed the rest of Nieves's story. I'd asked Rock to contact her, as he knew her better than I did, but I hadn't heard yet if he'd been successful. She was no doubt tending to her sister at the moment.

Who next?

Rock's biker friends, Hoss and Manny, came to my mind. Rock had sworn they were good guys, but I wasn't buying. They both skated between the lines of good ethics, especially Hoss.

We'd already established that. I had a hunch they were involved in this mess more than we knew.

Then of course, there was Father Jim.

Disgusting and psychopathic Father Jim.

Obviously, he couldn't be ruled out. Derek Wolfe had no doubt taken care of him over the years, but was the priest in a position to order a hit?

A hit cost money.

A *lot* of money.

Even more money to make sure several parties could be implicated, which had happened.

Father Jim might have had my father's contacts, but would he have had the required money?

I didn't know.

We'd already checked his financials. He made a modest income as the priest of St. Andrew's, but we knew better than to take that at face value. He probably had money hidden somewhere. Our PIs were looking into it.

Did Father Jim even have a motive? Dad had taken care of him all those years. Why would he want to off his meal ticket? And his ticket to both of their repulsive appetites? Surely Jim couldn't continue the "hunt" on his own.

Nausea crept up my throat.

How had we all been so blind to what our father was truly capable of?

Rock and Riley hadn't been blind.

Molesting our sister was horrible enough. None of us had foreseen what he was ultimately capable of.

Zee.

Sweet and beautiful Zee.

One of my father's many victims, and the only one—that we knew of—who had lived to tell the tale.

The tale we needed her to tell.

I'd said I wouldn't push her, and I meant it. Oddly, my siblings, especially Riley, didn't want me to push her either. I'd planned to seduce her and get what I wanted.

But those plans had gone to hell when I realized that...

I sighed.

That I liked her. I cared for her. I didn't want to do anything to make her uncomfortable. My father had already done enough to her for ten lifetimes.

I wasn't used to feeling this way. I loved women. Loved seducing women. Bedding women. But I'd never been *in* love. Women had always been playthings for me, and most of them were okay with that. I wined and dined them, and all was good.

Until Zee.

Zee, who refused my gift of expensive shoes.

Most women—at least the women in my circles—wouldn't have.

Zee was clearly *not* most women.

And I liked that.

I liked that a lot.

I yawned as I shut down my computer. I didn't need a lot of sleep, but it was time to call it a day. I had a meeting at eight with the contractor, and then I had brunch with Zee two hours later.

I brushed my teeth, undressed, and slid between the satin sheets of my king-sized bed.

Wishing a certain showgirl were snuggled up next to me.

19

ZEE

y stylist wasn't answering. I shoved my phone back into my purse as the limo navigated the streets of Las Vegas, delivering me to my brunch with Reid.

I'd slept well, which surprised me. No nightmares. No tossing and turning. And even though my alarm went off earlier than usual, I awoke with energy and a smile on my face.

Very unlike me.

I wasn't complaining. Reid Wolfe had kissed me last night. A sweet kiss. A kiss that said, "I won't push you."

I'd searched the internet a few times in the last couple days. Reid had no shortage of beautiful women at his disposal, most of whom probably jumped right into bed with him.

In truth, part of me wanted to do just that.

He was gorgeous, but I'd met many gorgeous men who wanted me. As a showgirl, I was pursued often. I always said no.

Reid was a billionaire.

Pretty cool, but if anything, that was a turn-off for me. I had nothing against money—I wished I had a lot more of it—but money couldn't change what had happened to me at his father's hand.

No, his looks and money weren't why I was interested.

I was interested because he was kind to me. I knew he wanted something from me, but he wasn't pushing me. Of course, he could be playing an elaborate game. I was far from naïve, mostly thanks to his father.

The limo dropped me off, and I hopped out, navigating my way into the lobby and then through the casino of the grand hotel to get to the restaurant for brunch. Reid stood, dressed casually and looking yummy in dark blue jeans and a white button-down, waiting for me. His blue eyes brightened when he met my gaze.

"Morning," he said.

"Good morning."

He grabbed my hand—tingles shot through me—and led me into the restaurant.

"Mr. Wolfe," the hostess said, "your table's all ready."

Once we were situated and our server had taken our drink orders, Reid smiled.

"How are you today, Zee?"

"Good, I guess."

"You guess?"

"Yeah. I was hoping to get in with my stylist today before my call, but she isn't answering her line."

"Oh." Reid picked up his phone and punched in a few numbers. "Hi there. This is Reid Wolfe in Suite 2700. I need a salon and spa appointment right away."

My eyes shot wide.

"Right. No, not for me. For a Ms. Zara Jones. An hour? Perfect." He ended the call. Then to me, "You're all set. Here at the salon and spa. Right after brunch."

My jaw dropped. Seriously, I almost had to pick it up off the table.

Finally, I found my voice. "I can't afford anything here."

"You don't have to. It's all on me. I do own this hotel, after all."

My mouth dropped open again.

"I know, I know," Reid said. "I'm being presumptuous again, right?"

"A little."

"I get it. You wouldn't accept the shoes, and I understand, but I want you to look at this a different way."

"How exactly is that?"

"My father put you through hell, and I want to help make up for it."

"But—"

"Please. I know nothing can make up for what he did to you. But let me try. Please. I need to."

"I… You don't have to. I…got a settlement."

"And if I know my father, he gouged you on that too."

"I didn't want much. Just enough to pay for the rehab and to start over somewhere new."

"You should have asked for the world. You had him over a barrel."

"I…"

"I'm sorry." He took my hand. "That didn't come out how I meant it to. I realize what he put you through. How much courage it took to ever look at him again. You're strong, Zee."

"I'm not," I said, staring at my menu.

"Look at me."

I met his gaze. His eyes were so beautiful. And so kind.

"Let me help. I need to. I know giving you things doesn't make up for what he did to you. What you'll always have to live with. But it's all I have, and I want to do it."

His hand was so big and so warm. I felt comforted—comforted in a way I hadn't felt since…

Maybe ever?

I certainly never got comfort from my mother. When she couldn't live out her showbiz aspirations through me, she kind of wrote me off. My father was never in the picture. I couldn't pick him out of a lineup.

Just when I was going places, had my college all set up...

Derek Wolfe had happened.

Then my spiral into drugs.

When I'd finally seen the light, I'd gone to Derek Wolfe. I'd had no choice. I needed money to pay off my rehab debt and start anew.

The sad fact? Reid was right. I should have asked for more. I could have gone public with my story. I could have ruined Derek Wolfe.

Why hadn't I?

I remembered so little about the actual negotiation. Derek had an attorney, of course, and I didn't.

Somehow, I got talked into...

It was all a muddle. I tried not to think of certain times in my life, and that was one of them.

"Okay," I finally said.

"Okay...?"

"I'll go to the appointment."

A wide smile lit up his face, making him even more gorgeous. "Great! Four hours for whatever you want. Hair, nails, facial, massage. You name it."

"I'm not sure I have four hours. My call's at three."

"Then you can go back another time for the rest."

"It's all very generous of you. Thank you."

Reid started to say something, but our server interrupted him.

"Are you ready, Mr. Wolfe?"

Reid gestured to me. "Zee?"

I quickly scanned the menu. I hadn't really given it a look. "I'll have the yogurt parfait, please."

"That's all?" Reid asked.

I smiled. "After I overate last night, it's all I can afford today. I have to fit into my costume tonight."

He didn't push. "I'll have the eggs benedict with a side of fresh fruit."

"Very good." The server rushed away.

After our coffee cups had been refilled, Reid's phone buzzed. "I'm sorry. I have to take this. Do you mind?"

"Of course not."

"Thanks. Excuse me." He rose and walked outside the restaurant.

A few seconds later, my own phone buzzed. My stylist, Cheree. No doubt returning my call about an appointment.

I didn't answer.

I already had an appointment.

And truth be told, I was looking forward to it.

Reid returned fifteen minutes later, and our food arrived. We didn't talk a lot as we ate. Reid seemed preoccupied.

"Is everything okay?" I finally asked.

He swallowed his bite of food. "Nothing for you to worry about."

"I'm not worried. I mean...you just seem a little different. Was that phone call bad news?"

"Not really."

He didn't sound convinced, though, and I didn't believe him. "Can I help?"

He regarded me, his gaze serious. "Maybe."

Uh-oh. I'd walked right into that one. He was going to ask again that I tell my story. I felt like I was going to puke all over my yogurt.

But I'd offered. "How?" I asked.

"Looks like I have to get back to New York earlier than expected. Can you come with me?"

Say what?

"No. Why would you need me to?"

"Zee," he said, "you're the only one who knows about my father's extracurricular hunting activities."

I gulped. "Yeah...but you said..."

"That I wouldn't push. And I won't. Neither will my brothers and sister. But something has come up in the case, and we need you now more than ever."

"Reid, I—"

"I'm leaving this evening. I want you to come with me."

"My show..."

"Do you have any PTO?"

"Paid time off? Yeah, but they like a little more than an hour's notice."

"I can take care of it for you."

"You don't know my director."

He smiled. "Your director doesn't know *me*."

I had no answer for that. He was no doubt right. The Wolfes made things happen on a daily basis. He might pay off my director. We had subs who were available at a moment's notice. This could definitely happen.

Still, I had a work ethic. This wasn't me.

"I'm not asking you to take time off for a luxury cruise or something," Reid continued. "This is important. My family is at stake here. One of us could go down for something we didn't do."

"I don't know, Reid."

"If you say no, I'll let it drop," he said. "But please, Zee. Please."

"It means a flight in our private jet," I prodded.

Then I wanted to punch myself. Money and luxury didn't matter to Zee. A simple life where she was safe and comfortable did.

That was the weapon I needed to use.

"Look," I said. "If you come, and we can get the other guy who hurt you behind bars, you won't have to be afraid anymore."

She still didn't look up at me.

Time to give up. I cared for her, and I'd promised I wouldn't push.

"Never mind." I forced a smile and squeezed her hand. "I understand. I'm sorry I have to leave so soon. I was hoping we'd get to spend a little more time together."

"I'd have liked that."

"Me too." I let her hand go and took a sip of coffee.

"I suppose..."

"What?"

"You don't want me to go to the spa appointment now."

Was she kidding? "Zee, of course I want you to go. It's a gift.

It's nothing compared to what you've been through with my father. Please. Go. I want you to go."

She nodded. "Okay. Thank you again."

"Don't mention it."

"When are you leaving?"

"This evening. Five p.m."

She nodded again.

If you change your mind... The words hovered on the tip of my tongue. I wanted her to change her mind, but not for the reasons she was thinking.

I wanted more time with Zee. Wanted to get to know her better.

Wanted to get her into bed, for sure, but if that didn't happen, I was okay. I actually didn't mind the idea of going slowly with her.

Not on brand at all for the Wolfe of Manhattan.

Really weird.

But I'd promised her I'd let it drop if she said no.

We finished our breakfast, and I signed the check. Then we stood and left the restaurant. I brushed my lips over hers. "Enjoy your appointment."

"I will. Thank you again."

She headed away, following the signs to the salon and spa.

My gut ached when I realized I wouldn't see her again before I left.

And maybe not ever.

I SAT ON THE JET, which was parked at one of the private terminals at McCarran Airport. The pilot was awaiting final instructions from the air traffic controller, when my phone buzzed with a text.

Zee's number.

I changed my mind. May I still come?

My heart jumped as I lunged out of my seat and ran into the cockpit. "Captain," I said to the pilot. "How long do we have?"

"About twenty minutes until we'll be cleared to leave the gate, but that could change."

"Great. We may have to delay. We're going to have another passenger."

"I've already filed the flight plan, Mr. Wolfe."

"I know, I know. I'll take care of the paperwork. Hold tight, will you?"

I quickly texted Zee.

Yes. Where are you?

At the airport.

Perfect. If she was already here, we could definitely make this work.

I had to buy a ticket, her text continued. *They wouldn't let me through security without one. I'll send you my flight information.*

I texted back. *Don't be silly. You'll fly with me. I'll send someone to escort you to the private terminal. Where are you?*

Heading toward my D gate.

Okay. Stay where you are. Someone will escort you to where I am.

I hastily made the arrangements and told the pilot to stand by. He didn't look too happy with me, but he nodded. He was well paid to be on call for our family.

My heart was pounding and my skin tingling like an adolescent schoolboy whose crush had just said she liked him too.

Really off brand.

She texted again. *How will I know if he's legit?*

Good question. Zee wouldn't go off with just anyone. She knew better from experience.

He'll have my number. Ask him to call me, and then ask to speak to me.

Okay.

Good. That seemed to work for her. No way would I let anything happen to her. That was why she was flying to New York with me and not on some commercial flight.

Ten minutes passed. The captain was updating the flight manifest and dealing with air traffic control. The flight attendants were seated, waiting for further instructions.

My phone buzzed.

"Mr. Wolfe, this is Ron James with airport security. I'm here with Ms. Jones. She'd like to speak with you."

"Yes, please put her on."

"Reid?"

Her voice. How happy I was to hear her voice.

"It's me," I said.

"So this guy's cool?"

"Yes, you'll be safe with him. He'll bring you to the jet. See you in a bit."

"Okay. Thanks, Reid. Bye."

I headed to the cockpit to let the pilot know our passenger was on her way. "She's in D concourse. A security guy is escorting her."

"That's about another twenty minutes, if they hurry," he said. "I'll update air traffic control."

"Thanks."

I conferred with the flight attendants quickly, ordering bottled water for Zee when she arrived.

The rest of the time passed slowly, as if I were a child waiting those last few days before Christmas.

Crazy, how Zee was affecting me.

Finally, she and her escort walked through the gate and onto the plane.

And my eyes nearly popped out of my head.

21

ZEE

everal hours earlier...

"Good morning, Ms. Jones," the receptionist at the salon and spa greeted me. "Have you had a chance to look at our brochure?"

"No, I'm afraid not."

"Mr. Wolfe said we're to give you whatever services you'd like over the next four hours." She smiled and handed me a paper. "Everything's listed here. Please let me know what you'd like, and I'll tell your stylist and therapist."

I raked my gaze over the brochure. "There aren't any prices listed."

"Correct. Mr. Wolfe has prepaid for anything you want."

"But I'd like to know..."

"He asked that we print up a list without prices."

"Why?"

She smiled again. "You'd have to ask him."

Because he didn't want me to feel like I had to choose something less expensive. I knew already why he'd done it. It was sweet, actually. He wanted me to have the services I desired without being constrained by price.

"So what looks good to you?" she asked.

"I definitely want a hair treatment. A color."

"The same color you have now?"

"No. I want to go back to my natural color, or as close as the colorist can get."

"What else?"

The sky was truly the limit. My only constraint was time.

"A manicure and pedicure?" I asked.

"Of course."

"That will probably take up all my time, right?"

"No. We have several staff members who can work on you at the same time, so you may choose something else. A Swedish massage, perhaps?"

I'd never had a massage before. Not even at Massage Avenue, despite the white lie I'd told Mo earlier. It always seemed too expensive and too decadent.

"All right," I finally said. "A massage it is."

"Anything else?"

"What else could I possibly have time for?"

"I'd recommend the salt glow before your massage. It will exfoliate all the dead skin cells from your body so the lotions can penetrate deeper. Also, our revitalizing facial. I believe we can fit all of that in."

What the heck? "Sounds great." I handed the paper back to her. "Let's do it."

"Absolutely. You'll be happy to know that Mr. Wolfe also added a generous gratuity for your services, so you won't need to worry about that when you check out."

Worry about that? I hadn't even considered the tip. For this number of services, at twenty percent, it would be outrageous. *Thank you*, I said silently to Reid.

A woman wearing a white coat led me to the locker room and provided me with a robe and slippers. Once I'd undressed, I sat in the "grotto" inhaling a lovely lavender aroma until another woman dressed in a white coat came for me.

"Ms. Jones?"

"Yes, that's me."

"I'm Eileen, your hair stylist. If you'll follow me, please."

We ended up in a private room. "This can't be right."

"It is. You've been booked in one of our solo suites. All your services will take place in here." She nodded toward a bubbling hot tub. "Feel free to relax in the tub between services."

This was ridiculously decadent. *Damn it, Reid Wolfe.* I didn't want to like him as much as I did.

I erased that from my mind. I'd never like someone just because he spent a boatload of money on me. I wasn't that woman.

"What can I do for you today?" Eileen asked, after I sat down in the chair.

"I want to go blond. It's my natural color."

"Not a problem. I'll have to bleach your hair to get the black color out."

"Yeah, I know."

"Don't worry, though. We condition thoroughly here, and your hair won't suffer any damage."

"Good."

"Take a look." She handed me a color chart. "Which color works best?"

Pretty crazy to consider. I hadn't actually seen my natural color in years, other than in my roots. I chose a honey blond, which was slightly lighter than what I imagined my natural color to be.

"Perfect," Eileen said. "Let's get started."

From there I was prodded and pampered for the next four hours.

By the end, I was blond again with glowing skin, freshly

waxed eyebrows in their natural brown, and fingernails and toenails painted a sparkly light blue to match my eyes.

I left the spa feeling brand new.

So brand new that I felt I might be able to tell my story after all. Especially if it would help Reid.

I had no alibi for the night of Derek Wolfe's murder, as my show had been dark. But I was innocent, even though I had a motive. I'd been here in Las Vegas. I wouldn't show up on any flight log, and I'd performed the night before and the night after.

I felt strong. Stronger than before.

Maybe I felt like *me* again. The Zee before all the turmoil. Looking in the mirror, I saw her. Tidbits of her before those horrible few days.

I inhaled and made up my mind.

I was going to New York.

REID STOOD, gawking at me. Did my new hair make that much of a difference?

"It's me," I said.

"I know. My God, you look beautiful, Zee."

"I should thank you. Your gift made it possible."

"But...why?"

I sighed. "I don't know. I guess I just wanted to look like myself again. Weird, really."

"You were gorgeous before, but now... Wow." He smiled.

How I loved that smile! When Reid smiled, I saw Reid. Not the son who looked so much like his father.

Just *Reid*.

That was who I wanted to see.

Two flight attendants—both gorgeous—fluttered around

me. "Anything to drink, Ms. Jones? Mr. Wolfe ordered bottled water for you, but would you care for anything else?"

"Bottled water is perfect," I said.

My massage therapist had told me to drink a lot of water today.

I was so relaxed. More relaxed than I'd been since…

It was the therapy, of course, but perhaps it was also the fact that I'd decided to go to New York. To tell my story. To help put away the priest and any others the authorities could find.

Perhaps it was being with Reid.

How was I falling so hard so quickly?

I never felt like this about men. In fact, I'd often wondered if I'd ever have a relationship. If I could ever be whole enough to.

Reid showed me to a lush seat and sat next to me.

"The captain says it's time to fasten your seatbelts," one of the flight attendants said. "He just got clearance to head to the runway."

The seatbelt had shoulder straps as well as a lap belt. Reid showed me how to adjust them.

"This is the safest jet you'll ever fly on," he said.

"It's beautiful." I gazed around at the lounge area, which included two long leather couches with plush pillows and blankets. I glanced at a door beyond. "What's through there?"

"The lavatories," he said, "and…"

"And what?"

He cleared his throat. "A bedroom."

"Oh." I looked down at my lap and fidgeted with the seatbelt buckle.

A bedroom. How many women had Reid Wolfe bedded in this jet? A lot. He was known as a womanizer.

Yet he'd been gentle with me so far. He hadn't tried anything other than a light kiss.

I wasn't the jealous type. I never had to be, as I wasn't interested in a relationship with any man.

Until now.

A lump formed in my throat.

Reid Wolfe.

The man most likely to *never* fall in love with me.

And I was halfway in love with him already.

22

REID

I couldn't take my eyes off her.

I forced myself to, though. Staring would make Zee uncomfortable, and I didn't want that.

Her blond hair cascaded over her shoulders. It was a few inches shorter, but still long and lush. Her cheeks glowed a natural pink, and her lips... God, her lips. Normally she painted them bright red, but now they were a soft pink, full and plump.

This was what she'd looked like when...

Hard as it was for me to go there in my mind, I had to. I had to remember what she'd been through at my father's hands. If I forgot, even for an instant, I might do something she wasn't ready for.

She'd freaked a little at my mention of the bedroom.

That bedroom had seen a lot of action. The norm for me was to bring a companion along on my business trips.

And we always joined the mile high club.

I was a lifetime member at this point.

I squirmed slightly, adjusting my boner without Zee knowing. At least I hoped she didn't know. That would freak her out even more.

As hard as I'd been for her before, I was even harder now. Seeing her the way she was meant to look...

This was the real Zee.

Not Zara Jones, but Zinnia Rehnquist.

Fuck.

I had to have her.

I *would* have her, one way or the other.

The plane taxied to the runway, and when it increased speed for takeoff, Zee grabbed her armrests.

A white-knuckled flier.

I covered her hand with mine. "Don't be nervous."

"I'm not."

"Your body language says otherwise."

"Oh, I'm not nervous about the flight."

"What, then?"

"It's not nervous so much as... Well, maybe it *is* nerves. I've made a decision that is going to change my life."

"The decision to go to New York?"

"Yeah. And to talk about...you know."

"You still don't have to."

"But...isn't that why you wanted me to come with you?"

Was it? Yeah, on one level.

On another level, I hadn't been ready to say goodbye to Zee.

I wanted to spend more time with her.

Funny, just a few days ago, I was ready to seduce her and use my womanizing charms—which were well tested—to get what I needed out of her.

Those aspirations were gone now.

I cared about this woman, and I wouldn't use her.

No matter how much my body wanted it.

~

WE ARRIVED at LaGuardia a little before eleven p.m. After we deplaned, my driver met us at the terminal.

"Home, James," I said to him.

His name wasn't actually James. It was Wayne. Now that I knew the truth about Father Jim, I vowed to stop the whole "James" thing.

Zee turned to me. "I need to book a room somewhere."

"That's not necessary. You can stay with me."

Her eyes widened.

"My place has three bedrooms," I told her. "I didn't mean…"

"I know," she said softly, though her demeanor negated her statement.

We arrived at the Wolfe building and I helped Zee out of the limo. "Thanks, Wayne," I said.

"Good night, sir." Wayne waved as he drove off.

Zee looked up and then stumbled into my arms.

I steadied her. "You okay?"

"This… This place…"

"Oh, shit," I said.

"I can't… I can't go in there."

"You remember."

"I ran out. Naked. A nice person helped me. And then…"

So much more to Zee's story than I knew. What had happened to her after she got away? I knew only that she'd gotten hooked on drugs and had eventually gotten through rehab.

That was something to be proud of.

"Do you want to tell me what happened?"

"I suppose I have to. I mean, that's why I came here, right?"

"You don't have to do anything you don't want to do. If you've changed your mind, no one, especially not me, is going to force you to tell us anything. I need you to believe that, Zee. I need you to trust that."

She nodded, still clearly nervous, her lips trembling.

"I also need you to trust that you *are* safe here. This is my building now, and I swear to God, I will never let *anything* happen to you."

My words surprised even me, and I meant them. I meant them with all my heart.

She nodded again. "Okay. Thank you."

"You have my word. Nothing will happen to you on my watch."

23

ZEE

My flesh was ice cold as Reid led me, his hand enclosed around mine, into the building, through the lobby, and toward a lone elevator that was in an alcove away from the other elevators.

He slid a key card through a slot, and the elevator arrived shortly. Then he slid the card into another slot once we were inside. "This goes straight to my place," he said.

"Do you *all* live here?" I asked.

"No. Just me. Rock will, eventually, but the penthouse where my father lived is still a crime scene."

"Where do Roy and Riley live?"

"They both live in other buildings, not too far from here."

"Why don't they live here?"

"Roy didn't want to, and Riley... Honestly, I don't know. I'm surprised my father didn't want her here, close to him."

"Why would he?"

"How much has she told you?" he asked.

"Not much. Just that you were all abused by him. Your father."

"I can't tell you her story," Reid said. "But if you ask her, I think she'll level with you."

I could already imagine what Riley had suffered, and I didn't like where my mind was going.

When the elevator door opened right into a living area, Reid said, "This is the second to top floor. The penthouse is at the top."

My stomach was jarred from how quickly the elevator had ascended. I felt a little queasy from the ride...and also from being here with Reid.

His place was huge and spacious, decorated in masculine black and green. I wanted to look, to take it all in, but I followed Reid.

He carried my small bag—I hadn't brought much—to a door and opened it.

I gasped. "Is this where you want me to stay?"

The room was huge and decorated in soft pastels. So unlike Reid Wolfe. A king-sized bed was covered in what appeared to be pink satin. Fluffy pink and white pillows lounged over it. The dresser and chest were white lacquer, and the window... Such a gorgeous view of the city lights. Nothing like the glitz of Las Vegas. The Manhattan skyline wasn't as colorful but was spectacular in a classy way.

"Don't you like it?" he asked.

"It's lovely, but I have to say. I can't imagine you having a pink and white bedroom in your house."

"It's a guest room," he laughed. "My own bedroom doesn't have a sliver of pink in it, I assure you."

A guest room. Of course. For female guests. Which he probably had a lot of.

Jealousy speared its ugly head into my flesh.

What did I have to be jealous of? Reid wasn't mine. Would never be mine, no matter how attracted I was to him. I was a mess, and getting involved with the son of one of my tormentors wouldn't help me heal.

Still, I couldn't help getting snippy. "Not all women like pink, you know."

He lifted his eyebrows. "Of course they don't. I have another guest room." He picked up my suitcase.

I sighed. How immature I was being. Pink wasn't my favorite color, but I had nothing against it. He was offering me a place to stay in this amazing apartment for free.

"This room is fine," I said.

"You sure? There's another, but it's closer to my master suite. I thought you'd feel safer being farther away from me."

"Why would you think that?"

"You seemed so...apprehensive about being near me," he said. "I want you to feel protected."

"Actually," I replied, "I think I'd feel safer if I were closer to you."

He smiled. "Good enough." He picked up my suitcase and led me down a hallway to another door and opened it.

This room was decorated in black and white—the furniture was black lacquer, and the bedding was zebra-striped. I gasped again. The room was roughly the same size as the other, but the view was even more spectacular from here.

"Is this better?" Reid asked.

"This is fine. Thank you. Where's your room?"

"Right across the hall."

Curiosity rolled through me. What might Reid Wolfe's bedroom look like?

He set my suitcase on the floor and led me to the bathroom, which was even more decadent than I could have imagined. "There are robes in the closet for your use. Lots of shampoo and conditioner and body wash. Towels and wash cloths. Everything you'll need, and if there's something else you need, just let me know. Lydia can get it for you."

"Lydia?"

"She's my housekeeper. Head of staff."

Staff? "Oh. Okay." I imagined a shapely woman dressed in a black and white French maid's uniform.

"Just push this button." He indicated a pad on the wall that looked like an intercom. "Lydia will come."

"She's not here now, is she?"

"She's off duty, but the night maid is here. Her name is Monique."

Monique. Yeah, definitely the French maid mini-uniform with black fishnets. "I don't want to bother anyone."

"They're paid to see to my guests. It's not a bother. What do you need?"

"Maybe just some water."

"Not a problem." He pushed the button. "Monique?"

"Yes, Mr. Wolfe?"

"We have a guest tonight in the second bedroom. She'd like some water, please."

"Right away."

I was still mesmerized by the view when someone knocked on the door.

Reid opened it. "Good evening, Monique."

I turned.

And nearly burst into laughter.

Monique was lovely, but she was an older woman with silver hair à la Helen Mirren, and she wore black slacks and a white shirt. Hardly a French maid's uniform.

"Here you go, Mr. Wolfe." Monique held out a bottle of Fiji water.

"Thank you, Monique. This is Zee. She'll be here for a few days."

Monique nodded to me. "Ms. Zee."

"Just Zee is fine. Thank you so much for the water."

"My pleasure." Monique smiled. "Is there anything else?"

"No, thank you," I said.

"All right. Good night, then." Monique left.

"Please make yourself at home," Reid said. "If you need anything, just buzz for Monique."

"She seems very nice."

"She's the best. I only hire the best people." Reid smiled.

I returned his smile shyly. "Thanks for all this."

"You're very welcome. Get some sleep, and we'll talk in the morning."

I opened my mouth to tell him not to go yet, but the words stayed stuck in my throat as he closed the door behind him.

I was alone.

I hadn't slept alone in a bedroom for years.

Part of me was scared silly.

How long had I been in the room with no windows? Someone in a mask had brought me food five times now, but without a clock or daylight, my internal clock was all messed up.

The meals were good, oddly. Whoever had kidnapped me didn't want me to starve, at least not yet.

Strange.

I gobbled up every morsel each time they fed me. After all, I never knew if it would be the last meal.

I slept and I ate. I went to the bathroom. I washed myself in the small sink.

And I waited.

Waited to...

To what?

Women didn't get kidnapped to just exist in sterile rooms and be fed. Something would happen. Someone would eventually come and beat me. Or rape me.

Or kill me.

One of those things would happen. Probably all three.

I existed on edge. Eating the meals they provided and always frightened of what would come next.

Why? Why had this happened to me?

I was supposed to be starting college. Orientation week.

Parties and mixers. Classes and new friends.

All that I'd looked so forward to.

I'd stopped crying a few days before. I had no clothes, no tissues. Only toilet paper, and I needed to save that. I had no idea if they'd replenish it, and the thought of not being able to...

Yuck.

I simply existed. Existed in a perpetual state of fear, my flesh crawling with invisible fingers, my mind numb yet always racing.

Racing with all the torture that could be coming my way.

But when it finally came, what actually happened to me had never crossed my mind.

24

REID

I t was late, but I called Rock. "Any news on the Nieves front?"

"None," he said. "I've tried to get in touch with her."

"What's up with Leta?"

"She's still in the hospital," he said. "Someone knocked her around pretty good."

"Any idea who?"

"The guys are looking into it. She knows something, and someone doesn't want her talking."

"She's already talked."

"Right. That might be the problem."

"Maybe you should go back to Montana and check things out," I said.

He harrumphed. "No can do, brother."

"Why?"

"All of us, including Lace, have been told not to leave the state of New York."

"You've got to be fucking kidding me."

"Nope. I just got that news while you were in flight. I was going to tell you first thing tomorrow."

"How are we supposed to do our work?"

"Beats the hell out of me, but Morgan says they're close to making an arrest."

"Then we've got to move faster," I said. "Which we may be able to do."

"What do you mean?"

"Zee is with me."

Silence for a moment.

Then, "Did you..."

"Of course not!" I raked my fingers through my hair. "I've hardly touched her, and she came to me. She said she's ready to talk."

"Nicely done," Rock said. "And thanks. For not..."

"Do you all think I'm nothing but a complete asshole?"

"No. But—"

"You do." I sighed. "I guess I haven't done a lot to prove you wrong. I learned from the best."

"Hey," Rock said. "None of us thinks you're a carbon copy of Dad."

"Right."

"We don't. But you learned at his side, so business-wise, you're used to getting what you want at any price."

I couldn't deny his words. "Whatever. We need to find out who made that call from my office to your place in Montana. I swear to God it wasn't me."

"We all believe you."

"Do you?"

"Of course. Your ass is on the line just like all of ours. We're in this together, Reid. We have to trust each other."

"Good."

"Once Zee tells her story to Morgan, they'll search our building from top to bottom."

"And they won't care what they destroy in the process," I added.

"Right. So we need to find Dad's shit first. He may have destroyed the bottom floor after Roy saw it. Which means he and Father Jim found a new place."

"Right."

"Damn." Rock rubbed his temple. "We need to find out what that sicko priest is hiding. But Morgan is keeping us all busy with this nonstop questioning."

"Why exactly is he talking to all of us again?"

"I don't know. Like I said, he didn't really ask anything new. But he's got something up his sleeve. I can feel it."

I felt it too. It was like an icicle had dropped into my shirt and freezing shards were spiking into me all over.

Something was going down.

And it wasn't going to be good.

"All right. Let's touch base in—"

I jerked when someone knocked on my door.

Monique would use the intercom, so it could only be...

"Hold on for a minute," I said to Rock.

I walked to the door and opened it. Zee stood, her body clad in one of the lush white robes, her feet bare and toenails painted blue.

My dick hardened. Really hardened. She looked so innocent, especially with her new blond hair. How easy it would be to take her in my arms, kiss her, say the right words, and seduce her. Take her into my bed and fuck her slowly, get her used to me, and then take her hard and fast, pounding her body all night.

"Is everything okay?" I asked.

She nodded. "I wanted to..."

"What?"

"Say goodnight."

"Oh. Okay. Goodnight, Zee."

"Goodnight..." She didn't move.

I waited a few seconds. Then, "I'm on a call."

"Oh! I'm sorry. I didn't mean to bother you."

"You're not a bother. Something is obviously disturbing you. Is it the room? Do you want to go back to the other one?"

"No, I... I'm scared."

"This is the most secure building in Manhattan. I swear you're safe here."

"But it's still the building where..."

I inhaled deeply. "I know. Would you like me to have Wayne take you to a hotel after all?"

"It's so late."

"Hotels are open all night."

"I know..."

"Would you excuse me for just a minute?" I asked.

She nodded.

I walked far enough away that I could mumble into the phone without her hearing me. "Rock, I have to go. Zee is... I'm not sure, but I think she wants to stay in my room with me."

"Don't," he said.

"I won't. Which is why she can't stay with me. I need to take care of this. We can touch base in the morning."

"Good enough. Stay strong, bro."

I tossed my phone onto the night table and walked back to Zee. "Sorry about that."

"I'm sorry I interrupted your phone call."

"So...a hotel?"

"No."

"Then tell me. What can I do for you? What do you need? Anything."

"I want to stay with you."

Yeah, I nailed it.

"All right. Come on in. I guess I can sleep on one of the chairs."

"No, I'll sleep on the chair. I won't take your bed."

"I insist."

"No," she said. "*I* insist. You gave me a perfectly lovely bedroom. It's not your fault I can't be alone in this building. Besides, you're a lot bigger than I am. You'll be uncomfortable on a chair."

"Zee—"

She walked to my two oversized wingback chairs. "We can push them together. I'll be fine."

She wasn't exactly short, but she was shorter than I was. Still, she wouldn't be able to stretch out fully, and I wanted her comfortable.

"Take the bed," I said.

Good God, this was going to be a long night.

25

ZEE

Reid pulled extra blankets out of his closet and pushed the wingback chairs together.

I bit on my lower lip.

This wasn't right. He had two other beds only steps away, and I was making him sleep uncomfortably in his own home.

And the truth?

I wanted to be in the same bed with him.

Sure, I was frightened beyond everything of having a man that near to me, but my apprehension about this building seemed to supersede that.

Or did it?

I was attracted to Reid. More attracted than I thought I'd ever be to any man. Even though he looked so much like...

Even though he was his son.

What was wrong with me?

Just ask him. Ask him to sleep with you.

I opened my mouth. "Reid..."

"Yeah?" A yawn split his handsome face.

"This isn't right."

"It's fine, Zee. You need rest."

"So do you."

"I'll be fine. I don't need a lot of sleep, and I've pulled more all-nighters than you can imagine."

"We can both sleep in the bed," I said.

"Zee, trust me when I tell you that's a terrible idea."

"I...trust you."

"Then trust me when I say again what a terrible idea that is."

"Why?"

He shook his head, his hair an unruly and gorgeous mess. "Do I have to spell it out for you? I'm attracted to you. I've wanted you since I first laid eyes on you."

My heart beat double-time. Sure, he'd kissed me. Wanted to kiss me. But to actually say the words... "Did you think that maybe...?" I hedged.

"Maybe what?"

"Maybe I'm attracted to you too?"

He wrinkled his forehead. "Are you?"

"Who wouldn't be? But..."

"What?"

"You look so much like...*him*."

Reid pushed his fingers through his hair, making it even more disheveled and sexy. "I can't change who fathered me. I can't change my looks."

"Why would you? You're gorgeous."

"Jesus Christ." His fingers trailed through his hair once more. "Are you trying to drive me insane? Or does it just come naturally?"

His tone. It wasn't anger so much as...frustration.

I wasn't being fair to him at all.

Still...for some reason—even though he looked so much like the man who'd tormented me—I felt safe with him.

Safer than I had in a long time.

I liked the feeling, and I needed it.

"I need to feel safe," I admitted. "And I feel safe in here. With you."

He sighed. "Fine. We'll share the bed." Then he mumbled something else under his breath.

"Sorry, I didn't hear you," I said.

"Nothing." He curled his hands into fists.

He was so handsome, with his unruly hair, his shirt halfway unbuttoned, and—

My eyes widened.

His black trousers were bulging.

Chills erupted over me. I wasn't sure why I was surprised. He'd said he found me attractive. Still…

Before I could change my mind, I walked swiftly toward the bed and pulled down the comforter. Then I turned to Reid. "Which side do you sleep on?"

"That one," he replied.

"Okay." I walked to the other side. Beneath my robe I wore white pajama pants and an old Iron Maiden T-shirt. Nothing sexy that would entice him. I removed the robe and slid under the covers.

"For crying out loud," Reid muttered just loud enough for me to hear.

I closed my eyes. The softness of the mattress and pillows made me feel like I was nestling into a cloud.

The sounds of Reid getting ready for bed gave me comfort as I lay there, waiting for sleep to come. Then the movement of the bed as he lay down, and the change under my eyelids when he turned off the lights.

No reason to fear the dark.

Reid was next to me.

Reid would protect me.

I fell into slumber.

≈

"They're ready for you."

Strong arms yanked me out of my bed.

How long had I been here? In this room?

They're ready for you. *The words played in my mind.*

It was time. I'd be beaten up. Or raped. Then killed. Today would be the end of my life. I'd thought about it these several days I was here, being held captive but fed oddly well. Funny. I'd become numb to the concept.

Until now.

Now, I had to face it.

This would be my last day on earth.

There was no escape.

The person grabbing me was masked.

"Who are you?"

"Doesn't matter," he said.

"Where are you taking me?"

"You'll find out soon enough."

He led me through what seemed to be a maze of hallways. From the corner of my eye, I spied cages. Women in cages. "Who are they?"

"Not your concern."

I hadn't been kept in a cage. Was that a good thing?

God, no. None of this was a good thing.

Saliva pooled in my mouth as my throat got ready to explode. "I'm..." I heaved on the man's arm.

"Fuck you, bitch!" He let go of me to wipe off my puke.

And I ran.

Where? I had no idea. This place was a carpeted maze. Doors here and there, hallways shifting off in strange directions.

Find a door. Find an escape. Run!

But there was no escape. Each door seemed to lead nowhere, and I had no idea from which direction I had started.

I ran, tears blinding me. Until—

My body hit something hard and I fell to the ground with a thud.

"Another one got away, I see," a voice said. "I told you it's a mistake to feed them so well."

"No, Jim," said another. "What good is a hunt without strong prey? There's no challenge."

I panted, trying desperately to catch my breath. When I looked up, two blurred figures stood above me. Both dark-haired, and one...

Was he wearing a clergy collar?

Thank God!

"Father, help me!" I screamed.

The one dressed in hunting garb laughed. "You'll get some help, but not from us. You're definitely worthy prey."

Pray. That was a good idea. I squeezed my eyes shut.

Help me, God. Please! Our Father, who art in heaven...

Strong arms lifted me to my feet.

"Stop the blubbering," one voice said.

...Hallowed be thy name...

"Look at the body on her."

"Tall too. Long legs. Definitely worthy."

...Thy kingdom come...

They dragged me, my toes scraping the carpeting.

...Thy will be done...

A door slammed, and someone pushed me onto a steel table.

...On earth as it is in heaven...

"Let's get her ready."

...Give us this day our daily bread...

Something cold and hard touched my flesh.

...And forgive us our trespasses...

I screamed as something punctured me.

And I never prayed again.

26

REID

I jerked upward.

"No!" Zee thrashed in bed next to me.

I rolled toward her and grabbed her shoulders. "Zee! Wake up!"

"No! Don't hurt me! Please!"

"Zee!"

Her eyes popped open. "Help me!"

"Shh. It's okay. You're safe."

"No, please!"

I moved away slightly so as not to alarm her. "It's me, Zee. It's Reid. You're safe here."

Her eyes changed then. They were still wide but she turned and looked at me. "You..."

"Yes, me. Reid."

"Thank God." She rolled toward me and plastered her body against mine.

This wasn't going to help my hard dick.

"Thank you," she said. "Thank you for keeping me safe."

"You must have been dreaming."

"Yeah. It happens sometimes. Especially if I'm in a new place."

I caressed her soft hair. "I'm sorry."

"I'm okay now. I rarely remember the dreams. Thank you." She nuzzled my shoulder.

"Zee..."

"Please," she said. "Just hold me. It's been so long since I've been held."

So much for sleep tonight. I couldn't turn her down, but this was going to slowly kill me. How was I supposed to deal with the blue balls?

I wrapped her in my arms and gently kissed her forehead. "Easy. Go back to sleep."

She closed her eyes.

Mine stayed open.

All fucking night.

MY PHONE ALARM went off as scheduled at six a.m. Had I slept once Zee got settled, I'd have gotten a little less than four hours. Because I'd stayed awake all night, though, with a perpetual hard-on, I got zero hours. Not even a damned millisecond.

Zee slept soundly beside me. Even my blaring alarm didn't wake her. I eased away from her as gently as I could so as not to wake her and turned off the alarm. I rose and padded to the bathroom. At least I could jack off in the shower. I'd considered taking care of it in bed after Zee fell asleep, but then decided that was a little too creepy.

Yeah. Way too creepy.

So I'd nursed the balls of blue all freaking night, and now I still had an erection and couldn't even take my morning piss.

For God's sake.

I relaxed—or tried to—and finally got my dick soft enough to pee. Then I got in the shower and masturbated to Zee's gorgeous body, how she'd looked with those bright red painted nipples in the show.

Fuck, she was sexy.

I stroked my cock as the shower pelted me in warmth, and with each stroke, I imagined Zee's lips around me.

Yes, good. Really good. I groaned aloud, backing up against the shower wall. The shower had four heads, so no matter where I stood, water drizzled over me.

I closed my eyes. "Yeah, Zee, just like—"

"Reid?"

My eyes popped open as I dropped my erection.

Seriously?

"Zee"—I cleared my throat—"I'm kind of indisposed at the moment." *Thinking about you giving me a masterful blow job. Yeah.*

"I'm sorry. I woke up, and you were gone. I got kind of...scared."

"Everything's fine. I'm just taking a shower."

"Yeah, I figured that out."

"Which I usually do privately," I continued.

"Yeah..."

Except the expected sound of the door closing with Zee's departure didn't happen. In fact, even with the shower noise, I heard her breathing. The glass doors were coated in steam, but still I saw her—a blur in white.

She was breathing...hard.

God, give me strength.

"If you'd like a shower," I said, trying to make my voice sound normal through gritted teeth, "there's a great shower in your guest room. Or if you need to go to the bathroom."

"I already went to the bathroom," she said.

"Okay, good. Why didn't you take a shower in there, then?"

"Because..."

"What?" *For God's sake, what?*

"I want to shower with you."

My hard-on swelled larger than ever. This was a damned test, and I was going to fail miserably.

How the hell was I supposed to shower with Zee and her amazing body without fucking her?

Answer—no way in hell could I, so she was *not* getting into the shower with me.

"That's not a good idea," I said.

"But...you..."

"What?"

"You calm me, Reid. I can't really describe it any better than that. I'm more relaxed with you than I've ever been, and I know it doesn't make any sense. I mean, you're his *son*." Silence for a few seconds. "I don't get it, but it's true."

"Fine. I'll finish my shower and then you can use this one. I'll sit in the bathroom if that's what you want, but you're absolutely not—"

She opened the glass shower door, clad in the white fluffy robe.

"For God's sake," I muttered.

She dropped the robe, and—

I sucked in a gasping breath.

Her body. I always knew it would be spectacular, but even I wasn't prepared for her magnificence.

Perfect breasts—which of course I'd seen before but not this close up—and the nipples weren't bright red, of course. They were dark pink. Dark pink and perfect.

She was tall and broad-shouldered, which of course was why she could handle those huge headdresses she wore in the show. She had just enough indentation at her waist to make her narrow hips shapely. And her rear end. I was never an ass man, but dancing had giving her a perfect booty.

My erection throbbed.

Her gaze dropped, and an audible gasp escaped her throat.

Well, what did she expect? *She* opened the shower doors. Did she expect me to be hanging flaccid?

And yeah, I was huge. Point one for me.

"Zee..."

She pulled her gaze up and met mine. "Please."

"You are testing me at every turn."

"What do you mean?"

"Come on. You're not that naïve. You know I'm attracted to you. I've told you. I'm not made of rock, you know."

Well, a certain part of me was at the moment.

She walked into the shower. "It's a huge shower. There's room for both of us."

"That's not the point, and you know it. I'm trying to be a gentleman here, and you're making it very difficult."

"Maybe... Maybe that's what I want."

No, Reid. You're not going to fuck your father's victim. Yeah, it was your first plan, but you promised Riley. You promised your baby sister.

No, you won't. You won't. You won't.

Before I could think anything more, I grabbed her and crushed my mouth to hers.

A kiss.

Just a kiss.

I was disciplined. I could stop at a kiss.

I probed the seam of her lips. *Open, Zee. Open for me.*

As if she read my mind, her lips parted, and I delved into her.

This kiss... All I'd done so far was give her quick pecks on the lips. Each time, I was left unsatisfied.

And this time...

Her tongue was velvety smooth and minty. She'd brushed her teeth, most likely. But it was more than just the stark mint of toothpaste. She had another flavor—like fresh winter snow and iced cranberries—that was uniquely her.

Fresh winter snow and iced cranberries... Who the hell talked like that?

Fuck, she made me insane.

I deepened the kiss, still determined that I'd go no further.

Our tongues slid together, and within a few moments, she became more active in the kiss, smoothing her tongue between my lips as well.

My dick was granite. Could cut a diamond as hard as it was.

Only a kiss.

Not a fuck.

A kiss.

A kiss I'd continue, until—

She pulled away, our lips separating with a smack, panting.

"Are you okay?" I asked, my voice husky with desire.

"I'm... I'm..."

"What is it?"

"I've never felt... Oh my God, Reid. Something's happening to me."

Shit. I'd gone too far. Too damned far. "I'm so sorry."

"No. It's not that. I've never... I mean..."

My father had hunted her. Was it possible he hadn't raped her? I'd be thrilled if that were the case. "Shit. I just assumed. Are you a virgin?"

"No. I mean, it's been a long time, but no. And before you ask, they didn't. Not during the hunt. I don't know if they would have, but I got away before..."

"Thank God." I breathed a sigh of relief. "Then what's wrong?"

"I've never... I feel so..." She pulled her wet hair back from her face. "I want you to make me come."

So that was it. She hadn't come in a while. Perhaps never. I was a master of the female orgasm. I could make a woman come with a look. Okay, not really, but pretty close.

She was ripe as a red tomato and probably just as juicy.

Damn it.

I could eat her, finger her, perhaps just suck on those luscious nipples, and she'd come.

But if I went that far...

Could I stop myself from jamming my cock into her and fucking her into next week?

"Please, Reid," she said again. "Please."

27

ZEE

My body wasn't my own. Except that it was. In a way, it felt more my own than it ever had. Something awakened in me—something hot and passionate and pure at the same time.

This man.

How did I want him so much, knowing who he came from? Knowing who he resembled?

But Reid was sweet. He had a good heart. He'd protected me. And that kiss...

I trembled beneath the pelting water. Seriously trembled, despite the warmth surrounding me. Yearning surged through me, and my core, that secret place that had sometimes sizzled but never boiled...

It was boiling now.

"Touch me," I begged. "Please."

"I can't."

"Please." I closed my eyes, letting one hand wander over my right breast. I shivered again.

Reid audibly sucked in a breath. "Fuck."

I gathered my courage. "Please. Touch me. Kiss me. Kiss my neck. My nipples. Please."

"Fuck," he said again, and then his lips were on mine once more.

I opened quickly this time, taking his tongue into my mouth and giving him mine.

I'd never kissed anyone like this before, and part of me knew I never would again.

So I wanted this. I wanted *him*. Reid Wolfe would give me enough for a lifetime, and I'd be satisfied. I could go back to Las Vegas and live out my life as a showgirl until I got too old. I was building up a nest egg. I'd be okay once I retired.

And I'd know I'd experienced perfection just once.

We kissed and we kissed and we kissed.

Still, his hands didn't stray. So I took the lead. I brushed one hand across his arm, taking his hand and leading it to my left breast.

Just the touch made me shiver even as the steam clouded around me.

He slid his finger over the top of my breast—over the scar. Then he broke our kiss.

"I'm so sorry he did this to you." Reid's voice cracked.

No! Don't want to think about that right now. Want to think about the man touching me, not the man who made the scar.

Who is the father of the man—

"No!" I said aloud.

Reid dropped his hand.

Quick as lightning, I grabbed it and brought it back to my breast. "I meant *no* as in don't stop. Please."

"But—"

"I want only this moment, Reid. Please. Only this moment with you and me. Without anyone else here. This is part of me, and I want you to touch all of me."

He trailed his fingers over the scar once more. "I'm sorry."

"Don't be sorry. Just touch me."

He moved gently over the scar and downward, cupping my breast. "So beautiful." He stroked his thumb over my hard nipple.

I gasped as pleasure jolted through me.

This is my body. I'm taking back my body.

Then the words dissolved into feeling in my mind. Words no longer mattered. Only the emotion coiling from my gut outward through my fingers and toes.

All tingles, all warmth, all hot lava.

Reid brought his hand to my other breast, fingering the scar again and then cupping and thumbing the nipple.

Both nipples stretched forward, and my breasts tingled.

I throbbed between my legs as vivid images coursed through my mind. Images of our bodies entwined, our lips fused, his dick...

It hung between us, erect and proud.

I sucked in a breath and grasped his length.

A groan vibrated from his chest.

I didn't know much about how to handle a penis, but I knew men liked just about anything down there. The warm water rained over us, and I worked my fist back and forth over him.

He groaned again, his eyes closed.

"Make me come," I said again.

He trailed one hand down my abdomen to my vulva. Then—

"Oh!"

When his fingers met my clit, I wanted to explode. Every particle of energy became my pussy. Empty, so empty. I never knew how empty I was and how much I longed to be filled.

Too much. Too soon.

But his fingers swirling over my clit...

Heaven, pure heaven.

My breathing became more rapid, and soft moans escaped my throat.

Please. Please. Please.

The only word I could manage.

Still his strong fingers circled that most intimate part of me that was sprouting all kinds of pleasure.

"Fuck it," he finally said and dropped to his knees before me.

He slid his tongue over my clit—so soft and slick—and then something crawled along my flesh. Something so fresh and vibrant...

A new feeling...

A new feeling I wanted more of...

Another swipe of his tongue. One more, and—

I crashed. I yelled. I broke into glorious pieces.

My fingers found their way to his hair, threading through the wet silk, pushing his face against my pussy, as words floated in the air around us. In my voice.

What words? I couldn't say.

More. More. More.

The feelings intensified, and the hot water showering me glittered like diamonds.

More. More. More.

Never want it to end. Never... Never...

Until Reid moved away, and the feelings became less intense, less magnified...

And I floated back down to reality, landing as if a soft blanket had been laid out before me.

I felt satisfaction in the most beautiful way.

He'd done what I asked. He made me come.

And I knew my life would never be the same.

28

REID

Her pussy tasted like her mouth, only more so. And all I'd done was lick her clit. I hadn't dived between those long, lean legs and shoved my tongue into her wet heat. I'd wanted to, but I held myself in check.

She asked me to make her come, and clearly she'd been ready.

I was good, but yeah, this had been amazing.

My dick pulsed between my legs.

I remembered...

How I'd felt when she grabbed it, worked it...

How hard I'd gritted my teeth together to keep from exploding from her mere touch.

How was it possible that I wanted her so much? More than I'd ever wanted another woman?

Her new blond hair was wet and stuck to her shoulders and neck. Her nipples were still hard and taut. And her pussy... So pink and swollen... An invitation if I'd ever seen one...

But she was done. Complete.

And I'd been left unsatisfied.

Oddly, I was okay with that. Making her come had felt good. Damned good.

Sure, I loved giving women pleasure, but I'd always thought of it as a prelude to my own pleasure.

Here I was, balls as blue as ever, and I felt *great*.

Unsatisfied, but great.

So strange.

I stood and pulled Zee into my arms. She was still trembling, almost crying but not quite.

"You okay?" I whispered loud enough to be heard against the shower.

"Better than okay. Thank you."

"You don't have to thank me."

She said nothing, just stayed plastered against me. The water rained upon us for a few more minutes.

Then she pulled back. "I don't think I'm done."

"What do you mean?"

"That was amazing. Better than anything. But I still feel..."

"What?"

"Empty. Yeah. Empty."

No. Not that word. Empty. My cock could ease that emptiness. I knew it instinctively.

I also knew she wasn't ready.

"You just need to relax. Settle down. Finish your shower, and you—"

She planted a kiss on my mouth and then met my gaze. "You know what I need."

To the contrary, I had no idea what Zee needed. I did, however, know exactly what *I* needed, and it wasn't a tender hand or a slow fuck.

It was a hard fuck. A fuck where I pounded her against the slick walls of my shower. An animal fuck.

"You're not ready," I said.

She took one of my hands and led it to her pussy. "I am."

Fuck, she was slick as my herbal shampoo. And warm. Make that hot.

Without thinking, I slid a finger into her.

She moaned softly.

"Feel good?" I asked.

"Better than good."

I fingered her gently, finding her G-spot and giving it a good press.

"Oh!" She nearly lost her footing.

I steadied her with my free arm. *Get hold of yourself, Reid. You aren't going to fuck her.*

But my dick had a mind of its own. I slid my finger out of her, hoisted her slick body into my arms, and set her down on my hard cock.

Fuck. There was no going back now.

She and I were fucking. In my shower. And my God, I felt like I'd come home.

So tight and ridged. So perfect around my hardness, as if she'd been created for me.

I stayed embedded inside her for a few precious seconds, trying to get her used to me, but then I could hold on no longer.

I moved her off of me and then plunged her back down again.

She screamed, but it was a good scream. Her eyes were closed and her breasts flushed from more than the water, which had become lukewarm.

"Yes, yes." The words left her throat in a gasp.

Yes. That was all I needed.

I pushed her against the shower wall and thrust up into her. Again. Again. Again.

I clenched my teeth, grasping every last shred of control I had to make this last. To make it good for her.

But stick a fork in me. I was done.

I plunged into her as far as I could, my balls scrunched and aching for release.

And I gave in.

The orgasm ripped through me with explosive force, and for the first time, not just my cock was involved.

Every cell of my body seemed to hum with the climax.

I shuddered all over.

The release went on and on, and I stayed inside Zee, pinning her to the shower wall, complete in a way I'd never experienced before.

My cheek was flush against her neck and shoulder, and I made my legs go rigid so I wouldn't collapse and bring us both to the hard shower floor.

We panted against each other, our bodies still fused.

After timeless moments, my dick slid out of her and I gently released her as her feet touched the floor.

I had to look at her. Tell her I hadn't meant to go so far.

Apologize.

"Wow," was all I said, though.

Seemed to sum it up pretty perfectly as far as I was concerned.

But more of my concern was for the woman who grabbed a shampoo bottle and squeezed some into her palm. She spread it on my hair, digging her fingertips into my scalp.

"Zee..."

"Shh," she said. "Don't say anything. I don't want to think about any consequences right now. I just want to live in this moment. With you."

Okay. I'd take it. At least until the water got so cold we had to turn it off. The steam was dissipating.

She massaged my scalp for a wonderful minute and then moved me toward one of the pulsating shower heads, where she helped me rinse it out. She shampooed her own hair then, and though I wanted more than anything to do it for her, all I could do was stare.

Stare at this beautiful woman who I'd just fucked hard against a wall.

This woman who deserved a much gentler hand. A much gentler touch.

She washed her body then, so I did the same, and by the time we were ready to leave the shower, the water had indeed turned uncomfortably cool.

I opened the glass door, grabbed two fluffy black bath sheets, and wrapped one around Zee. Such a shame to cover her up, but she'd catch a chill otherwise.

I kept my teeth from chattering as I dried off with the other sheet and then wrapped it around my waist.

Her hair was wet and sticking to her forehead and neck, but God...had she ever looked more beautiful?

"I'm not sorry," she said abruptly.

"I'm glad."

"Are you?"

"Sorry?" I sighed. "It's not how I meant for it to go."

"Really? It was amazing."

"Well...yeah. It was great. But I didn't mean to do it at all."

"Why not? We both wanted it."

"But you... I didn't want it like this with you. I shouldn't have done it."

"You're the Wolfe of Manhattan," she said, looking down. "It's what you do."

"Not with you," I countered, more harshly than I meant to.

She looked up, her eyes glassy, sad. "I'm no different than any other woman."

"Yes, you are."

"I'm not. Do you think other women don't have pasts?"

"Not like yours."

"Maybe not exactly like mine, but you'd be surprised. You should see the bruising and scarring I see on some of my cast mates. And Reid, some scars aren't visible."

"You're different, though. My father—"

She placed her hand over my mouth harshly. "Don't go there. I didn't."

No, she hadn't. If she had, none of this would have happened.

"Part of me will always go there," I said. "Do you think it's been easy for me? You're beautiful. I promised my sister I wouldn't touch you."

"Your sister? What does she have to do with this?"

"She... Well, all of us were victims of our father, but not like you were."

"I try not to dwell on it. Some days are better than others, but for the most part I've put it in the past." She took the second towel I handed her and swept her wet hair into a turban.

"And today?" I asked.

She smiled shyly. "Today was the most amazing day of my life."

29

ZEE

My words rang so true.

I'd steered clear of relationships—clear of men, honestly—because I didn't imagine myself ever being so attracted to a man to become intimate.

I had a boyfriend when I was a teenager. I was homeschooled by a tutor, but he went to the local high school. We met through a local church group. He took my virginity, and then, once we broke up, I had a one-nighter at a party—one of the only parties I attended at that age—with a jock from the local high school. Both were enjoyable, but neither was anything close to my experience with Reid Wolfe.

After the hunt—I could say it now —I was a mess. I turned to drugs, and after I struck a deal with Derek Wolfe to pay off my rehab bills and finance a new start, I still wasn't interested in men. I was clean, I had a good job that kept me in great physical shape, and I didn't have to worry about anyone except myself.

It wasn't exactly heaven, but it was good. As good as I figured things would ever get for me.

Then Reid Wolfe catapulted into my life, asking me to be his date for his family's double wedding in Las Vegas.

And feelings I never thought I was capable of surfaced.

Raw feelings. Raw yet pure in the most devastatingly wonderful way.

The Wolfe of Manhattan wasn't in love with me, and I could live with that. I'd been around the block enough to know I wasn't in love with him either. I could easily mistake the pure emotion I felt for love, but I was skeptical. I'd been beaten down more than most, and I didn't believe in love at first sight, or even love at first feeling.

Just didn't happen.

Still, today had been the most amazing day of my life so far, and it had only just begun.

Reid cupped my cheek. "I can't lie to you, Zee. It was pretty damned amazing for me too."

A soft sigh escaped my throat. Reid was the Wolfe of Manhattan. He'd probably uttered those same words to dozens of women. Make that hundreds.

But I chose to believe them. This wouldn't last forever, so I'd take what I was given.

This had been special for him. I'd take him at his word.

"Are you hungry?" he asked. "I can have the chef make you some breakfast."

Chef. He had his own chef. Wow. "I could eat. What do you like for breakfast?"

"The breakfast will be for you," he said. "I have a meeting to get to."

"Oh." The disappointment was apparent in my voice, but Reid didn't seem to notice.

"So what will it be? Eggs and bacon? Pancakes?"

Pancakes sounded good. Sort of. I'd just burned a lot of energy, but my appetite had waned in the few seconds after Reid told me he wouldn't be joining me.

"Zee?"

I bit my lower lip. "Coffee. Black. And a few pancakes would be nice. Thank you."

"I'll get it ordered." He grabbed a towel and rubbed it over his short hair. When he hung the towel back up, his hair was spiky and nearly dry.

"So"—I cleared my throat—"when will I meet with your detective?"

"He's not my detective," Reid scoffed.

"I didn't mean—"

"I'm sorry," he said kindly. "I didn't mean to get short with you. It's just that this guy has been the bane of my existence since the murder. He's gunning to get one of us to go down for it."

"You don't think..."

"Think what?"

"That he'll try to pin it on me?" My voice came out like a squeak.

Reid touched my shoulder. His hand was warm. "I don't. I've discussed that with my brothers and sister. Your show was dark the night of the murder, but we can easily prove you weren't anywhere near New York. Flight logs will show you weren't on a plane, and it would take days to take the train or drive. Plus, you don't have the kind of money or connections to have it done."

I knew all this, but his words flew at me and pricked me as if they were little shards of metal. His voice seemed so distant and cold, in contrast with his hand so hot on my flesh.

"I suppose you're right," I said.

"Trust me. I've been through this with my lawyers ad nauseum. You won't be charged. I guarantee it."

"How can you guarantee it?"

"I just can. You may have a motive, but you've had that motive for ten years, Zee. Why now? And you weren't even in the state of New York."

His words still pricked me like talons, but he made a lot of sense.

"So when, then?"

"When what?"

"When will I meet with him? The detective?"

"Oh, right." Reid squirted a tiny amount of gel into his palm and then whisked it through his hair. "Sometime today, I imagine. I have to go in for more questioning as well."

"Will you be with me when I'm questioned?"

"You're not being questioned, Zee. You'll simply make a statement."

"But after that, they'll question me, I assume."

"Not if I have anything to say about it." He touched my cheek lightly.

His words no longer pricked me like tiny nails. He was sweet Reid again.

"Okay." I attempted a smile.

He let his towel drop to the floor. I kept my eyes from widening. I'd already seen all of him, but he was still magnificent every time. Tan and muscled and spectacular.

"I'm going to call in your breakfast and then get dressed. I'm already running late."

Okay. Back to distant Reid.

But was this truly distant Reid?

Perhaps this was businessman Reid. Billionaire businessman Reid. A billion-dollar empire didn't run itself, and Reid had been his father's right-hand man.

God, his father...

I'd learned to compartmentalize over the years. Some days I was more successful than others.

Right now, though, my mind didn't really know which way to go. I was here with the son of my tormentor. I'd just slept with him, and now I had to tell the story of what his father had done to me.

So it was pretty difficult to compartmentalize, especially when I was in love with his son.

Except I wasn't in love. I'd already been through that in my head. It was simply emotion spurred by physical reaction.

It had to be. No other explanation made any sense.

I unwrapped my towel, hung it over the shower door, and donned one of the lush white robes, my hair still bound in the turban. I left the bathroom and found Reid already in boxer briefs and black dress socks. Not really a good look on a man but he pulled it off astoundingly well.

"Food's on the way. I figured you'd be more comfortable eating in here." He opened his closet door.

I gasped.

This wasn't a walk-in closet, it was another bedroom. Suits hung, separated by color. Then shirts, again by color. Five different racks of ties. And...

I couldn't hold back a gasp.

One wall was all shoes.

I never imagined a man could own so many shoes. No wonder he sent me shoes. They were obviously his thing.

He chose quickly and dressed with similar speed. I couldn't take my eyes off him. Within minutes, he was ready to grace the cover of *GQ*.

Then a knock on the door. He opened it, not seeming to worry that I stood right within eyeshot in a robe.

"Breakfast, Mr. Wolfe."

"Thanks, Lydia." He took the plate and carafe of coffee.

"Better than room service," I said.

"I have a great staff." He set the items on the small table by the window. "It's all yours."

"What should I do with the dishes?"

"Leave them. Lydia will clear them when she does the room."

This was better service than the poshest of hotels. Not that I'd know, of course.

"I'll be in touch when I know more about when you'll be giving your report. In the meantime, make yourself at home." He adjusted his tie.

"But when—"

He brushed his lips over mine quickly. "Sorry. I'm already late. I'll let you know as soon as I know anything." Then he left his bedroom, closing the door behind him.

I plunked down in the chair where my breakfast waited on the table before me.

And I wasn't hungry at all.

30

REID

My elevator took me straight to the private entrance to Wolfe Enterprises. I checked my watch once more. Ten minutes late. Ten minutes.

I was never late.

I opened the door to our private conference room.

"So he joins us," Rock said.

"Sorry."

"Never thought I'd see the day. You're usually all over *my* ass for being late."

"Sorry," I said again.

Terrence slid a cup of steaming black coffee in front of me.

"Thanks," I murmured.

"Morgan is due here in less than an hour," Rock continued. "So let's get our ducks in a row."

"Zee is ready," I said. "She's just waiting for me to tell her when and where to be."

"Good."

Lacey swept into the room with Charlie behind her. "Sorry!" Then she looked around. "I guess we're not the only ones."

"The others don't work here or live here," I said.

"You're the one making excuses?" Rock lifted his eyebrows. "Am I in the right universe today?"

Lacey swatted his arm as she took the seat next to him. "How's Zee doing, Reid?"

I cleared my throat. *Oh, she's great. I gave her a good hard fucking.* "She's good. Ready to talk. I've told her I don't believe she'll be considered a suspect."

"It's unlikely," Lacey said, "but I honestly don't know. Somehow I'm a suspect and I have no motive at all."

"We're going to take care of that, babe," Rock said soothingly.

Lacey was scared, though. She tried to hide it behind her lawyerly demeanor and a slight bit of humor, but I knew.

And so did Rock.

"I'm texting Roy," Charlie said. "I don't know what's keeping him and Riley."

"Riley's still in her honeymoon phase," Lacey said.

"I got married the same day she did," Charlie countered.

"Yeah, but you and Roy were together longer."

"About a week longer." Charlie laughed.

I had to hand it to all of them. They were taking this better than I was. Rock and Riley both had more of a motive than I did, but they didn't seem as concerned.

Rock had a decent alibi, of course.

But Riley?

No way would my little sister go down for this. No way would any of us go down for it.

Not on my watch.

"We need to take this seriously," I said.

"We are," Rock said. "But a little humor never hurt anyone."

Lacey cleared her throat. "Actually, Reid is right. Things are coming to a head, so we have to be ready."

"Turns out I *was* in the office the day that phone call was made to your landline, Rock," I said. "I doubled checked everything against my calendar. I hope you believe me when I tell you I didn't make that call."

"I do believe you," my brother affirmed. "But now we need to find out who did."

"Dad was still alive," I said. "My bet's on him. All of our voices are similar enough that he could have made the call to you with enough confidence that you'd believe it was me."

Rock nodded. "And then when Nieves intercepted the call, she just assumed it was you, never having heard your voice."

"Right." I inhaled deeply. "Which means we'll never know *why* he made the call, since he's not here to tell us."

Rock sighed. "Which also means none of this helps at all."

"We do know one thing, though," Lacey said. "We know your father *knew* a hit was out on him. Or he wanted you to *think* there was a hit."

"I'm still not ruling out that he orchestrated the whole thing," I said. "It's off brand for a megalomaniac, but I swear, I get a niggling at the back of my neck every time I consider it. I've learned never to ignore that feeling."

"I hear you, brother," Rock said. "The news from your men who searched St. Andrew's should be in sometime today."

"Did they search Father Jim's living quarters too?" Charlie asked.

"Yep. All of it." I took a drink of coffee. "They're the best. No one will know they were ever there."

"Where was Father Jim? And the staff?"

"They took care of it," I said. "I've learned not to ask those kinds of questions."

"Just out of curiosity," Lacey said, "are these people who worked with your father?"

I shook my head. "No way. I hired all new people. I don't trust anyone who worked with him."

"Good call," Rock said.

"We're paying through the nose," I went on, "but we can afford it."

Roy rushed into the conference room. "Sorry!"

"Why are you so late?" his wife inquired.

"I got a phone call right as I was leaving," he said. "A gallery got an offer on one of my older pieces. I felt I should consider it."

"When all our lives are at stake?" I asked.

"Easy," Rock said.

"Fuck easy. This is important!" I had to physically stop myself from pounding on the table.

"Reid," Roy said, "I understand, and I'm sorry I'm late. What's gotten into you? Until now, you've been... I don't know. Cool and collected. Pretty business-like."

He was right. I had been. I hadn't worried too much about all of us being implicated because I knew damned well none of us had done this.

Now?

The game had changed.

Zee was involved.

Zee.

And I vowed to protect her just as I vowed to protect the rest of my family.

One way or the other, I'd get us out of this, but I needed all of their cooperation.

Riley shuffled in, finally, and my anger softened a bit. What she'd gone through at that monster's hands...

What Zee had gone through...

Fuck.

"All right," Rock said. "So are we going on the assumption that Dad made the call to me pretending to be Reid? Or do we investigate further?"

"I've got one of my men investigating on the inside," I said. "Someone I trust. I hired him myself a few years ago."

"Are you sure he was never tainted by Dad?" Rock asked.

"I'm sure. Besides, we're in charge now. What good would any loyalty to Dad do him?"

"Fair point." Rock nodded.

"So yeah, I'm investigating, but I'm still pretty convinced Dad made the call himself."

"Good enough." Rock glanced down at his notes. "Nieves Romero. She still hasn't answered my calls, so I'm going to have someone in Montana go in."

"Who?" I asked.

"Just someone I know who can get things done quickly. He'll scare her into telling the truth."

Riley's lips trembled. "I don't want anyone else to be hurt."

"He won't hurt her," Rock said. "Just scare her a little. Look, sis, either *we* go down or someone else does. I'm all for it being the guilty party."

Riley nodded. "You're right."

"I'm with you too," I said to Rock. "That little bitch got her hands in this because she thought she and her sister could make a buck. Maybe they did. I don't rightly give a shit. But if she knows something, she has to come clean. All our lives depend on it."

Charlie's phone buzzed on the table. She glanced down. "Great news. Detective Morgan has arrived."

"I suppose we should be grateful he's not dragging us all down to the station," Lacey said.

"Are you kidding?" Rock guffawed sarcastically. "Free donuts here. Bagels too."

"Christ." I raked my hands through my hair.

Charlie stood. "I'll go get him. I doubt he'll go for questioning us together in here, but we can hope."

"He'll never do that," Lacey said. "He can't risk us communicating with each other in nonverbal ways."

"No, he won't," I agreed. "But I *will* be in the room when he talks to Zee."

"Zee isn't a suspect—not yet, anyway—so he shouldn't have an issue."

"As soon as he hears her story, though..." Riley bit her lip nervously.

Lacey shook her head. "We've already gotten the flight logs. She performed the day before and the day after the murder. If she wasn't on any flight, she couldn't have done it."

Although this wasn't surprising news, a cement block seemed to float off my shoulders.

Zee was safe.

She wouldn't be arrested or even implicated.

Thank God.

But fuck.

I cared way more than I thought I did.

I knew I cared, but now?

I was in love.

Fucking in love with a woman whose life my father had tried to destroy.

God help me.

31

ZEE

I felt...useless.

I wanted to do something. Something to help Reid. Something more than just tell the story of what I'd been through long ago at his father's hands.

The priest's hands.

There were others there too, but I didn't recall any of them chasing me. Were they chasing others? I tried to remember, but I couldn't. I'd been focused only on one thing.

Survival.

Funny, how the mind works. The instinct for survival is greater than anyone can imagine. I didn't know how strong it was...

Until I'd had to face it.

I'd been ready to do anything—absolutely anything—to prolong my life for one more second.

If I'd had a weapon, I'd have used it. I'd have maimed or killed to save my own life.

I'd have spread my legs and let the two of them rape me.

But they weren't interested in rape. Only in the hunt.

The hunt to kill.

Strange that I hadn't thought about it in so long. After rehab, I'd gotten therapy and trained myself to compartmentalize.

I'd done pretty well until now.

Now, when my feelings for Reid Wolfe brought it all together in my mind. He was Derek Wolfe's son, which blew the compartmentalizing thing into outer space.

It just wasn't possible anymore.

Yet I couldn't bring myself to feel too sad about that. I wouldn't trade my time with Reid for anything. It was so special, and I wanted it to last as long as it could, which wouldn't be long.

Once this murder was solved, he and I would never cross paths again.

I kept to myself, despite having four roommates. I was closer to Mo than the other two, but though Mo shared some deep stuff with me, I'd never reciprocated. I was happy to be there for her, but I never felt the need to divulge anything.

I didn't have a lot to share, other than my story, and until now, I'd never shared that with anyone. Not even my therapist. She didn't know the whole truth.

I needed to share now, though, and with someone other than this detective.

I wanted to vent.

To explode.

But who could I trust?

When I was younger, I talked to a pastor sometimes. My mother and I weren't overly religious, and after my first communion at St. Andrew's in Manhattan we never went to that parish again. I went to a protestant church with a neighbor every now and then and talked to the pastor there. He used to say the *Lord's Prayer* with me. I got into the habit of saying it nightly, until I prayed it that fateful day...and then stopped praying altogether.

A pastor would be trustworthy. A pastor *should* be trustworthy.

But one of my hunters had been a priest. A priest who mocked his collar by wearing it while tormenting another human being.

The priest who gave an innocent little girl her first communion, and ten years later, hunted her.

Nope. No pastor or priest.

Unless...

St. Andrew's. I was stronger now. I grabbed my phone and did a search.

Father James Wilkins. St. Andrew's. I had a credit card with a small line. I could take a cab...

I could confront my demons.

Once and for all.

I dressed quickly. Now what? Reid had my number. He'd call when they needed me, and I'd come back. After all, I hadn't told him I wouldn't leave the building.

It was time.

Time to take back my life in more ways than one.

32

REID

I sat in my office while Hank Morgan questioned Rock. I was next, but in the meantime, I wanted to check in with my man on the inside.

I looked up when someone knocked on the door.

"Yeah. Come on in."

A young man entered.

"Speak of the devil," I said. "I was just going to call you. Have a seat."

Leif Ramsey, a former Navy SEAL who'd been discharged due to a hip injury in the line of duty, sat down to face me. I'd hired him a few years ago as a kind of in-house spy. He was on the company's payroll as an administrative assistant, but he was also on my personal payroll.

"Anything new?" I asked.

"I've asked around as well as I can without raising suspicion. No one remembers seeing your father access your office that day, but it was weeks ago and no one would really think twice if he went into your office."

"Right. Why would they?"

"But there's one thing that doesn't quite jibe."

I raised my eyebrows. "What's that?"

"Your assistant. Terrence."

Terrence? He'd been with me a while and did an incredible job. The guy got things done that no one else would be able to. He got me those great seats at Zee's show in the middle of the night. He had contacts.

I inhaled deeply. "Spill it."

Leif cleared his throat. "Terrence claims he doesn't remember seeing anyone access your office on the day in question, but his calendar tells a different tale."

"How so?"

"Luckily, I hacked into several personal calendars before I started questioning. I wanted to see if anything stood out before I asked questions. Otherwise, they might do some deleting. Not that I couldn't recover deletions, but it would take time and energy that we don't really have right now."

"Got it. Go on."

"His calendar indicates, or at least it *indicated*, that he was out of the office that day."

"Where?"

"It didn't say. Just said he took a personal day. So I figured when I questioned him, that's what he'd tell me. But he didn't. He said he didn't remember seeing anyone access your office that day."

Hmm. Strange. I wrinkled my forehead.

"Does Terrence take a lot of personal days?" Leif asked.

"No more than anyone else." I opened my phone to my own calendar, pulling up the date of the phone call. "Strange. If he'd taken a personal day, I'd have had to approve it, and it would show on my calendar."

"Do you always approve his personal days?"

"I can't think of a time I haven't," I said. "Like I said, he doesn't abuse the privilege."

"This could mean nothing," Leif said, "but it stood out to me. Seems like a red flag."

"Yeah, it does."

Terrence. Really? I paid him handsomely, but like most others in the world, if he saw dollar signs elsewhere…

"Also," Leif continued, "remember that your father was still head of the company at that time, so if he asked Terrence to do something—"

"He trumped me." I nodded. "Yeah. You're right. Something about that stinks. Did you ask Terrence about what his calendar indicated?"

"I didn't, because he appeared to pull up his calendar when I talked to him. So he would have seen that he wasn't in, and he would have said so."

"So one would think."

"Yeah. Red flag."

"All right. What's Terrence's calendar say now?"

"As I suspected, it no longer shows a personal day that day."

"Did you screenshot the original, showing the personal day?"

Leif smiled. "Of course I did."

"All right. It's possible that he meant to take a personal day and then decided not to but forgot to delete the entry in his calendar."

"It's possible," Leif agreed.

"Still…"

"How long has Terrence been working for you?"

"A few years. I hired him—"

I stopped with an abruptness that surprised me.

I did hire Terrence. He had impeccable qualifications and his references gave him glowing reviews. He fit right in and even started a bromance with my father's assistant, Jarrod, who now worked for Rock.

But...I hadn't found him myself.

Oh, God.

I remembered clearly now.

My father had brought his resume to me.

Sure, I'd been looking for a new executive assistant, as my former one had moved to Hawaii after her husband got transferred. Him handing me a resume hadn't seemed odd.

Until now.

Still, it could all mean nothing.

"Anything else?" I asked Leif.

"That's all I've got for now. It's small, but it could be significant."

"Yeah, it could be." I twisted my lips as my mind raced. "Thanks, Leif. Keep looking."

"Will do, boss."

"And stop calling me boss."

He laughed as he stood. "Okay, commander."

Still a SEAL to his core.

Leif was a good guy. Someone I'd brought in myself. I'd thought I trusted him, but I realized something important after our conversation.

I could no longer trust anyone but myself.

33

ZEE

St. Andrew's was a beautiful old building of gray stone. I almost felt like I was visiting an ancient cathedral in Europe. Not that I'd ever gone to Europe, but situated in the heart of the city, the church made me feel like time was flowing backward. Funny, I hadn't noticed any of this when I was a kid and my mother brought me here. It was just church.

I walked up the stone steps and through the ornate doors into the narthex attached to the sanctuary. One wall held a bulletin board with notices of events, times for mass, and charitable drives.

I opened the door to the sanctuary and walked in. The noonday sun cast flickers of color through the stained glass windows. A lone woman knelt at the altar holding a candle.

I walked slowly toward the altar, mesmerized by the beauty of the golden crucifix standing there.

I gasped when someone touched my arm.

"May I help you with something?"

A young priest stood next to me, clad in black with his white collar. "Are you..." My nerves fluttered and my stomach churned. "Father Jim?" I knew well he wasn't, but my mouth ran off on its own.

"No, I'm Father Amos Baca. I'm interning here."

Father Amos dark skinned and handsome, and he had a very kind face. He seemed a little old to be an intern, though. He had laugh wrinkles around his brown eyes.

"What's that woman doing?" I asked.

"She's lighting a candle for a loved one."

"Oh. Of course."

"Parishioners come in and out during the week. To light a candle. To pray. To attend confession."

"It's been a while since I've been to church," I said truthfully.

"Indeed," he said. "Then may I ask why you're here?"

Why *was* I here? I'd been thinking about how I used to talk to a pastor. Thinking I wanted to take my life back. Then here I was. The parish where one of my hunters worked.

"I'm not sure I know," I replied.

"Do you want to talk about anything?"

I sighed. Such a loaded question. "I don't have a good past. With priests, I mean."

"I'm sorry to hear that." He smiled. "We're not all bad."

His smile was genuine, but still, I panicked.

Cold fear welled up in me, and I turned swiftly.

"Miss?" the priest said.

I didn't turn around. "I have to go. I'm... I'm sorry." My steps quickened until I was outside the sanctuary.

Sanctuary. This was supposed to be a place of sanctuary.

I sped through the narthex and out the door until I was completely outside the church.

No longer did I adore its beauty.

Now it was a hostile place. A place that made me feel the way I'd felt all those years ago.

My breathing came rapidly. Too rapidly. My legs turned to jelly, and my vision blurred.

No. No. No. Not now. Not here.

What had I been thinking, coming here? Take back my life? I could do that without facing the priest who tormented me.

"Miss?"

I stumbled, and strong arms caught me.

The intern priest. Father Amos Baca.

"Are you all right? Should I call someone for you?"

I willed my body to work. "No. I'm fine."

"You don't look fine. Let's go back in. I'll get you some water. Or some herb tea."

"No. Please. Just let me go." I shrugged him away.

He dropped his hands from me. "Of course."

"You should..."

"I should what?" he asked.

"You should get rid of Father Jim," I said. "He's not who you think he is."

Then I ran.

I ran until I was somewhere behind the church, in a rose garden. The roses were in bloom, and their scent infused the air. I breathed in deeply. Rose was supposed to calm, but it did anything but. I stared at the ground. A piece of white paper lay between the bushes. I knelt down and absently grabbed it, not knowing why. I crushed it in my fist and tried to stand.

I breathed in again, but the air forced itself outward as quickly as I could get it into my lungs. Panic. Sheer panic.

I fell to the ground. Among the leaves and thorns. *Help Help Help.*

Then bells ringing.

Bells. A church bell?

I shifted back to reality. It was a phone. My phone.

I breathed in hard and grabbed the phone out of my purse,

not bothering to look at who was calling. "Hello?" I said breathlessly.

"Zee."

Reid's voice. Reid's soothing voice.

"Are you okay?"

"Yes," I said, trying not to stammer. "I'm okay. Now."

34

REID

"You don't sound okay."

Worry for Zee edged through me. She sounded out of breath. Maybe she was working out. But I knew that wasn't the issue. I wasn't sure how I knew, but I did.

"I'm fine."

I didn't believe her, but I'd called for a reason. Morgan was done with me—just a bunch of badgering about things I'd already told him—and I had to prepare Zee. "I'm going to send someone up to the apartment to get you. The detective will be ready for you in about an hour, and our attorneys need to prep you.

"I... Okay."

"Lydia will answer the door and come get you. Are you still in my bedroom?"

"Oh. No, I'm not."

"In the home gym, then?"

"Uh...no. Why would you think that?"

"You're out of breath. I thought you might be working out."

"No. I'm... I'm not at your place."

Ice gripped the back of my neck. "Where are you, then?"

"At a church. St. Andrew's."

"Fuck," I said under my breath. "Why are you there?"

"I wanted... I don't know what I wanted."

"Are you okay? Did anyone..." What was I going to say? *Did anyone hurt you?* Why would she intentionally go to Father Jim's parish?

"I'm okay. I'm in the rose garden."

"Listen to me, Zee," I said. "Leave the rose garden. Go back to the street and find a café. Do it now while we're on the phone together."

"Yes. All right."

Rustling met my ears. She was leaving the rose garden. It would take her a few minutes to get off church property and back to the street. There was a Starbucks nearby. She could go there.

"Do you see the Starbucks?" I asked.

"Yes."

"Go there. Have a seat inside. The driver will be there as soon as possible. Stay on the phone."

"I am."

I left the office quickly, yelled at Terrence to make sure Wayne was waiting for me downstairs, and pounded on the elevator button until the doors split before me.

"Reid?"

"I'm here, Zee. Just stay at the Starbucks."

"Okay." Her voice didn't tremble as much now. Good.

As soon as the elevator doors opened, I ran out through the lobby to the waiting car. "The Starbucks by St. Andrew's," I said to Wayne. "Hurry."

Hurry. Yeah, in Manhattan traffic.

"You still okay?" I asked Zee.

"Yeah."

"Get yourself some tea or something."

"I'm fine. I don't want anything. Especially not tea."

"Oh?"

"The priest. He offered me tea."

"The priest?" Damn. Had she actually talked to Father Jim?

"Yes, he was nice, but he scared me."

"Father Jim?" I demanded.

"No. The other one."

There was another one? How would I know? I wasn't exactly a churchgoer, and I'd never set foot in St. Andrew's again, now that I knew what Father Jim was all about. Sitting through my father's memorial and listening to the priest sing his praises had been about all I could handle.

"You're safe now," I said, trying to sound soothing when my nerves were a fucking mess.

"I know." Her voice was monotone.

Hurry, Wayne. For God's sake, hurry!

Twenty minutes to go a couple blocks. Fucking crazy shit. I should have walked. In fact—

"Stop," I said. "I'm getting out. Meet me at the Starbucks."

Wayne nodded as I wrenched open the car door and sprinted the last block to Starbucks.

Zee sat at a table outside, her phone still glued to her ear, her left hand clenched in a fist. She gasped when she saw me.

"Are you all right?" I panted.

"Yeah. I am now. When you stopped talking, I..."

"Never mind. I'm here now. Wayne will be here in a few minutes and we'll drive back to the office." I sat down next to her. "Zee, why did you go to St. Andrew's?"

She stuffed her phone into her purse. "I'm not really sure."

"Tell me."

"I was thinking about when I was younger. You know, before...everything."

I lifted my eyebrows.

"There was a pastor at home I used to talk to sometimes. He always made me feel better."

A pastor? Did she know there were dozens of other churches around? Churches that weren't St. Andrew's? "Why that church?"

"It was the only one I knew."

"Zee..."

"Okay." She sighed. "I wanted to be strong. I thought if I could go there, it would be like taking my life back."

I shook my head. "Oh, sweetheart."

"Stupid, I know. But you have to understand. I thought I'd put all that to bed, but now it's all come back to me in vivid color."

Because of me.

"When you've been through something so terrible," she went on, "something you think you might never get over, sometimes you're willing to do just about anything to merely survive."

"I do understand. And I promise you. You will take your life back, Zee, but St. Andrew's isn't the place to do it. Telling your story is. Owning it. Going public so we can take Father Jim and any other tyrants still out there down. So we can show the world who my father truly was."

"And talking to the detective is the first step."

"Yeah. It is." I cupped her cheek and looked up as the black car weaved through traffic to stop in front of the Starbucks. "Here's Wayne now. Let's go."

She stood, and I took her left hand. It was still clenched into a fist.

"Hey," I said. "Relax."

She released her hand. A small piece of white card stock was crumpled in her palm.

"What's this?"

"I don't know."

"You must. You're holding it."

She closed her eyes a moment, as if trying to recall something important. Then she opened them. "I think I found it in the rose garden. Behind St. Andrew's."

I took the crumpled card from her and straightened it. Then I widened my eyes. "You found this on church property?"

"I guess so. If the rose garden is church property."

It was a business card—a business card that had clearly been in the rose garden for a while. It was weathered, had probably been rained on. But the printing was still intact.

Lacey Ward.

It was Lacey's business card for her former law firm.

Either Lacey had been in that rose garden…

Or someone wanted us to *think* she had been.

35

ZEE

Reid didn't look happy.

Finally, my mind seemed to be returning to normal. I remembered now. I'd knelt down to pick up the piece of paper and then I became lightheaded. I'd stumbled and fallen.

"What is it?" I asked.

He didn't meet my gaze. "Just an old business card."

"Whose business card?"

"No one's. Come on." He led me to the car and then slid in beside me.

Reid stared at the card for another few seconds before placing it in his wallet.

He'd said it was "no one's." If that were the case, though, why didn't he just toss it in the trash can at the Starbucks?

I let out a sigh.

My mind was back to normal, but I was on my way to meet with a police detective. A police detective to whom I had to tell my story.

"Reid?"

"Yeah?"

"Does this detective know what I'm going to say? I mean, have you told him about the stuff you've found out about your father?"

"We have. Roy has told his story, but because it came up during a session of guided hypnosis, the police are skeptical. Your story will corroborate his, and then they'll be able to investigate Father Jim."

"What about the others?"

"What others?"

I cleared my throat. "There were others. The person who brought me food. Others I saw in the hallways..."

"Can you describe these others?"

"Not really. Sometimes they were masked, other times they weren't, but I didn't get a good look at any of them. When you're locked up and scared to death, or when you're running for your life in the dark, you don't really stop and take notice."

He nodded. "I understand. Just tell the detective everything you remember, Zee. In fact, if you've held back anything up to this point, now is the time to let it out."

I hadn't held anything back. Not really. I just hadn't gone into specific detail. That was difficult. The stuff my blurred nightmares were made of.

But I'd be strong. For Reid. For Riley and the others. I had to get the focus off of them. I felt strongly that none of them had killed Derek Wolfe.

Plus...at this point I'd do anything to protect Reid.

I'd fallen hard.

Too hard. It made no sense, and part of me was fighting it as if I were in a gladiator arena, but that didn't make it any less true.

I'd never felt these emotions. Their purity and their strength. They made me brave.

For the first time, I would tell my story to someone who

might be able to get justice for me and the countless others who hadn't made it out of that hunting compound alive.

Reid's phone buzzed. "Yeah?"

His face went pale as he listened to whoever was on the other side of his phone.

I ached to touch him, to give him some sort of comfort, as he was obviously distressed.

But I didn't. I sat, staying still. Gathering all my courage for what I must do when we returned to the Wolfe building.

After nearly a half hour in stop-and-go traffic, Reid's driver pulled in front of the building. Reid was still on the phone and hadn't said anything other than a few "mmm hmms."

The driver, Wayne, opened the door and Reid slid out. Normally he offered me a hand, but not this time.

He was distracted, and not in a good way.

I walked with him—his phone still glued to his ear. Finally, he said, "We're here. We'll talk in a minute." Then he ended the call and slid the phone into his pocket.

"Is everything okay?" I asked.

"Yeah," he said absently.

I didn't believe him. Not for a minute.

We headed for the elevator...and my breath caught.

The elevator. Which one did I run out of? I couldn't remember. Not quite. But it was one of the elevators facing the lobby, because I ran straight to the lobby, to the revolving doors. Someone gave me a blazer—I have no idea who—and offered to help me.

I took the blazer but I didn't stay for the help. I ran.

I ran and ran and ran until I couldn't run anymore.

Then blackness.

Nothing else.

Not until I woke up in a hospital ER, with stitching and bandaging over the wounds at the top of my breasts.

I held my own and walked into the elevator with Reid.

I wanted to help him. Wanted to get the focus off him. But how could I, when there was so much I still didn't recall?

Whether I'd blocked it out or whether I'd fainted, as I must have done in the streets of Manhattan wearing nothing.

Had I been in the news?

No, or I would have read it or heard about it.

How could that happen? Why wouldn't some paper or network pick up a story about a woman running through the streets of New York clad in only a blazer?

I shook my head.

I had as many questions for the detective as he had for me.

36

REID

My body still felt like ice from the news I'd just gotten.

Our architects and elevator mechanics had finished their investigation into the building where I was now ascending with Zee.

No floor existed below the bottom mechanical floor.

However, they hadn't ruled out that such a floor had existed and *had* been filled in. The concrete beneath the building's foundation was suspect, and they were continuing their investigation.

I'd talk to my brother in a few minutes—and I wasn't looking forward to telling him that Zee had found his wife's business card on St. Andrew's property—but first I had to see to Zee.

She stood rigid beside me.

She was frightened, for sure, but I had the feeling something else was bothering her as well. I decided not to press her, though. I couldn't take the chance that she'd change her mind about talking to Hank Morgan.

I just hoped like hell Morgan didn't freak her out. He was an asshole, to be sure, and bound and determined to pin this on one of us.

Zee was the one who could clear our names. Well, not technically, but she could make the case that there were a lot more people out there with motives to off Derek Wolfe. People other than disgruntled colleagues who he'd fucked over in business, although there were hundreds of them as well.

I grabbed Zee's hand. It was cold as a winter day. "Hey," I said. "It's okay."

She nodded, though I wasn't convinced.

We walked through the reception area and down a long hallway to the small conference room where Morgan was doing the questioning. Moira Bancroft and Zach Hayes, two of our attorneys, sat across the table from Morgan.

I cleared my throat. "Zee, this is Moira Bancroft. She'll be acting as your attorney during the questioning. And Zach Hayes, he'll be acting as the attorney for Wolfe Enterprises.

Moira and Zach both rose.

"Nice to meet you." Moira smiled. She was an older woman with silver hair and warm brown eyes. Very motherly, which was why we'd chosen her to represent Zee's interests. She'd help put Zee at ease.

"Thank you," Zee said.

"We're glad you decided to talk to us today." Zach held out a chair for Zee. "Moira and I are here to make sure you're comfortable."

Zee nodded and took the chair he offered. "Can't Reid stay?"

I glared at Morgan. I'd had every intention of staying, but he wouldn't hear of it, no matter how I balked. I'd be suing his ass later, but for now, I wanted Zee to tell her story, so I made sure she had an attorney like Moira who could make her feel comfortable.

"I'm afraid not," Moira said, "but we'll take good care of you."

Detective Morgan stood then. "I'm Hank Morgan, NYPD."

Zee simply nodded.

Morgan sat back down. "We'll get right to it as soon as you go, Mr. Wolfe."

My feet seemed to be glued to the carpet. I had some kind of alpha wolf instinct to protect my mate.

Zee wasn't my mate, of course, but...

Damn. I had feelings for her that I didn't want to have.

She deserved far better than me.

"Mr. Wolfe..." Morgan said again.

"Yeah. I'm going." *Asshole.* I turned to Zee. "Moira and Zach will take good care of you, but if you need me, I'm only a text away."

She nodded.

"I'm serious," I said. "You just tell Moira you need to see me, and she'll make it happen. Right, Moira?"

"Yes, of course, Mr. Wolfe."

Zee nodded again. "I'm all right."

"Okay." I forced my feet to move from their glued spot. "Take it easy on her," I said to Morgan. Then I left.

Rock was waiting for me outside the door. "We need to talk."

"We do," I concurred. However Rock wasn't going to want to hear what I had to say.

"This hunting ground thing," Rock said. "Lace and I think he must have gotten rid of it after Zee escaped."

"Probably."

"Which means he either stopped his little game, or—"

"He just started doing it somewhere else," I finished for him.

"Right. That's my bet."

"Mine as well. Such a narcissist wouldn't let the potential of being caught stop him. He'd continue his power-trip games. Just in a different place."

"Has the report come in from the guys who searched St. Andrew's? That's my best bet for where it continued."

"Mine too. That building is old and no doubt has crevices no one even knows about."

"Definitely. And even if it doesn't, Dad could have built a new playground."

Rock shook his head. "Could he have? People are in and out of that church every day. I doubt he could have built anything. But it's likely a place could already be there."

"Maybe. When do you expect to hear from them?"

"Any time now."

I cleared my throat. "Zee went to St. Andrew's today."

Rock's eyebrows rose. "Why the hell would she do that?"

"I'm not quite clear on that one. Jim did her first communion, but then she said she used to talk to a pastor when she was a teen. Why go to St. Andrew's when she knows what Father Jim did to her?"

Rock didn't reply.

Fuck. Now or never. I pulled out my wallet and removed Lacey's business card. I handed it to him.

Rock regarded it. "Lacey's old card."

"Yeah."

"Why are you giving me this?"

"Zee found it," I said. "In the rose garden behind St. Andrew's."

Rock's face went pale. "Could mean nothing."

"I know that. In fact, no one even needs to know I found it."

"I'll ask Lace about it. Care if I keep this?"

"Speak of the devil..." I said.

Lacey turned the corner and came toward us. "Good, there you are," she said to Rock. "I need your signature on a few things. Charlie couldn't find you and Jarrod and Carla didn't know where you went off to. I figured you'd be down here keeping an eye on the detective."

"We need to go to my office," Rock said. "Now."

"Sure, what's up?" Lacey asked.

"Not here," Rock said. "Reid, you come too."

I followed my brother and his wife through the twists of the hallway to his corner office—the one that had been my father's.

"You ever have this place checked for wires? Cameras?" Rock asked me.

"This was Dad's office, so no, I didn't."

"Fuck. We're going downstairs, then. Outside."

I opened my mouth to respond, but Rock whisked past me, taking Lacey's hand and dragging her along with him. I had no choice but to follow.

Ten minutes later, after a silent elevator ride and a brisk walk about a block away to an outdoor café where we got a table far away from any prying ears, I finally had the chance to speak.

"Dad wouldn't be surveilling himself," I said.

"Doesn't mean he didn't have equipment installed. I wouldn't put it past the fucker to have it all ready and an order to turn it on if anything happened to him."

I couldn't fault my big brother's logic. For someone who hadn't been around for the last two decades, Rock seemed to know our father as well as or better than any of the rest of us.

"What's going on, Rock?" Lacey asked, her lips trembling slightly.

"Lace, have you ever been in the rose garden in back of St. Andrew's?"

"No, I haven't," she said. "I'd never even been to St. Andrew's until the funeral."

"Fuck." Rock shoved the weather-beaten business card across the table to his wife. "Zee found this in the rose garden. Today."

Lace picked up the card. "I didn't put it there. Looks like it's been there a while, though. This has been stepped on and rained on."

"Which means it could have been there before Dad's death," Rock said.

"Circumstantial," Lacey said. "Just because it's my business card doesn't mean I put it there. Also, as far as anyone else knows, the church and Father Jim have nothing to do with the murder."

Rock raked his fingers through his hair. "I still don't like it."

"Neither do I." Lacey let go of the card as if it were burning her.

I picked it up and stuck it in my wallet. "No reason anyone needs to know about this."

"Give it back to me," Rock demanded.

"Why?"

"Because I'm going to fucking destroy it."

I looked to Lacey. She was an attorney, and she knew destroying potential evidence was not a good idea.

Still, she nodded at me slightly.

Good enough. My sister-in-law had not killed my father, and if this card could tie her to the murder, I was fine with getting rid of it. I took it out of my wallet and handed it back to my brother. He tore it in two. Then four.

"I need to get back," I said. "They're questioning Zee and I don't want to be too far away in case she needs me."

Rock nodded. "Go ahead. Lace and I have got this."

I stood and walked back to the building. Though the day was clear, a cloud hovered over me, invisible but dense. Something was brewing.

Something bad.

37

ZEE

I really wanted to throw up.

Detective Morgan creeped me out with his bad blond comb over and polyester tie, but he was nice, sort of. He didn't ask a lot of questions at first, and he let me go at my own pace. In a voice that didn't seem quite like my own, I told the story.

The story of how I'd woken up in that dark and windowless room. How I'd received good and hearty meals. How my clothes, my purse, my ID were all gone.

How one day, a masked man came for me.

How someone cut the tops of my breasts with a sharp blade.

The pain of the incision came back to me with a vengeance, and I had to stop talking.

"Do you need a break?" Moira asked me gently.

I shook my head. "I need to keep going. If I leave this room, I may never return."

She nodded. "All right. Just take your time, Zee."

"They cut me," I said. "They said it was to lessen my advantage. They considered me worthy prey. Those were the exact words they used."

"When you say 'they,'" Detective Morgan interrupted, "who do you mean?"

"Derek Wolfe and the other one. The priest."

"And by priest you mean Father James Wilkins?"

"Yes."

"You're sure?"

"Of course I'm sure. Why else would they have both forced me to sign a non-disclosure agreement when they paid me off?"

"As I understand it, none of this story is stated in the agreement."

"I don't remember."

"Derek Wolfe would have been pretty stupid to spell out what he had done to you in any written agreement," Morgan said. "But tell me. Why did *you* sign it?"

"It was the only way he'd give me the money I needed."

"Why not go to him before then? You went five years after the incident took place."

A lump lodged in my throat. Now his not-so-nice side was showing. His "I'm determined to pin this on one of you" side.

"Detective," Moira said, "Ms. Jones is here of her own volition to tell you her story. This isn't an interrogation."

"Noted," the detective said. "Ms. Jones?"

"What?"

"Could you answer my question, please?"

"Don't answer," Moira said. "It's irrelevant."

"It's very relevant," Morgan countered. "I need to make sure Ms. Jones didn't make up this story and then threaten to go public with false allegations as a way to blackmail Mr. Wolfe into giving her money."

Zach stood, his eyes fiery and angry. "Are you serious?"

"Calm down, Hayes," Morgan said. "We both know it wouldn't be the first time that a money-hungry young woman blackmailed an older man with money for her own gain. The allegations are usually false."

Tears threatened, but I inhaled, willing them away. No way was this guy going to make me cry.

"For the life of me," Moira said, "I have no idea why you're asking this question. She's telling you that there are others besides his children who had a motive for killing Derek Wolfe."

"All she's telling me is that *she* had a motive," Morgan said icily.

"We've already established that Ms. Jones was not in New York at the time of the murder," Zach said, his tone adamant.

"Zach is right," Moira agreed. "I think this meeting is over."

"No," I said softly.

"Zee," Moira said. "You don't have to do this."

"I do have to. I have to for all those women who didn't survive. And I also have to for myself. To put this to bed in my own mind. I've carried it around for far too long."

Moira smiled. She reminded me of my grandmother, who died when I was ten. Very nurturing but also a spitfire who didn't let anyone push her around. "As you wish."

I cleared my throat. "I didn't come forward earlier because I was afraid, Detective. I was a mess. Men had kidnapped me, cut me, and then hunted me with the intention of killing me. That's not something you get over quickly."

"I never meant to suggest that it was," Morgan said.

"Well, you kind of did. What woman in her right mind would go straight to the person who violated her and demand money to keep her mouth shut?"

"You could have gone to the police."

"I should have. But I was kind of catatonic for a while. I have no idea how I got to the ER. I have no idea how I got home. I was a mess, and my mother wanted me to get back into modeling right away."

"Why didn't you?"

"I hated modeling. I wanted to go to college."

"Why didn't you go? You said you had a scholarship."

"Because I couldn't."

"Why?"

Rage swirled through me like a black storm. "It's all so easy to sit in judgment of me, isn't it? But you've never been through what I've been through. I was a mess. I needed an escape."

"So you turned to drugs."

"I did. I'm not proud of it."

"She got help," Moira said. "She took responsibility."

"And then you went to Derek Wolfe."

I gulped. "Yes. To pay off my rehab, and to get some money to begin a new life somewhere far away."

"Las Vegas."

"Yes."

"You dance in a topless show."

"I do."

"Why didn't you just prostitute yourself? It's legal there, you know."

Moira and Zach both stood. Gone was the nurturing Moira. Now she was a lioness protecting a cub.

I was never so thankful to be a cub.

"This meeting is over." She held her hand out to me. "Come on, Zee."

"I agree," Zach said. "The Wolfes will hear about this."

"The Wolfes don't scare me," Morgan shot back.

"Maybe they should," Zach said.

"Are you kidding me? Half my colleagues were on—" He stopped abruptly.

Zach's eyes darkened. "Go on," he said through clenched teeth.

"Nothing," Morgan said. "Ms. Bancroft, please have your client take a seat."

"No way," Moira said.

"Yes," Morgan said, "because if you don't, I'll have her arrested and dragged down to the station."

I gulped audibly as my heart pounded.

Moira whipped her hands to her hips. "On what grounds?"

"Failure to cooperate in an ongoing criminal investigation."

"Try it," Moira said. "I'll tie you up in court for years."

"You'll regret that."

"I'll take my chances. Let's go, Zee."

I walked, sandwiched between Moira and Zach, out of the conference room.

Two lawyers protecting me.

But they wouldn't always be there.

Had I done the right thing? Telling my story to the detective?

One thing I'd learned in my relatively short life—the what-if game served no purpose. *What if I'd stayed at a different hotel in Queens? What if I hadn't gone to New York? What if I'd driven straight to Smith?*

I'd be a doctor now.

"I'm so sorry," Moira was saying.

"I am too," Zach agreed. "Mr. Wolfe will take care of this. Plus, you've given Morgan enough to call Father Jim in for questioning about the murder."

Had I? Would justice truly be served?

I'd given up on justice long ago.

"I'll take you to Mr. Wolfe," Moira said, smiling.

Mr. Wolfe. Reid.

Yes, Reid would protect me. I felt certain.

But who would protect him?

38

REID

Back at the office, I called in a team to thoroughly search Rock's and my offices for surveillance equipment of any kind. I'd had my own searched after we all became implicated, but it didn't hurt to be sure.

Besides, I was rapidly learning to trust no one but my family and Zee. I looked around. Terrence. Any of the others. A fucking mail clerk, for God's sake. My father could have gotten to any of them. Already Terrence was a suspect, given the issue with his calendar.

This was a nightmare that was getting more horrific each day.

I was lost in thought when my phone buzzed. Good. It was the PI who'd searched St. Andrew's, a colleague of Leif's.

"Give me some good news, Buck," I said into the phone.

"Got lots of it," he said, "but also some bad."

"Fuck."

"I don't want to talk on the phone. I'm heading to your office."

Trust no one. The words emerged in my head seemingly of their own accord. "I'd rather go somewhere public. The café a block over. It has outdoor seating. I was just there with Rock and Lacey to discuss some stuff."

"Are they still there?"

"I have no idea."

"Let's go somewhere else," Buck said. "I need to talk to you alone first."

Icy fingers gripped the back of my neck. This couldn't be good. "All right. Text me with a location. I need to check on something first."

"Good enough."

Buck was a good man. He'd never worked for my father and he came highly recommended by Leif, who I trusted.

First, though, I had to check on Zee.

I walked swiftly to the conference room where she was meeting with Hank Morgan but wrinkled my forehead. Morgan sat alone in the conference room.

I entered. "Where's Zee?"

"She left."

"That's obvious. What happened, Morgan?"

"I don't owe you any explanation."

Hank Morgan was an enigma. At first, he'd seemed highly cooperative. He wanted to get to the truth, and he seemed to believe that none of us, especially Rock and Lacey, had been behind the murder of our father.

Each day, though, he seemed more distant. More ready to pin this on someone just to get it out of his hair.

Was he crooked?

I wasn't sure.

"Fine," I said. "If you're done here, get off our property."

He slammed his file folder shut. "I'm leaving, but I'm far from done here." He picked up his files, shoved them into his briefcase, and then brushed hotly past me.

Yeah. Not good.

I walked out the door only to run into Zach Hayes. "Hey, Zach. What the hell happened in there?"

"It was ugly," Zach replied. "He asked Zee why she didn't get into prostitution in Vegas."

Anger erupted through me like hot lava from a volcano. "That mother—"

"He's a dick," Zach interrupted, "but something else bothers me even more."

"What's that?"

"He said something out of anger. Or he started to."

"What?"

"He said the Wolfes didn't scare him, and then he said, and I quote, 'half my colleagues were on...' and then he just stopped."

"My father's payroll?"

"That was my first thought."

"What an idiot. Why would he even let something like that come out of his mouth?"

"I don't know," Zach said. "He knows better. He's not brilliant, but he's not stupid either."

"I was just thinking about how he's been less cooperative each day," I said.

"I've noticed that as well. Would he say something like that to throw us off track?"

"Who the fuck knows what he'd do?" I scoffed. "Is Zee all right?"

"Moira's taking care of her. They're probably in her office. Zee was a little shaken. Moira was awesome. She became a beast in there."

"Moira's a wolf in sheep's clothing," I agreed. "I figured Zee would be comfortable with her. I'll go check on her, but I only have a few minutes. I'm headed out to a meeting. Thanks for everything, Zach."

"No problem. That's what you pay me for." Zach saluted and walked quickly toward his own office.

I headed to Moira's office. The door was closed. I knocked softly.

"Yes?"

"It's Reid."

"Come in, Mr. Wolfe."

I opened the door. Moira didn't sit behind her desk. Instead, she was seated on her burgundy velvet couch next to Zee.

Zee smiled listlessly when she saw me.

"Hey," I said. "You okay?"

She nodded, but I wasn't convinced.

"Zach tells me you were kind of a pit bull in there, Moira," I said. "Thank you."

"Not a problem. That detective was way out of line."

I met Zee's gaze. "I have to go to a meeting. Do you want me to take you up to the apartment first?"

She shook her head. "I'll be all right."

"She can stay with me as long as she wants to. I have some paperwork to do."

"She doesn't need a babysitter, Moira."

Zee laughed softly. "No, I don't, but Moira seems to know how to calm me down."

"You remind me of my daughter," Moira said. "I think the two of you would like each other."

I looked hurriedly at my watch. "You sure?"

Zee nodded. "I'll stay here for a little while, since Moira doesn't mind, and then I'll ask Rock or Lacey to take me back to your place. Will that work?"

"As long as you're comfortable. I don't know how long I'll be in the meeting, but if you need anything—I mean anything—you call or text me. Got it?"

Zee nodded again, her smile faltering a bit.

I couldn't help myself. I reached forward and brushed my fingers over her soft cheek. "I'll be back soon."

39

ZEE

My cheek burned from Reid's touch.

Moira, still sitting next to me, must have noticed. She'd have had to be blind not to.

"He's a good man," she said.

I nodded. "I really don't know him very well."

"By that blush on your cheek, I'd say you know him well enough." She smiled.

"He... I like him a lot. But he looks so much like..."

"His father. Yes, he does. But Reid *isn't* his father, Zee. He never was."

"How long have you worked for the Wolfes?" I asked.

"About ten years," Moira replied. "I was in private practice for twenty years, and this opportunity kind of stumbled into my lap."

"Oh?"

"Yeah. My daughter—the one you remind me of—did an internship here between her junior and senior year at Columbia. The Wolfes were expanding their legal department at the time, and she suggested I apply."

"So you did."

"I did."

"You must be grateful to her."

Moira laughed. "She was only an intern. I doubt she had anything to do with my getting hired. But she knew I was growing displeased with my firm and the decisions the partnership was making, and she knew a position here would pay well. I never thought they'd hire me."

"Did Derek Wolfe hire you?"

She shook her head. "No. Lester Gardner did. He's the chief counsel here. He runs the legal department."

I nodded. I felt a lot better knowing Derek Wolfe hadn't hired Moira. She was so nice.

"Tell me," she said. "What made you decide to come here and tell your story?"

I inhaled and let the air out slowly. "I guess Reid did."

She smiled. "I see."

"I know in my heart he didn't kill his father."

"I believe that as well."

"I don't think the rest of them did, either."

"Nor do I. The elder Mr. Wolfe had his share of enemies in the business world." She sighed. "And in his personal world as well, I now know. I'm so sorry for what he put you through."

I simply nodded. She was being so kind to me, and I was near tears.

"It's okay." She grabbed a box of tissues from the end table next to her and handed them to me. "You can cry if you want to."

I took a tissue and wiped away a tear before it fell. "I'm trying to be strong."

"I know you are. It's a terrible thing, what he did to you. What he did to the others whose names we'll never know."

"That's why I'm doing this. Not just for Reid and his brothers and sister, but for *them*. The others. Derek Wolfe is already dead, but if we can put Father Jim away..."

Moira's countenance went rigid. "To think. All that nice stuff the father said about Derek during his memorial. It makes me sick."

I didn't even want to think about what Father Jim might have said at the service. At some point, if he was arrested, I'd have to come face-to-face with him at his trial.

I couldn't bear the thought.

Moira squeezed my forearm. "I have to get to some paperwork. Would you like a book or a magazine or something?"

I shook my head. "I'd just like to lie down on the couch, if that's okay."

"Of course it is. I have a blanket around here somewhere."

"I don't need one. I'm not cold."

She rose and walked toward her desk. She returned with a fleece throw. "I get cold sometimes when I'm working late."

"Thank you."

I lay down, and Moira covered me as if I were a child. A tall child, of course. My feet stuck out.

"Just relax," she said. "I'm right here if you need me."

40

REID

Buck Moreno was another ex-Navy SEAL, which was how he and Leif knew each other. Now he made money fighting MMA. No one knew he worked for me on the side. I financed his MMA fights and paid him hourly as well.

"My man on the inside is watching Jim like a hawk," Buck said.

"Right. The priest?"

"Yeah, Father Amos Baca. He and I served together. He was a chaplain."

"How'd you get him into the church?" I asked.

"The less you know about that, the better," Buck said. "Plausible deniability and all."

I nodded. "Got it." I already knew more than I wanted to. Buck's methods were foolproof. And also very illegal.

"You were right," he said. "There's a system of tunnels under the church."

My throat ached. I knew what was coming. "And..."

"They're cave-like, built of stone. Legend has it they were part of the underground railroad back in the day."

"New York was in the north. How can that be?"

"Churches were sanctuaries for runaway slaves. Manhattan was close to Maryland and Virginia, which were both slave-owning states."

"Wow. This place has a history."

"Yeah. A really awesome history. The tunnels were used to hide runaway slaves until papers could be forged for them. Except that now those tunnels are probably being used for something horrific."

Nausea crawled up my throat.

"Was there"—I swallowed back bile—"anyone down there?"

He shook his head. "It's all been cleared out, as far as I can tell. But there's a stench."

"What do you mean?"

He inhaled, wrinkling his nose. "You don't serve as a Navy SEAL for ten years and not know the stench of dead human flesh. And that smell is down there."

I swallowed audibly, literally gulping back puke. "What else?" I finally said.

"There's an antechamber that all the tunnels lead to." He paused a moment, closing his eyes.

"Just get on with it," I said. "For God's sake."

He pulled his briefcase onto the table. "I found some things. Things that you aren't going to like."

"Fuck."

"Nothing implicates you, so relax."

"Relax? That means nothing to me. What about my brothers? My sister? Zee?"

"Zee?"

I shook my head. "A story for another time. What is it? Just spit it out."

He pulled a folder out of his briefcase. "I took a lot of photos. It was dark down there, so the photos aren't great, but I enlarged them and printed them out." He pushed the file toward me.

I instinctively looked around. I was about to see something that would disturb me. That much was apparent, so I needed to make sure no one was looking over my shoulder.

A server glanced at me slyly out of the corner of his eye.

Red flag. *Big* red flag.

I pulled my own briefcase off the floor and shoved the folder into it. "We're leaving."

Buck nodded. "I saw him too. He's looked suspicious for a few minutes. Let's bolt."

We walked slowly out of the café, each carrying our briefcases, until we found an unoccupied bench. We sat down.

I pulled open my briefcase and pulled out the folder. I drew in a deep breath. "Care to give me some idea of what I'm about to look at?"

"Pictures speak louder than words, Wolfe. Just prepare yourself."

I closed my eyes and drew in another breath. He'd mentioned stench. I could be holding photos of dead bodies. Of severed limbs. Of...

God.

Of my father doing things to...

I swallowed hard.

I opened the folder.

And I gasped.

"You're kidding. Fuck."

No severed limbs greeted me. Thank God. But I'd have preferred nameless and faceless bodies to what the first photograph showed.

It was another of Lacey's old business cards, and this one hadn't been stomped and rained on.

"Circumstantial," I said robotically.

"Keep going," Buck prodded.

I fought back the puke threatening to erupt from my throat

and slid the photo of Lacey's business card over, revealing the next photo.

I swallowed hard. It was a blue scarf with the initials LW clearly embroidered on it. I swallowed again. "Still circumstantial."

"Agreed. Keep going."

More and more photos of Lacey's belongings. Or what appeared to be Lacey's belongings.

"Did you take these items?" I asked.

"Of course I did. I have them all in a safe place. But that's not what concerns me."

"What, then?"

"These things could be extras. Stuff implicating Lacey could have already been planted."

"Why her? Why Lacey?"

"I'm not sure," Buck said. "She was Derek's estate lawyer, but that's no reason to frame her."

"No," I said, swallowing again. The lump didn't move. "My father would implicate his kids before he implicated his attorney."

"Right, which means..."

"It means Father Jim—or someone else—is implicating Lacey. But why?"

Buck didn't need to answer. I already knew. Father Jim was trying to lead the authorities on a wild goose chase so *he* wouldn't be implicated. He was afraid my father had left a loophole somewhere that would lead to him.

Derek Wolfe didn't leave loopholes. I knew that better than anyone, but Father Jim, apparently, did.

"I think we can use this to our advantage," I said to Buck. "Jim is afraid. So afraid that he's framing an innocent woman for a murder he might have had a hand in."

"Framing an innocent lawyer is nothing compared to what the bastard has already done," Buck reminded me.

"True. He's evil. But now we know what he's up to, and we can fight it."

"You don't know everything," Buck said. "You haven't seen the last photo yet."

41

ZEE

I ran, blood dribbling from the cuts at the tops of my breasts. Something to stop the bleeding. I needed to find something I could use as a bandage. Was that part of their game? To help me?

I felt like I was living in the world of the Hunger Games.

Only the strong will survive.

Was anyone else being chased? Or were they focused on me?

I'd been running and hiding for a while now. I had no idea of the time, as time had seemed to suspend itself since I'd awoken in the cement room.

My stomach growled. So far, they'd fed me well. But would they continue to do so, now that they'd let me out and the game was on?

Survival of the fittest.

They'd considered me fit, so they'd given me a handicap by cutting me. The cut was deep enough to hurt, deep enough to bleed, yet not deep enough to slow me down. Already my blood was beginning to clot.

They wanted me in pain. They didn't want me bleeding out.

Could I outsmart them?

Maybe, on an even playing field. But this was far from an even *playing field. I didn't know where I was. I didn't know what I'd find down here. I didn't know where my next meal was coming from. I didn't know where I could go to the bathroom.*

I knew nothing.

Nothing except my life was in jeopardy and would most likely be over soon.

Instinct required that I survive.

They must have given me a head start, as I didn't hear anyone following me. I found a secluded corner, sat down, and applied pressure with my hands to the cuts on my breasts. I couldn't afford to wait here for long, but if I could stop the bleeding altogether, I'd be able to move faster.

"Help me."

I cocked my head at the soft voice. No one was here.

I was imagining things. I had to be. And why not? I was fighting for my life. Fighting for my future.

And my future was the next minute.

If I was lucky, the next hour.

"Help me."

"Stop it," I said aloud. "You're imagining things."

"I hear you," the voice said. "Help me. Please."

Still my imagination. A boobytrap, probably. I wasn't falling for it.

When I finally had stopped the bleeding, I rose. I couldn't run now or the precarious clots wouldn't hold. Which was, of course, the point.

I inched slowly against the wall, the cement rough against my back. I turned a corner, and—

I clasped my hand to my mouth.

"Help me."

A young woman lay curled in a fetal position. She was naked, as I was, and her head had been shaved. And she looked young. So young. I was only nineteen myself.

I knelt down. "Hey. Who are you?"

"Please help me."

"Get up. Come on. Get up."

"I can't."

"You can. You have to." I shook her gently.

She sobbed quietly. "That hurts."

I looked closely. I didn't see any blood, so she was in better condition than I was. "You can. Now get the hell up!" I grabbed her shoulders.

"Aauuuggghhh!" she shrieked.

I broke my hold quickly. "What did they do to you?"

"My shoulders. They're both dislocated."

"Damn. I'm so sorry."

"Can you pop them back in?"

"I can't. I'm not a doctor." And if I didn't get out of here, I never would be. "I might do more damage."

"Then please. Kill me."

My heart dropped to my stomach. Kill her? I couldn't kill anyone.

"Please," she said again. "I'd rather die here than have them torture me anymore. Please."

"I..."

"What's your name?"

"Zinnia. Like the flower."

"I'm Katelyn."

"Katelyn. I'm so sorry."

"Please, Zinnia."

"My friends call me Zee."

"Please, Zee."

"You can't ask this of me. How will I live with myself?"

She scoffed softly. "Live with yourself? You won't live through this, Zee. You won't have to live with yourself for long."

I considered her words. Yes, I actually considered them. But not for long.

"I'm so sorry," I told Katelyn. "I'm not a killer."

She closed her eyes, groaning. "Then run. I hear them coming."

I turned my head. Sure enough, faint footsteps.

"Maybe it's not them," I said.

"It's always them. Now do as I tell you. Get the hell out of here."

"I can't leave you."

"If you can't pop my shoulders back, and you're not willing to kill me, there's nothing more you can do."

"I can carry you."

"Then we'll both die."

My survival instinct flew into overdrive as the footfalls got louder. Katelyn was right. Survival of the fittest. I hated myself for leaving her, but I fled.

And I never saw her again.

42

REID

I slowly slid the last photo into view. It wasn't an item belonging to Lacey. No. It was a document.

A marriage certificate.

I gulped.

"No," I said. "This can't be."

"It is."

Derek Wolfe—my father—had married another woman.

And according to the date on the certificate, they got married before he married my mother. He was young. Really young.

"What does this mean?" I asked.

"It could mean nothing," Buck said. "It could be a forgery that Jim was going to use to blackmail your father."

"No." I shook my head. "My father had way more resources than Jim. No way would Jim be stupid enough to even try."

"How do you suppose," Buck began, "your father got Jim to take part in his games?"

"Sickos attract sickos," I said. "They'd known each other since they were kids. I'm sure they went around killing small animals and getting off on it." God, I was going to throw up right here in broad daylight sitting on this damned bench.

"True enough. But have you ever considered that perhaps Father Jim was the instigator?"

"Over Derek Wolfe?" I scoffed. "No way. This has my father's stink all over it."

"Does it, though?"

"The man molested my sister from the time she was six years old. You don't get much more disgusting than that."

"Oh, you do. Your sister didn't deserve what happened to her, but she's alive. Many women aren't. I've pulled the clippings."

"They weren't all buried?"

"The women disappeared inside New York city limits in the five years before Zee did. I have names, but I can't find any more information. No next of kin. Nothing."

"Buried," I said. "He paid them off. They're dead?"

"Most likely. No remains were ever found."

"But the smell..." I wrinkled my nose.

"Yes. Rotting flesh. The odor was down there, but no bodies. Which means they continued killing, but again, they disposed of the bodies."

"Are there any news stories after Zee's time?"

Buck shook his head. "They upped their game after Zee escaped, but given what they put Zee through, I can imagine it got worse. A lot worse."

I sighed. Buck was right, of course. Absolutely right.

"So anyway," Buck went on, "we have three possibilities here. The marriage certificate is a fake. Or it's not a fake, and Jim was holding it over your father's head. Or it's not a fake, and Jim was hiding it for your father."

"My father could have easily had it destroyed himself if he'd wanted to."

I read the certificate. Irene Lucent. Was she still alive? Did she even exist? Easy enough to find out.

"He could have. But he didn't. Or at least he didn't destroy this one."

"Which makes me think it's a fake."

"Think about it, though," Buck said. "If your father *was* actually married to a woman before your mother, like you said, he could have destroyed all the evidence long ago. In fact, he probably *would* have."

"So you agree it's a fake."

"No, I think we're attacking this from the wrong angle. Father Jim is about the longest relationship your father had, other than his parents, who both died when you were a kid."

"True."

"Jim and Derek were childhood friends. They probably trusted each other implicitly. So it's feasible that Derek trusted Jim with the biggest secret of his life."

"Why would a first marriage be such a secret?"

"I don't have the answer to that question," Buck said. "It's something we need to find out."

"My mother," I said.

"That was my first thought, but she likely doesn't know."

"Why do you say that?"

"You really think Connie Wolfe wouldn't hold this over your father's head?"

"Good point, but that could be why he destroyed all evidence of it."

"It could. But I did some digging. There's no record in any government database of this marriage. But...there *is* a record in the church's logs."

"Okay..."

"And here's the kicker," Buck said. "This particular church also keeps records of all marriages officiated there that have been annulled or dissolved. This marriage doesn't appear in any of those records."

"Fuck me," I said. "Are you telling me my father was a bigamist?"

"I'm not telling you anything. I'm saying it's a possibility we need to investigate."

I exhaled. Inhaled. Exhaled again. "Easy enough to figure out. I can find out if my father was sending money to some kind of unknown entity. Keeping this Irene woman."

"I'd bet you'll find something."

"Who the hell is she?" I shook my head. "Why would she stay with such a psychopath? Surely she knew what was going on with him and my sister, even if she didn't know about his hunting games."

"I couldn't tell you," Buck said.

"Right. Shit. First, we have to make sure Lacey doesn't get implicated any further."

"As I told you, I took all the items I found. Doesn't mean there aren't others out there."

"No, it doesn't. Fuck." I raked my fingers through my hair.

"Honestly, I'm surprised Jim—or someone else—hasn't begun planting them yet."

"Me too."

Unless he had, and we'd missed it. Or...unless he knew we'd find the church underground and he left them there on purpose.

Then there was Hank Morgan, who seemed determined to pin this on one of us.

He was dirty.

I felt it in my bones.

"Thanks for everything, Buck." I stood. "I've got to run. Time to pay a visit to dear old Mom."

∾

CONNIE WOLFE LIVED UPTOWN in a lavish apartment. Her spousal maintenance, which had stopped after Dad's death, had kept her living the high life. How long would she be able to stay in this place? I had no idea. Didn't really care, either.

"I'm here to see my mother, Dexter," I said to the doorman.

"Very good, Mr. Wolfe. Is she expecting you?"

"Honestly, I don't give a rat's ass." I slipped him a couple Benjamins.

"Fair enough." He opened the door. "Go ahead."

I fetched the keycard to my mother's place out of my wallet. She didn't know I had it, but my secret would be out in a few minutes. I walked briskly to her private elevator, slid the keycard, and ascended.

The elevator doors opened into my mother's lavish apartment. One of her servants nearly dropped the tray she was carrying. "Mr. Wolfe!"

"I'm sorry to startle you. I need to see my mother."

"She's having a massage right now," the woman said.

"Ah, I suppose I shouldn't interrupt that."

"That would be best, sir."

"I'm sure it would be. However, I'm in a hurry." I scurried through the foyer and living area, up the stairs, and down the hall to my mother's meditation chamber. Yeah, that was what she called it.

The aroma of lavender and chamomile crept through the doorway. *Blech.* Some people found the scent relaxing. I found it putrid. Or maybe it was just this whole situation that was putrid. I touched the door handle. It could very well be locked, but I had a hunch.

I turned it.

Voilà! I opened the door and made my way through the chamomile fog to—

Oh, God. No way would I ever be able to unsee what laid before my eyes.

My mother's massage therapist—if you could call him that— had his head between her spread legs.

If I weren't already a mess, this would have put me over the edge.

My mother was still a beautiful woman with a great body.

I'd never wanted to see this much of it, though.

I cleared my throat. Loudly, over the Native American flute music.

The head between my mother's legs shot up.

"Good afternoon, Mother," I said.

The therapist threw a sheet over my mother's nudity. Good call. I'd be sure he got a bonus, though eating my mother might negate that. Did he fuck her too?

And why was I even asking myself that question? Of course he did.

"You're dismissed," I said to him.

"Yes, sir." He moved quickly to exit the room.

I didn't get a good look at him, but he was tall and well built. I wouldn't have been able to pick him out of a lineup, though. I probably should have looked at his face.

I just didn't want to see my mother's lubricant on his chin.

I'd been feeling sick all day, and this was the clincher. I swallowed. Hard.

My mother popped up into a sitting position. "Reid! What are you doing here?"

"You do know solicitation is against the law, right? I could have you arrested."

"I wasn't paying him."

"Connie, you were there when I was born, so you know damned well it wasn't yesterday. Of course you were paying him for sexual services. I won't hesitate to have you *both* arrested."

"Really? You might want to talk to you brother before you make those kinds of threats."

"My brother backs me completely."

"Does he?"

Was she talking about Rock or Roy? Probably Rock, though it didn't really matter. "Yes," I said confidently. "He does."

"Then ask yourself why he agreed to continue paying me seven figures a month, Reid."

"Rock?" That didn't sound like Rock.

"Of course Rock. Roy has no access to business coffers. Surprised, are you?"

"No," I lied. "You're our mother. We're not going to let you flounder." Another lie. I'd never let my mother live on the streets, but she sure as hell didn't need to live like this.

"I see."

Did she believe me? Rock and I would be having a conversation later, but I hadn't come here to let my mother pit my brother and me against each other.

"Rock, Roy, Riley, and I are all on the same side, Mom. So don't try your little mind games. I came here for another reason."

"I hope it's good enough to interrupt my massage."

"That was hardly a massage," I said, "and yeah, I think it's more than good enough."

"All right, for God's sake. Let me get dressed and order some lunch or something."

"Not hungry."

"At least let me get dressed."

Talking to my mother wearing a sheet wasn't really on my bucket list, but at this point, I could never unsee what I'd seen. So no way was I going to let her out of my sight to figure out a way to get out of this.

"Wrap it up like a toga," I said. "We're going to talk now."

She huffed. "This isn't proper."

"That ship has sailed, Mom. Just wrap up the damned sheet and then turn off that wretched infuser. The chamomile is going to make me lose my breakfast."

"For Christ's sake, Reid."

I looked away as she knotted the sheet around herself. Once I heard her get off the table, I turned back around. She was covered totally, thank God. She walked to the infuser and turned it off.

"The aromatherapy won't go away just like that," she snapped.

"I'm not a moron, Mom." I breathed in through my mouth.

She nodded to a couple of chairs in the corner. "Have a seat. I have to go to the bathroom."

I shook my head. "No, you don't."

"My bladder says differently."

"You're a big girl. Hold it. I know you better than you know yourself, Connie. You're looking for an out. I'm not giving it to you."

"I can have you arrested for trespassing."

"You want to go there? I'll grab Fabio the masseur and he'll hum like a hummingbird for the right price. You want to go down for soliciting? And that's the least I'll do to you."

"You kids never had any respect for your mother," she huffed.

"Why would we? After you let Dad molest Riley all those years."

She dropped her mouth into an O. "I had no idea!"

"Stuff a sock in it, Mom. She already told us the whole story. How you told her to close her eyes and think of diamonds, Queen Victoria."

"You have no idea what I've been through myself." She

forced a sniffle. "Riley didn't go through anything I haven't gone through."

Was she telling the truth? Perhaps. Unfortunately, any sympathy I might have had for her had been snuffed out long ago. "Then you, of all people, should have protected your daughter."

"Yes, I suppose I should have."

"Quit bucking for sympathy, Mom. The fact is that you didn't, even when you knew damned well what was going on. We all know why you didn't."

"Do you? Do you really know why?"

"Of course we do. You let it all happen for the money."

She fake sniffled again. "You truly don't know me. None of my children do."

"Stifle it. We know you better than you know yourself. I'm not falling for this fake crying bullshit. If you truly went through something as horrible as Riley went through, I'm sorry. I don't wish that on anyone. But you gave up your right for us to care long ago. None of that is why I'm here, anyway."

"Why are you here, then?"

"I want you to tell me," I said, "about Dad's first wife. Irene Lucent."

43

ZEE

I jerked my eyes open.

Moira stood over me, gently shaking my shoulder. "Zee, honey. I'm ready to leave for the day."

Where was I? Right. Moira's office. I'd fallen asleep after that horrible questioning from Detective Morgan. "What time is it?"

"It's four o'clock. I'm leaving early because I have an appointment. I suppose you can stay in here if you'd like, but I figured you wouldn't want to be alone."

I sat up. "Right. I don't want to be alone."

"Can I call someone for you?"

"Yeah. Reid, please." I wiped the sleep out of my eyes. Several hours had passed, and they'd seemed like seconds to me. I'd slept hard.

Moira walked to her desk and tapped a button. "Henny, could you get Reid Wolfe for me, please? Thank you."

A few seconds passed.

Then, through the intercom, "I'm sorry, Moira. Mr. Wolfe isn't answering."

"Try his cell."

"I did. He didn't answer that either."

"All right. Thank you." Moira turned to me. "I can find someone else. Lacey, maybe?"

I nodded. "Lacey's fine. Riley would be better."

"Riley doesn't work here, but I'm sure Lacey is around. Let me check." She called Henny on the intercom once more.

"I've got Mrs. Wolfe," Henny's voice came through the intercom.

"Thanks, Henny." Moira pressed another button. "Lacey? It's Moira in legal. I've got Zee in my office, and I have to leave for an appointment. I couldn't get hold of Reid, so she asked for you."

Pause.

"Brilliant. Thank you." Moira hung up and turned to me. "Lacey will be here in a few minutes."

"Thanks."

"I do need to leave or I'll be late, especially in this traffic. Will you be okay until Lacey gets here?"

I nodded. "Thank you for everything, Moira."

"You're most welcome. Perhaps I'll see you tomorrow, if you're in the office."

I smiled. "I'd like that."

She returned my smile and left her office, leaving the door open just a crack. I stood and stretched my legs. I felt good, oddly. Nice what sleep could do for a body.

I walked to Moira's desk and gave it a cursory glance. She was a lawyer. Was she working on the Wolfes' defense? I slid my fingers over a few folders on her desk. Nothing that looked important. I sat down in her comfortable leather desk chair and absently opened the top drawer of her desk. Paperclips and some lip balm. A safety pin. A measuring tape. And a short stack of business cards. Lacey Ward, and the name of a law firm. Lacey's old firm, probably. Why would Moira have those? One, maybe, but a stack of ten or so?

I shoved the door closed and sighed. Nothing to see here.

I stood quickly. If Lacey showed up and saw me sitting in Moira's chair, it wouldn't look good. I stretched my arms over my head and walked out from behind the desk.

Something on top of Moira's file cabinet caught my eye. A pink handkerchief. Did anyone use handkerchiefs anymore? I could easily see Moira using one. She was an older woman, a mother. Seemed like the handkerchief type. I picked it up and smoothed my fingers over the soft cotton.

Then my eyes popped.

The handkerchief was monogrammed.

LW.

Those weren't Moira's initials.

"Knock, knock." Lacey's voice slid through my thoughts. "Hey, Zee. What do you have there?"

I held out the hanky for her to see.

Her forehead wrinkled. "Is that..." She grabbed it out of my hand. "That's one of my monogrammed handkerchiefs. Where did you find it?"

"On top of the file cabinet." I gestured.

"Seriously?" Lacey fled quickly to the file cabinet. "Right here? On top? Out in the open?"

"Yeah."

"Where did Moira get it?"

"I don't know. She was already gone when I found it."

"Strange. I didn't even know it was missing." She bit her lower lip. "This isn't good."

"I'm sure Moira just found it somewhere and was keeping it for you."

"Probably. Except I haven't used these in ages. The set of four was a gift from my godmother years ago. They're lovely, but handkerchiefs are kind of old-fashioned."

"What are you saying?"

"I'm saying that someone took this from my place."

"You don't think Moira—"

"No, but someone did, and it ended up here." She wrinkled her forehead. "Someone wanted me to think Moira took it. I need to talk to Rock."

"But I—"

"I'll see you get back to Reid's, Zee. Don't worry. But we need to make a detour to my husband's office."

I SAT, quiet, in Rock's office, the door closed and locked, as Lacey told him about the hanky.

"Where do you keep them?" Rock asked.

"In the bottom of my top dresser drawer," Lacey said. "I haven't packed that drawer yet. I don't keep anything in there that I need, so I figured, until the penthouse was ready—"

"I don't like this. Not one fucking bit." Rock glanced at me. "Sorry, Zee."

"About what?"

"The profanity."

I burst into a sarcastic laugh. "Please. I've heard more of that than anyone in the showgirl business. It doesn't bother me."

"All right. Good, I guess." He turned back to Lacey. "Have you noticed anything else missing? Lately? Or before now?"

"No, not really."

"What about that business card in the rose garden?"

I had no idea what they were talking about, but I listened closely anyway.

"I threw out all my old business cards."

"How many did you have?"

"Well, honestly, quite a few. I'd just ordered a new batch right before..." Her face went white.

"Right before what, Lace?"

"Right before Derek's murder."

"Fuck." Rock swept his fingers through his hair. "We need to go to your apartment. Now."

"Excuse me…" I began.

"Right," Lacey said. "I have to get Zee to Reid's."

"We'll take her with us. She's trustworthy. Right, Zee?"

"Of course. The only reason I'm here is to help all of you. But I—"

"Surely we have time to take her to Reid's," Lacey said.

"We don't, Lace. We need to get to your apartment and take inventory. I don't want to waste one second."

"Can I please finish my sentence!" I hadn't meant to yell, but I was frustrated. Scared, and freaked, and frustrated.

"I'm sorry," Lacey said. "I'm anxious about all this. What do you need?"

"I don't need anything." I drew in a breath. "Moira has some of your old business cards too."

"What?" Lacey's eyebrows nearly flew off her forehead.

I nodded. "In her top desk drawer. I didn't mean to look. I just… She left, and I was waiting for you, and…"

"It's okay, Zee. Thank you for telling us. I'll take care of that right now." Rock raced out of his office.

Lacey slumped into a chair.

"Moira seems so nice," I said.

"She is." Lacey shook her head, rubbing her forehead. "And she's also not stupid. If she were trying to frame me, she wouldn't leave a handkerchief out in plain sight."

"And the business cards?"

"If they were in her top drawer, that's pretty close to plain sight."

"So Moira's not involved."

"No, I doubt it. But someone wants us to *think* she is."

∽

A HALF HOUR later the three of us arrived, via Rock's limo, at Lacey's apartment.

"Nice to see you, Lacey," the doorman said. "We've missed you around here."

Lacey nodded without responding, and we hurried into the building and up to Lacey's door. She unlocked it quickly and raced inside.

It was a lovely place, better than anything I'd lived in, but very modest compared to Reid's apartment.

"Have a seat," Rock said to me.

"I'd like to help if I can," I said.

"All right." Lacey rummaged through a kitchen drawer and handed me a pad of paper and a pen. "Write down what I tell you."

I nodded and followed her and Rock into the bedroom. She opened her top dresser drawer harshly, nearly landing it on the floor. She pulled out scarves and garments, throwing them to the floor. "Here they are." She pulled out a handkerchief identical to the one from Moira's office. "Only three. In a set of four."

Rock riffled his fingers through his hair. "Someone was here."

Lacey nodded. "We need to get a PI in here to dust for fingerprints."

"We can," Rock said, "but I'd bet whoever did this was a pro and knew better than to leave fingerprints. What else is missing? Anything?"

"I don't know. I'm going to have to go through this place with a fine-toothed comb."

"No time like the present. One pink hanky from a set of four. Write that down, Zee."

I nodded and complied.

"When was the last time you used the hankies?" Rock asked his wife.

"Like I said, I really don't know. I don't think I've ever used them."

"Not at the memorial?"

"Especially not at the memorial. I wasn't crying. Were you?"

"True enough," Rock said. "Write down never used, Zee."

Again, I obeyed.

Lacey continued to open drawers and throw things onto the floor.

"Easy, baby." Rock gripped her shoulders. "If you keep making a mess like this, we're not going to be able to figure out what's missing."

Lacey's lips trembled. "You're right. You're right. I just feel so..."

"Violated," I finished for her softly.

"Yes. Yes, that's it." She clasped one hand to her lips. "I'm so sorry, Zee. This is nothing compared to what you've been through."

"You're entitled to feel the way you feel," I said.

She smiled weakly and then turned back to a pile of scarves on the floor. "I never wear scarves. Most of these are from Secret Santas at the firm. For some reason, everyone thinks female attorneys want scarves."

"Anything missing?" Rock asked.

"Yes. One I got from my mentor, Robert Mayes. It was blue." She gulped. "And monogrammed."

"I'm seeing a pattern," Rock said. "Whoever did this was going for monogrammed things that could be easily traced to you."

"Still circumstantial," Lacey said dully, not sounding convinced.

"Circumstantial is all they need to tie you to the murder."

"What the hell is my motive?" she shrieked. "I hardly knew the man!"

"Think," he said. "Is there something you're forgetting? Did my asshole father ever come onto you?"

"Of course he did. Derek Wolfe came onto every available female."

"There's your motive."

"No." She shook her head. "He didn't push it. I told him no, and that was that."

"What about the guy who referred my father to you?"

"That was Robert Mayes. My mentor."

"You trust the guy?"

"Of course I do! He was always good to me."

"Maybe we should talk to him."

Lacey sighed. "Another scarf is gone."

"Monogrammed?"

"No, not this one. Maybe we're on the wrong track."

"I don't think so. It'd look pretty suspicious if someone robbed you and only took monogrammed items."

"This whole thing already looks suspicious. Who the hell breaks into someone's place and takes only scarves and handkerchiefs?"

"Someone who doesn't want a person to realize she's been robbed," I said quietly.

"Zee, you're right on target," Rock said. "Did you write down blue monogrammed scarf?"

I nodded. "Lacey, can you describe the other scarf that's missing?"

"I can, only because it's so ugly I'll never forget it. It was a gift from one of the senior partners, Blaine Foster. It was brown and olive green paisley. Kind of the color of baby puke."

I quickly made a note, leaving out the baby puke part. Then I sat, numbly, noting everything Lacey discovered was missing. All items that wouldn't be missed, but enough to know she hadn't just misplaced them. Especially things she never used, like scarves and hankies. A few pairs of costume earrings.

"Makes sense," Rock said. "If they took a piece of expensive jewelry, you'd notice it was gone. And you have a ton of earrings, Lace."

"This is going to take all night," Lacey said. "I have to go through everything. Zee should go."

Rock nodded and took the notepad from me. "Thank you for your help. I'm sorry we didn't just take you to Reid's, but I didn't want to delay getting here any longer than we had to. Now we're here. I'll tell my driver to take you to Reid's. Can you get in?"

"I...don't know."

"I have Reid's key. I'll take you up," Rock said. "Will you be okay here for a half hour or so, Lace?"

"I'll be fine, but get right back, will you? Please? The fact that someone was here has me freaked."

"I will, baby. Let's go, Zee."

I stood. "Where is Reid? Moira said he wasn't answering his cell phone."

"I don't know," Rock said. "He usually responds. Must be in an important meeting. Come on."

44

REID

"Irene Lucent?" My mother's eyes popped wide. "*I'm* your father's first wife."

"You sure about that?"

"Of course I'm sure. Don't you think I'd know if my husband had been married?"

Her tone sounded almost sincere, but I was so used to her lies I didn't believe her for a second.

"Nice try, Connie. Maybe if you weren't such a pathological liar, I might give you some credence."

"Look, Reid. I have no idea who this Irene is. Your father and I were young when we married. He couldn't possibly have been married to someone else."

"I have a marriage certificate that says otherwise," I said.

"Then it's a forgery."

"Could be."

"It is. Where did you find it?"

"None of your business."

"Of course it's my business. What if it's real? That means..."

Her face went white.

"Right you are, Mom. It means your marriage to Dad was never legal, and the four of us are bastards."

Oh, she wanted to reply to that with some smartass comment. So apparent in her eyes. But I'd give her credit. She let it pass.

"Even if it *is* legal, he obviously divorced her."

"Did he?"

She stood. "This is completely ridiculous. I'm done here."

"Sit, Mother."

To my surprise, she sat.

"Don't you think it's odd," I said, "that all four of your children are implicated in Dad's murder but you, his ex-wife, are not?"

"I don't find it odd at all," she said. "I didn't kill him."

"Neither did I, and neither did Rock, Roy, or Riley."

"Talk to Rock," she said with a sly smile.

"We have. He told us everything, Mom. How he caught Dad in Riley's room and tried to off him with a kitchen knife. How the two of you sent him away to Buffington Military School and how he had to keep from being molested himself."

Mom kept her face rigid. Good. This got to her.

"Rock has an alibi. I figured it out. You conned him into continuing to pay you off by saying you'd go to the cops with your story of his youth. Too late. We've already been to the cops. They know everything, and so much has gone on in such a short time that Rock hasn't even thought about rescinding his payments to you."

"You'd see your mother starve?"

"Of course not. But I don't think my mother needs to be paying for cunnilingus, either."

"I didn't pay—"

"Please." I rolled my eyes. "Let's not go there again."

She harrumphed.

"Now, I want the truth. Tell me about Irene Lucent."

"Reid, I honestly don't know anything about her."

"How about if I make it worth your while. A couple hundred mill in the bank, and you can go live happily on some Greek isle with as many whore masseurs as you want."

She bit her lower lip. She wanted to take the offer. Would she make up a story to do it? Or would she stick to her guns, in which case she probably didn't know anything about the first marriage.

"All right, all right," she said, finally. "I want it in writing."

"The money? My word is good, Mom."

"Fine." She huffed. "Irene Lucent was your father's first wife."

"Nice try." I couldn't help a bristling laugh. "You really didn't know."

"I—"

"Save it. The Connie Wolfe I know would never have married a budding billionaire knowing another woman was out there who could get a hand on his fortune. I gave you an offer you couldn't refuse, and you took the bait. Now I know the truth. You actually weren't lying when you told me you didn't know anything about Dad's first marriage."

She shook her head. "You are definitely your father's son, Reid."

"Don't insult me, Mom."

"That's not an insult. He always saw right through me, and so do you. I give up."

"No, you don't."

"Okay, I don't. But please. I *did* give birth to all of you. I don't deserve to live like a peasant."

"You won't. But we need your help, Mom. If you ever cared even the tiniest bit about your children, please find it in your heart to help us."

"I've always loved all of you. I did the best I could."

I regarded my mother. For the first time, a look of pure defeat swept over her face. Did she love us? Maybe she did, in her own warped way. Maybe she *had* been molested as a child. I didn't know, and she'd given up any chance of sympathy from me long ago.

"Then help us, Mom," I said. "Help us find out who killed Dad."

"All right, Reid. I'll help you."

I nodded and grabbed my phone out of my pocket. I'd missed several calls and texts because my phone was on silent. I didn't silence it. I must have done it by mistake. Calls from the office and from Rock. Texts from Moira, Rock, and Zee.

The latest from Rock.

I'm taking Zee to your place. She's fine. I have news. Call me.

"I have to go," I told Mom. "I'll be in touch tomorrow."

A LITTLE OVER a half hour later I was back at the Wolfe building riding up to my apartment. The elevator doors parted, and I walked in. "Lydia," I said loudly. "You here?"

Lydia bustled out of the library. "Good evening, Mr. Wolfe."

"Good evening. Is Zee here?"

"Yes, she's in your bedroom. Your brother brought her home about an hour ago."

"Thanks."

"Mr. Rock wants you to call him."

"I will. Thank you."

"Deirdre wants to know what you want for dinner."

I shook my head. "Not hungry, but Zee might be. Order some Italian or something. Tell Deirdre she can call it a day."

"Will do." Lydia bustled away. She'd be off the clock soon as well.

I headed up the staircase and to my bedroom, my heart increasing in speed.

So much going on, but still the thought of seeing Zee made my heart race. I smiled despite myself. If we couldn't get out of this, I could very well spend the rest of my life in prison for a crime I didn't commit.

In the meantime, shouldn't I be happy? Shouldn't I experience joy? Shouldn't I make love to the woman who, despite her past at my father's hand, seemed to want me?

Shouldn't I use the time I had to feel these emotions that were so new and amazing to me?

I clicked the door handle to my bedroom and opened it slowly.

My master suite was large, and the bed itself wasn't visible from the door. I expected to see Zee sitting in one of my wing-back chairs in the bay window alcove, or maybe she was in the bathroom. But the bathroom door was open and no whooshing of the shower sounded in the air.

God, the shower.

I'd fucked her up against that shower wall. I grew hard just thinking about it.

Easy, Reid. Zee had been through questioning with Morgan today, so the last thing she needed was the Wolfe of Manhattan sniffing around.

I drew in a deep breath, willing my cock to behave. It didn't, but at least I'd relaxed slightly.

Very slightly.

I continued my walk into the bedroom, and when my bed was in sight—

"Oh my God," I growled.

45

ZEE

He was here. Finally. Reid's hair was disheveled and his dark blue tie loosened around his neck. His gray suit even looked slightly wrinkled.

This wasn't normal Reid.

I lay atop his bed, waiting, my nipples hard and ready, my core a throbbing mass of melting jelly.

Had I made a mistake?

This wasn't in character for me at all, but after the day I'd had, I knew the only thing that would make me close to whole again was Reid. Reid, inside my body, helping me take back what had always been mine.

I'd only forgotten for a while.

He raked his fingers through his hair, his eyes widening. Something sounded softly through the air. Not his voice, exactly. A low hum. A groan? A growl?

Whatever it was, it made me yearn even more as the tickle between my legs intensified.

He stalked toward me, reaching the bed so quickly I thought he might have arrived instantaneously in a flash of light.

"What are you doing to me?" he demanded, his voice low and husky.

I swallowed, my body blushing at his nearness. Chills pricked the back of my neck and traveled to my breasts, forcing my nipples to harden further.

I opened my mouth, but nothing emerged but a soft moan.

"Listen," Reid said, "this is your only out. Leave now, Zee."

"I... I don't want to leave."

"I'm warning you. If you don't get off that bed right this minute, I'm going to fuck you all night long."

"Maybe that's what I want," I replied softly.

"Maybe?" Reid removed his suit coat and threw it across the room. He started with his buttons. "Maybe? Fuck *maybe*, Zee. Maybe tells me nothing. I don't care what comes out of your mouth. If you don't get the hell off my bed this instant, that's your consent. And I will hold you to it."

I breathed in, letting my courage and my yearning flow through my veins like boiling honey.

"You have my consent, Reid. Do it. Do it all."

"Fuck it." Reid stopped unbuttoning his shirt halfway down and then pulled the two sides apart. Buttons snapped off with his strength and flew outward, one hitting the night table near me with a soft clatter. Reid kicked his shoes off and then got rid of his pants and boxer briefs. He stood by the bed, holding his cock in his right hand.

It was huge. It was marbled with one purple vein. It was beautiful.

It was ready.

I longed to touch it. I'd never touched a man's cock before. Never wanted to.

Until now.

A drip of fluid emerged at the tip. An urge to lick it off surged through me, but I didn't. I had no idea what I was doing.

"I'm going to fuck you," he said. "Hard and fast."

I nodded nervously.

"Then, when I'm done, I'm going to do all that other stuff I want to do. I'm going to kiss those breasts, suck and bite those hard little nipples, eat that pussy, Zee. I'm going to shove my tongue between your legs and feast on your cream."

I shuddered as he sat on the bed and then moved on top of me. He hovered above me, his forehead already slick with sweat. He paused, and for a split second, I wondered if he was going to ask for my consent again—

"Ah!"

He slid into me, burning a trail through my channel.

"Fuck. You're so tight," he groaned.

Yes. Wet as I was, I was also tight, and his cock trailed flames into me. Good burn. Fast burn. Perfect burn.

His gaze never left mine as he pulled out and then thrust in again. The burn lessened this time, and pleasure erupted through me as he eased my emptiness.

Took it away completely.

"Yes," I said softly.

"Good?" he groaned.

"God, yes." I closed my eyes to revel in the magic.

"Open your eyes, Zee. Open those beautiful blue eyes and watch what I do to you."

I obeyed, meeting his own sapphire eyes. They smoldered. All of Reid smoldered.

For me.

Reid Wolfe, the most beautiful man on the planet, smoldered for *me*.

It no longer mattered how much he looked like his father.

Now, I saw very little resemblance because I knew this man. I knew his heart. He was nothing like Derek Wolfe.

He was Reid. Simply Reid. And he was fucking me.

He thrust into me again and again, harder each time. With each plunge he abraded my clit, and this time... This time...

A new spark surged across my skin, skittered across my flesh and pulsed into my clit.

This was it.

This was—

I shrieked! No words, just sounds of pleasure and gratitude.

For I was grateful.

Grateful to be taken away from this day. Grateful for his help taking my body back.

Grateful for this most amazing pleasure I'd ever known.

I soared with the vibrations tunneling through me, around me, above me.

Still he pumped. Still he thrust.

"That's right, baby. Keep coming. Grab hold of that big cock. Come, baby, come. That's—Fuck!" He thrust deeply.

So deep I wondered if he could feel my heart racing.

So deep I knew I'd never be the same.

As he released, I grabbed onto his butt and held him inside me, pushing him, hoping to get him deeper and deeper into my body.

His eyes were squeezed shut, but my gaze never wavered. A minute or so later, when he opened those eyes full of flames, they softened as they looked upon me.

"Fuck," he said, softly this time.

Then he rolled off me, sliding out of me. I felt the loss deeply, but we weren't done. He'd promised all those things he'd do to me, and I'd see that he kept that promise.

He lay on his back, one arm over his forehead. "Fuck," he said again.

What is it? I wanted to ask. Was he okay? Had he enjoyed it? Of course, he'd enjoyed it, but was he happy? Or did he have regrets?

"Condom."

"I'm on the pill," I said on a breath. "The director requires it."

Reid shot up into a sitting position. "What? That's illegal."

"I know, but he provides them, so I take them. It doesn't cost me anything, and I haven't been with anyone in—well, since before."

"Thank God. I'm good. I'm always safe. Except, apparently, with you. What the hell is the matter with me?"

I stayed silent, still cloaked in a haze of nirvana as my body reeled in the aftermath of the orgasm.

And I never wanted to move again.

So I lay there, finally closing my eyes. When a breeze drifted over me and I felt a chill, I pulled the covers up from the foot of the bed over both our bodies.

I couldn't sleep. Reid's eyes were closed, but I doubted he was sleeping. What about his promise?

Of course I had to let him rest. Men were different than women. They needed recovery time. Fine with me.

We had all night.

46

REID

Damn. I'd needed that more than I'd ever needed sex. Ever needed a woman.

Sure, this day had been majorly fucked up, but that wasn't the only reason I'd desired this. Needed this. Yearned for this.

I was feeling something so completely foreign to me. Something I'd never wished for or wanted.

Was I in love?

My God, was it something in the Wolfe genes that made us fall in love so quickly? I'd watched both my brothers and my sister fall in love within weeks.

A fluke, I'd thought. It won't happen to me. Never in a million years.

Except it had.

I loved this woman. A woman who, though she obviously wanted me and was attracted to me, could never love me. Never, because of what I represented.

The man who'd kidnapped her, tortured her.

Hunted her.

But I was also the brother of the man who'd saved her. Rescued her.

My release into her body had taken me to another planet. Nirvana and ecstasy tripled, like nothing before.

But now I lay next to her, covered, my eyes closed.

And these thoughts consumed me.

Did I have the right to drag her into my mess of a family after all she'd been through?

Did I have the right to ask her to be with me? The son who most resembled the man who'd hurt her so deeply?

She wanted me, yes. But could she ever *love* me?

I opened my eyes and looked at her, first peripherally but then I turned onto my side. She was resting, her eyes closed, her pretty cheeks flushed. Her blond hair was splayed over the pillow like a curtain of honey. Her full pink lips were parted just slightly.

Just the perfect amount for me to slide my tongue between them.

My cock woke at the thought. Semi hard and then hard again, just from the thought of a kiss. A beautiful kiss between the lips of the woman I loved.

Lips.

I hadn't paid any attention to those luscious lips between her legs.

She was sleeping, but she'd already consented to everything I told her I'd do.

I moved slowly, removing the quilt she'd covered us with and—

I simply looked at her.

I took in her flushed cheeks, those pink, parted lips. That look of pure innocence. Her innocence had been stripped from her long ago by my psycho father and that priest, but regarding her now, flushed and sleeping, I could see what had been.

A beautiful naïve girl who only wanted to get to college.

That pureness. That loveliness.

She was still lovely. Very lovely, and that body... A dancer's body for sure, with lean but muscular arms and legs, a flat belly, and those breasts... Luscious and large and perfect. Her nipples were like velvet, and though they weren't painted red, they were even more beautiful in their natural state. I'd kiss them. Soon, but not yet.

I raked my gaze downward to her shaved vulva.

Shaved, no doubt, because of the skimpy costumes she had to wear. Or did she shave because she wanted to?

Most women I'd been with had been shaved, but some weren't. I didn't mind the hair, but something about a shaved pussy was sex on a stick to me. I loved being able to see the slight swell of pink when a naked woman stood before me. Then when I spread her legs...

I spread Zee's legs gently.

And beheld the beauty of the paradise between them.

Already I'd felt this paradise. Felt it on my dick. She was still slick from my come. I gently eased myself from the bed to get a warm washcloth from the bathroom. Once I'd wiped the last of me from her, I smiled between her legs.

She opened her eyes.

"Hey," I said lazily.

"I felt something."

"Just cleaning you up," I said.

"Oh?"

"Yes. So I could do this." I slid my tongue over her folds.

She moaned softly.

God, she tasted like honey. So pretty, all pink and swollen, the sides of her inner thighs still slick with wetness. I kissed one thigh and then the other. Then back to her pussy. I slid my tongue through her folds again and then moved to her clit. She shook with the smallest touch of my tongue. The nub was still hard from our sex. She'd come hard, and I'd felt every contraction of her channel around my cock.

Fucking paradise.

Paradise I wanted to experience again and again.

"Zee," I said, "you have the sweetest pussy I've ever tasted."

No lie, and I'd tasted many pussies in my lifetime. I loved eating pussy. Other than fucking, it was my favorite part of sex. Every woman was different, and finding that sweet spot was a game to me.

A game I never lost.

Some women were tart, others sweet, others a combination, and others pure musk. All delicious, but Zee was the most delicious by far.

She lifted her hips, granting me better access. Below her pussy was her other entrance to paradise. Her ass.

Would she ever be ready for that?

God, my cock. Already I was itching to slam into her again.

No. Go slowly. I'd made a promise to her, and I'd keep it.

I sucked on her clit gently, and she undulated beneath me, soft moans humming from her throat and into my ears. Each sweet sound fueled my desire, and I licked her faster, sliding my tongue over every millimeter of her sweet pussy.

Her hips rose higher, and I couldn't help myself. I slid my tongue downward over her puckered asshole.

Fuck. It. All.

She gasped slightly but didn't tell me to stop.

So I didn't. I rimmed her with relish. Some men didn't like rimming.

Some men weren't me.

A woman's asshole was a delicacy to be savored, and Zee's was nearly as sweet at her pussy. I gripped the cheeks of her bottom and settled in for the feast, my cock throbbing between my legs.

I swirled my tongue around the tight hole, easing her into the sensation.

She moaned above me, sliding her hips in tandem with my questing tongue.

When the tight muscle relaxed, I forced my tongue into a point and probed her the slightest bit.

She gasped this time, but again, didn't tell me to stop.

Fuck, she was hot. Would she rim me? I loved a soft tongue on my ass. Not all women were into it, but when they were, I was in heaven.

Probably wouldn't happen with Zee. She was too inexperienced. But a guy could dream.

While I loved rimming, pussy was still my flavor of choice, so I slid upward to her glorious slickness. I met her gaze between her legs.

Damn. Those light blue eyes were flaming hot. She'd liked it. She'd liked the rimming.

Fuck. Maybe she'd let me...

Didn't matter. Right now I'd eat her out and make her come. She made the most delectable little noises when she came, and I wanted to hear them again and again.

I was hard. So damned hard for her right now.

But I hadn't sucked on those nipples yet. Hadn't bitten her flesh and marked her.

First an orgasm. I licked her clit and then sucked it, shoving a finger into her.

That did it! She screamed and clamped around my finger, milking it as she came. And I swore to God I felt the orgasm as profoundly as she did. Each contraction around my finger surged through me like electricity.

I loved making a woman come, but this was on a new scale of pleasure in someone else's pleasure.

A brand new scale.

I dropped her clit from my lips. "That's it, baby. Come all over my face. Drench me in that sweet cream." I went back to her pussy, rubbing my cheeks over her wetness, making my face shine.

God she was so hot.

When the throbbing around my finger lessened, I removed it. Yeah, I wanted those tits. I wanted so much more, but my cock was ready now.

I thrust into her and crushed my mouth to hers.

I loved it when a woman tasted herself on my tongue. It was so hot, and Zee was so sweet.

I shoved my tongue into her mouth, my cock into her pussy. I thrust with my tongue in tandem with my cock. Two fucks at once as I took her.

Took her.

Took myself.

Took us both to fucking heaven.

It was glorious.

And I knew...

I knew I couldn't live without this woman in my bed.

She was mine now.

47

ZEE

I woke from a hazy dreamland.

Reid was sucking my nipple.

Pinching the other.

Two orgasms so far, and by God, I might just get another from this breast play alone.

Reid's lips were lethal weapons, and never before had I wanted anyone so much.

Never before had I imagined wanting any of this with anyone.

He tugged harshly on one nipple with his fingers while sucking the other gently between his lips. The contradiction between the two sensations drove me slowly insane.

We'd already had sex twice, and I wasn't even close to done. This was crazy. Unreal. Completely unreal.

"Beautiful tits, baby," he rasped against my flesh. "You like this? You like when I suck your pretty nipples?"

"God, yes," I breathed, my hips rising of their own accord.

"So hot," he said. "So sexy. So beautiful, Zee."

Zee. I loved to hear my name in his low and erotic voice. It was like music, like a musical groan.

"I could play with your nipples for hours," he said.

"Nothing stopping you."

"Only my hard cock," he said. "Twice it's been inside your pussy, Zee. Twice, and I want you again. I could fuck you all night and keep getting hard for you. That's how much I want you."

I gasped softly at his words. "I want you that much too."

"Do you?" He plucked a nipple between his thumb and forefinger. "Do you really? Because I'm ready. I need you again."

"Yes. Please."

Then his cock was inside me, and he was thrusting, thrusting, thrusting...

So hard. So good.

No more emptiness.

Only Reid.

Reid.

And me.

I wasn't sure when the climax hit me this time, but I was jumping inside, jumping toward the peak of the highest mountain. Fluffy clouds surrounded me, and I flew. I flew, the spasms hitting me hard and catapulting me into pleasure unknown.

"Fuck," he gritted out. "Fuck!"

This time I felt his release. His dick filling me. As we flew together, I gripped his shoulders, pulled him toward me so I could kiss him.

Our tongues tangled together in a mass of panting and teeth and lips.

A kiss that was so much more than a kiss...

It was a meeting of hearts. Of souls.

Time seemed to suspend for a moment as we kissed and came together.

As our bodies melded into one.

Pure peace.

Pure peace that I never thought I'd experience.

Finally, Reid broke the kiss, and we both gasped in a breath.

He rolled off me, breathing loudly. "I can't even..." he said quietly.

Can't even what? I didn't ask. I couldn't yet form words. I wasn't sure I'd ever be able to speak again.

The buzz of Reid's intercom knocked me out of my revelry.

He shot his eyes open. "Dinner."

Dinner? Food? Was I even hungry? Every part of my body except my pussy seemed to have gone on hiatus.

I should be hungry. I hadn't eaten lunch, and—

Reid hopped off the bed and answered the intercom. "Yeah?"

"Mr. Wolfe, the dinner you requested is here. Do you want me to bring it to your room?"

He turned and looked to me, his eyebrows lifted.

Was this my call? I had no idea how to respond, so I didn't.

"Yes, please. Thanks, Lydia."

Reid walked to his massive closet and pulled out two robes, donning one. He brought the other to me. "Put this on."

"But she'll..."

"Know we've been having sex in here?" He chuckled softly. "They already know that, baby. We weren't exactly quiet."

"Oh?"

He chuckled again. "Some shrieking comes to mind."

Right. That had been me. Warmth crept into my cheeks and chest as I sat up and wrapped myself in the fluffy robe.

"You've had a lot of women in here," I said matter-of-factly.

He sighed. "If I told you otherwise, you'd know I was lying."

I nodded. No reason to feel bad about that fact. So why did I? Reid was a known womanizer. The Wolfe of Manhattan.

I was one of many.

I couldn't blame him for what had occurred. I'd wanted it. Heck, I'd been lying here naked, waiting for him, and even so, he offered me a chance to leave.

I didn't want to leave, so I hadn't.

And I couldn't regret what had happened. It was the most intense pleasure I'd ever experienced. I never imagined sex could be like that. Could make me feel like that.

Though I wasn't a virgin, I was pretty close to one. Reid made me feel like I'd never been touched before...and that I'd never be touched that way again by anyone else.

No man could possibly compare to Reid Wolfe. No man on earth or in heaven.

Lydia delivered the food—I averted my gaze the whole time she was in the room setting it up—and we sat down at the small table between the two wingback chairs in the bay window alcove.

The sun was just beginning to set, and the pink and orange hues over the skyline were beautiful indeed. I couldn't help a satisfied sigh. "It's a gorgeous sunset."

"Believe it or not, the Manhattan smog makes it quite pretty."

I shook my head. "It's beautiful to me. I don't get to see the sunset much, as I'm always working during that time."

"What about the nights your show is dark?"

"I'm not usually outside. You've seen where I live. Not really a good view anyway."

Reid picked up the bottle of wine that had come with the dinner. "Would you like a drink?"

I shook my head. I didn't want anything to detract from the natural high coursing through me. "I really don't drink much. Not after being so dependent on drugs for so long."

"You drank Champagne at the wedding."

"I did. It was a special occasion." Plus I'd been nervous as hell, meeting the Wolfes and having just told them my story.

"Tell me about your addiction," Reid said.

I averted my gaze. It wasn't something I talked about. "Alcohol was never the problem. It was meth."

His eyes widened. "Meth? For how long?"

"Years."

He regarded me as I took a bite of salad, his gaze focused on my mouth.

I chewed and swallowed. "The settlement from your father," I said.

"What do you mean?"

"You're wondering why I don't have meth teeth. I have good teeth, so I had minimal problems from the drug use, but the problems I had I got fixed with some of that money."

"I see."

Did he think less of me now? He hardly could. He already knew my history of addiction and rehab. He just didn't know I'd been a meth head. I took another bite of my salad. Even though we'd just had sex for a couple hours, the appetite I'd worked up had waned quickly.

I didn't like to think about my past.

"You're a strong woman, Zee," Reid said.

I lifted my eyebrows. Not what I expected.

"You took the bull by the horns," he continued. "You got clean. You did what you had to do to survive."

"I could have turned your father in," I said.

He shook his head. "It was better that you didn't. He would have made your life a living hell. He would have gotten out of it somehow."

"But I might have been able to save some of the others."

"Don't play the what-if game," Reid said. "I'm a master at it, and it never changes a damned thing."

I'd told myself the same thing many times, and Reid was right. I'd made the decision I thought was best at the time.

And it had all led me here.

To this man.

Reid Wolfe.

I was falling hard.

48

REID

After making sure Zee was comfortable after our evening and subsequent night together, I headed down in the elevator to the meeting Rock had called. All eyes went wide when our mother walked in.

"What the—" Rock started.

"I invited her," I said. "She's promised to help. Right, Mom?"

My mother, looking pale and a little bit green, nodded. "Yes. I know none of you killed your father. I didn't either."

"You wouldn't kill off your gravy train," Rock said snidely.

Lacey slid him a stink-eye for the comment. No one else said anything.

So I spoke up. "We all have our problems with our mother. We need to put them aside for now, at least until this case is solved. We need to work together to make sure the guilty party is found."

Riley bit her lower lip. Matt sat next to her, holding her hand.

I stood and made introductions. Mom hadn't yet met Matt and Charlie. It was awkward, but I got it done in two minutes flat.

"Lace and I have come up with a working theory," Rock said. "There's no evidence that anyone other than Dad himself made the phone call to me from Reid's office, posing as Reid."

"You do all sound a lot alike," Mom observed.

"Right, so here's the theory." Rock drew in a breath. "Dad was planning to stage his own death implicating all of us, but someone got wind of his plan and actually killed him, knowing they'd get away with it because Dad had put the whole plan in place to implicate us."

"Interesting," I said. "Have you—"

"Yes," Rock said, appearing to read my mind. "The body we cremated was definitely Dad. The body the police found was definitely Dad. He is *not* alive. We've checked it out and gone over and over it with a fine-toothed comb."

Riley nodded, trembling. "I identified the body in the morgue. It was Dad. I swear to you."

"Suspects, then," I said. "Father Jim, of course. Hank Morgan?"

Rock nodded. "Lacey and I believe he is a suspect. Dad had a considerable amount of pull in the NYPD. And then there's Irene Lucent."

My eyes shot wide. "You've talked to her?"

"No. We haven't found her yet, if she exists at all." He turned to Mom. "What do you know about her?"

"Nothing," Mom said quietly.

"I believe her," I said. "She wouldn't have married Dad if she'd known there was someone else who could possibly have split his pie with her."

"Fair enough," Rock said. "We need to find her. But would she really be behind Dad's murder? Why not take care of him years ago?"

"Maybe," Roy, who was usually quiet, began, "Dad had decided to go back to Irene."

"Give up his billion-dollar enterprise?" Rock said. "Doesn't sound like him."

"Are you kidding?" Roy continued. "He probably planned to live the high life on some Caribbean island while getting reports of the chaos his will had caused. Forcing you to come here and run the company. Watching Reid have to give up what should have been his birthright. Watching us all be implicated. He had all the hoops set up and ready for us to—"

"Oh my God," Riley broke in.

"What?" Several of us asked in unison.

"I don't know why I didn't think of this before," she said. "Actually, I do know why. I've kind of erased it from my mind. Dad has an island. A *private* island."

My heart threatened to jump out of my chest. "How do you know?" I asked.

She gazed down at the table. "I've been there."

Silence for what seemed like more than a few seconds. We all knew what Riley had experienced on her trips with Dad. And on a private island? Nothing would have been off limits.

"Do you know where the island is?" Rock asked.

She nodded. "It's not in the Caribbean. It's somewhere in the Pacific. We'd fly out of Honolulu. Or take a boat. Honestly I don't remember how we got there most of the time."

Why didn't you tell us this? I wanted to demand.

But I didn't. I already knew the answer. Riley tried very hard not to think about those times, and none of us could blame her. She honestly hadn't thought of it until now.

"Records," Lacey said. "There'd be a record of the purchase somewhere."

I held back a snorting scoff. Lacey was still new to this family. She didn't understand that Derek Wolfe could make any record disappear. "He probably covered it up," I said. "But there would have to be a flight manifest for the jet." I turned to my sister. "I'm sorry. I know this is hard for you to talk about, but when you went to the island, did you take the jet?"

She nodded, swallowing visibly.

"If he can hide a property investment," Rock said, "he can easily forge a flight manifest."

"Those have to be filed with the FAA," Charlie said.

"The FAA is a government agency," I said. "Government employees are often underpaid."

"So they're ripe for bribes," Charlie said. "Got it."

"Still, it's worth a look." I made a note. "I'll have Buck investigate."

Rock nodded. "I wonder..."

"What?" I asked.

"If this Irene Lucent lives on that island."

"Maybe," I said. "Why would Dad keep a first wife on the side, though? Why not just divorce her and marry Mom?"

"I may know why," Mom said quietly.

All gazes flew to her.

"I signed a contract before our marriage," she said.

"A pre-nup?" Lacey asked.

"No. I refused to sign a pre-nup. In retrospect, that was a mistake. I could have protected myself as well as your father. But I did sign a confidentiality agreement."

"Why?" Lacey asked. "Why would you need to keep anything confidential before you were married?"

Mom cleared her throat. "I had some money. Not just some, actually. A lot of it."

"We know that," I said.

Our mother had come from rich Massachusetts politicians. She'd been worth millions, until her father lost it all in a sham oil investment overseas. This wasn't new information. Still, she'd had a hefty trust fund when she married Dad.

"Your great-grandfather, who you never knew, was corrupt as

they came," Mom said. "He laundered all his money through Europe, and somehow, it ended up in a trust fund for yours truly."

"What?" Rock said. "You're not talking about your original trust fund?"

Mom nodded.

"What money?" Rock went on. "How did he—"

"He was a politician in cahoots with the mafia," she said. "Your grandparents—my mom and dad—never talked about it. Somehow, all his laundered money ended up mine."

"Why would he give it all to you?" I asked.

She sighed. "I was his favorite. Unfortunately."

"Oh my God," I said. "It wasn't your father who…"

"No," she said sullenly. "It was my grandfather."

"Close your eyes and think of diamonds," Riley said quietly, her eyes full of anger.

Mom cleared her throat. "Anyway, Derek found out somehow about the nearly a billion dollars that would come to me on my twenty-fifth birthday. Mind you, even *I* didn't know about it at the time. My parents never told me."

"Did they even know?"

"Maybe they didn't. I have no idea. Once they found out how corrupt Grandpa Larson was, they cut him out of our lives."

"How old were you then?" I asked.

She breathed in. "I was fifteen, Reid. Fifteen. My grandfather had been molesting me since I was seven."

Silence for a few moments.

None of us wanted to think about what a degenerate had done to our mother, but personally I couldn't forgive her for not helping Riley.

Neither could Riley, evidently.

"Fuck you, Mom." Riley stood, her fists clenched.

"Hey, honey," Matt soothed. "It's okay."

"What about *any* of this is okay, Matt?" Riley yelled.

"None of this is okay," Matt said. "But we need to get to the bottom of your father's murder. After that, you can decide how to deal with your relationship with your mother."

Riley sat down. "You're right. I'm sorry."

"You never have to be sorry," I said. "You're right to be angry with her. We all are."

Riley nodded as Matt entwined his fingers with hers.

"How are we just finding out about all this now?" I asked my mother.

She scoffed. "How do you think? I signed a confidentiality agreement promising never to tell where the money came from, and your father made it all go away. He had my trust fund, nine hundred and fifty million dollars. Easy enough to wipe out stuff he didn't want anyone to see. Then, with the rest, he built up Wolfe Enterprises into a billion-dollar company."

"And you've kept this from us all these years?" I shook my head.

"I didn't have a choice. I signed a contract."

"Were you forced to sign?"

She laughed lightly. "I was not. I thought I was in love with the bastard."

"What about your divorce?"

"He took care of me. I hated him by then, so I didn't care about the marriage. He paid me off, and I was just as happy to be rid of him."

None of us could dispute that.

"And you really never knew about Irene Lucent?" Rock asked.

"No, I didn't."

"I believe her," I said. "We talked at length about this yesterday."

"All right." Rock drew in a deep breath. "Our working theory is that Dad wanted to fake his death. Nieves Romero intercepted the call he made to me pretending to be Reid. Somehow she and her shady sister got involved, and they went to Hoss and Manny. Which means..."

"Fuck," I said. "It means that was the leak. That's how Father Jim—or whoever ultimately offed Dad—found out about his plan."

"Why would he want you to know, though?" Roy asked Rock. "Why would he call you, pretending to be Reid, and tell you about the hit?"

"Easy," Rock said. "To implicate me. To implicate all of us. Jesus Christ."

"But—" Lacey began.

"You have to think like Derek Wolfe," Rock said. "It was a cover-your-ass thing."

"You lost me there somewhere," Roy piped in.

"First," I said, "the phone call"—air quotes—"proves that both Rock and I knew about the hit. Then we have the will that Lacey drew up, naming Rock as CEO instead of me. Giving it all to Rock. So by me telling Rock about the hit, that sets Rock up to be implicated because he knows he'd be taking over. It sets me up as well because I'd be angry Rock was taking over instead of me."

"But none of us knew that," Roy said.

"No, but *Dad* knew. About the will. He was sowing the seeds to pit us all against each other and try to implicate each other."

"Motherfucker," Rock said. "His fingerprints are all over this, and there's no fucking way to prove it."

Someone pounded on the door to the conference room.

"What is it?" I yelled.

"It's me." Terrence's voice. Terrence whom I no longer trusted.

"What do you want, Terrence?"

He opened the door. "I'm sorry."

"Sorry for—"

Two uniformed NYPD officers followed Terrance into the room. "Lacey Ward Wolfe?"

Lacey's face went pale. "Yes?"

"You're under arrest for the murder of Derek Wolfe." One of the officers entered and grabbed Lacey out of her chair.

Rock stood. "Hands off my wife, asshole."

Lacey's eyes were wide with fear. "Rock, please... You'll just get yourself in trouble."

The officer cuffed Lacey's hands behind her back.

"Come on," I said. "You're really going to parade her out of here in cuffs? The wife of our CEO?"

"I'm only following orders, sir," the blue said.

"You have the right to remain silent," the other officer began. "Anything you say can and will be held against you. You have the right to an attorney. If you can't afford an attorney, one will be provided for you."

"She'll have the best fucking attorney," Rock said. "What is the basis for this arrest?"

"Detective Morgan has determined probable cause and the DA agrees," the blue who cuffed Lacey offered. "That's all we know."

I glared at Terrence.

I didn't know for sure if he had anything to do with this, but somehow my father had gotten into my office to make that phone call to Rock.

"I'm going with her," Rock said. "Don't worry, baby. I won't rest until you're cleared."

"I'm innocent," Lacey said softly.

"We know," I said. "We'll prove it."

Even as I said the words, though, I knew how difficult proving her innocence would be. Dad had put this whole thing in motion, but somewhere along the way, his plan had been derailed.

His original plan must have been to fake his death to implicate Rock and me. Riley would be implicated simply because of her past with Dad, and Roy because he had seen Dad's hunting antics with his own eyes. Derek had all of us.

Whoever got wind of it and had him killed for real had found it easiest to implicate Lacey.

The tape of her entering and leaving her place the night of the murder had disappeared. Items of hers were found in strange places.

And she was Rock's wife now, so Rock was still being punished.

Someone had thought this out very well.

Someone with a brilliant criminal mind.

Someone who was able to outsmart Derek Wolfe.

I looked around the room as the cops led Lacey out and Rock followed.

The guilty party was not here. Call it instinct, but I was sure of it.

No. Our mastermind was out there, and he was still calculating.

Which meant, even though a suspect was in custody, none of us were safe.

49

ZEE

I 'd showered and dressed, drunk two cups of coffee, and was sitting in Reid's master suite alcove, when someone knocked on the door.

"Ms. Jones?"

I walked to the door and opened it. Lydia stood there.

"Yes?"

She fidgeted nervously. "I'm sorry, Ms. Jones, but there's a police officer here to escort you to the precinct for questioning."

My skin went numb. "What? Did you call Reid?"

"I didn't."

I grabbed my phone and called Reid quickly.

"Zee?" he said breathlessly.

"Reid, I need you. Lydia says there's an officer here to take me in for questioning."

"Fuck. This too?"

"What do you mean?"

"They've just arrested Lacey."

My heart dropped. "Lacey? You said she had no motive."

"She doesn't. But someone thinks she does. Or rather,

someone wants the police to think she does. But don't worry about that. Do *not* leave. I'm coming up."

I nodded, though of course he couldn't hear me through the phone. "Okay." But the call had dropped already.

"Reid's coming up."

Lydia nodded. "The officer said you should come out."

I shook my head vehemently. "Not until Reid gets here."

"Where is he?"

"I don't know. He said he's coming up, so he's probably just in the office."

God, I hoped I was right. I couldn't do this without Reid. I just couldn't.

Relax, I told myself. *You're not a suspect. You have an alibi.*

Lydia nodded and left me in Reid's bedroom. I trembled, and my bowels churned. Shit. Literally. I ran to the bathroom and took care of that necessity, and then I washed my hands and ran a comb through my hair.

"Why do I care what my hair looks like?" I said aloud.

I set the comb down, my hands shaking so badly that it fell to the bathroom floor with a clink.

"Zee?"

Thank God. Reid was here. Everything would be okay now. Right? I ran out of the bathroom and into his arms.

"It's okay, baby." He kissed my forehead. "It's all going to be okay."

"But Lacey..."

"She'll be fine. We won't let anything happen to her."

"Why do they want to question me again? I already told that detective everything."

"I don't know, sweetheart."

Sweetheart. The endearment coated me in warmth like a blanket on a brisk day.

"You're not going alone. Zach is waiting downstairs to go with you."

"Zach? I want Moira."

"I understand, but when you found that handkerchief and those business cards of Lacey's in Moira's office—"

"Not Moira!"

"I don't think so either, but we can't take the chance. I had my people sweep all the attorneys' offices during the night. Zach's was clean."

"But that doesn't mean—"

"Baby, I'm not sure who to trust right now. But Zach's a good man. He's been with the company for three years, and I hired him myself."

"Moira told me the head of legal hired her."

"He did. Zach is kind of my attorney on the inside, and that's who I want representing you."

I nodded into his shoulder.

I had to trust Reid.

I had no other choice.

REID WASN'T ALLOWED in the room where Detective Morgan questioned me, but Zach sat next to me. His presence reassured me. Sort of. I'd have been much more comfortable with Moira.

"Tell me," Morgan began, "about your relationship with Reid Wolfe."

My mouth dropped open.

"Don't answer that," Zach said. "It has nothing to do with this case."

"I beg to differ, counsel," Morgan said. "Reid Wolfe is a suspect in this case."

"You've already arrested Lacey Wolfe," Zach replied.

"Doesn't mean there isn't more than one suspect. We have evidence, Mr. Hayes, implicating all the Wolfes."

"Then why not arrest all of them?" Zach asked angrily.

"You know the system as well as I do."

"Don't answer," Zach said to me again.

"I can compel her to answer."

"Not without a subpoena."

"So I'll get a subpoena."

"Get it, then." He stood. "This is over."

"Sit down, Mr. Hayes," Morgan said. "I assure you this is far from over."

"With all due respect," I interjected. "I have nothing more to tell you. You got my whole story yesterday."

"Are you sure?" Morgan asked.

"Of course, I'm sure. I told you everything so I wouldn't have to talk to you again."

"You did know you'd probably be called as a witness in the trial," Morgan said.

I hadn't thought of that. "I live day by day, Mr. Morgan," I said.

"That's Detective Morgan." He glanced down at the papers in front of him.

"Do you have anything new for Ms. Jones?" Zach asked.

Morgan continued reading his notes for a moment before he looked up. "This case will go to trial, Mr. Hayes," he said. "It's just a matter of how many defendants and how many trials."

"You know Ms. Jones is not a suspect. She has an alibi."

"Does she?"

Morgan's words stopped me cold. I wanted to stand and yell and defend myself, but I was frozen. Frozen to the chair.

"That's already been determined, as you know," Zach said.

"Her relationship with Reid Wolfe changes things."

"There *is* no relationship with Reid Wolfe," Zach said.

My eyes shifted. He was lying. Zach was lying to the detective, which wasn't right, but he was my attorney. He knew what he was doing.

Right?

"Then why did Ms. Jones spend the night at Reid Wolfe's residence last night?"

"She's staying with him," Zach replied, "while she's in town."

"Staying in his bedroom?"

I gasped.

Zach gave me a side-eye. "It's irrelevant where she's staying."

"It's far from irrelevant, and you know it. She has access to Reid Wolfe's apartment, which means she has access to his files. His bedroom."

"I'd never look at his files!" I exclaimed.

"Mr. Wolfe doesn't keep business files in his home," Zach said. "If you want files, you'll have to subpoena them, not rely on hearsay from Ms. Jones." He stood for the second time. "This is over. Let's go, Zee."

I stood, still trembling, and allowed Zach to lead me out of the room.

"This isn't over," came Morgan's voice.

Reid was waiting outside. "Everything okay?"

"We need to talk," Zach said. "Now."

"What is it?"

"Not here," he said. "The coffee shop around the corner."

We walked out of the precinct and then a little less than a block to the coffee shop. We took an outdoor table.

"They're not done," Zach said. "I think Lacey's arrest is a ruse to make the rest of you a little more lax. They want you to trip up."

"Fuck," Reid said.

"All Morgan wanted to ask Zee about was you. About your relationship."

"There isn't a relationship."

Though Reid's words cut through my heart like a sharp blade, I showed no bodily reaction. I was still numb, though tears were flowing inside me.

There isn't a relationship.

After last night... All we'd shared...

But this was Reid Wolfe. Known rake. The Wolfe of Manhattan.

Of course there was no relationship.

"That's not what Morgan thinks," Zach said. "Apparently he knows she spent last night in your bedroom."

Reid dropped his gaze to the table, but only for a split second. "That's not his business."

"Of course it's not, and I told him that. But if this woman means something to you, he's going to try to get to you through her."

This woman? I huffed. "I'm sitting right here. I have a name. Stop talking about me like I'm not here."

I waited then. Waited for Reid to say I meant nothing to him. That I was just his current bed warmer and I'd be heading back home to Las Vegas soon. After all, I had a job—a job a lot of dancers in Vegas would kill for. I couldn't be gone forever or I'd risk losing it.

But Reid stayed silent.

"Reid..." Zach prodded. "I need to know. I can't help you protect her if I don't."

Reid inhaled slowly. "She means something to me."

I gasped, my body still numb but warm numb this time. It wasn't confession of love, but it was a start.

Or did he just not want to say the opposite in front of me?

Surely he wouldn't lie to his attorney.

"Is that the truth?" Zach asked.

Reid looked at me, his rigid jawline softening. "It's the truth.

If it weren't, I'd have asked to speak to you alone to tell you. I wouldn't hurt Zee in front of you."

Zach nodded. "Then I have a solution."

"What's that?"

"You two need to get married."

50

REID

Get married? Had I heard Zach correctly?

I must have looked confused, because Zach started talking again.

"You're aware of spousal privilege, right?"

"Yeah, I've heard of it."

"It means they can't compel Zee to testify against you in court. Or anywhere."

I rubbed my jaw. Man, I was tired. So tired. "But I haven't done anything."

"I know that, but they're trying to implicate you, and they're willing to put Zee through the wringer to do it. You can protect both of you by getting married."

I cocked my head. The idea was far from distasteful. I'd already fallen in love with Zee. But this wasn't how I wanted it to go. I wanted to woo her. Court her. Ask her when we were both ready. Get down on one knee and all that.

My thoughts surprised me. Perhaps I was a romantic at heart. Perhaps I'd just never met the right woman.

Was it even possible to meet the right woman when I was in the middle of dealing with my father's murder and its fallout?

Sure it was. Obviously. It had happened for all my siblings.

Still, a marriage of convenience wasn't what I was after.

"No," I said.

Zee's lips dropped into a sad frown.

"It's not that I don't have feelings for you, Zee," I said.

She dropped her gaze. "You don't have to explain. We barely know each other."

"It can be a temporary solution," Zach said. "You can have the marriage dissolved once this has all come out with the wash."

I took Zee's hand. "Would you be up for it?"

"I don't know."

"If it means protecting you," Reid said, "I'll do it. I promised I'd protect you, Zee."

"You don't need to protect me," she said. "I'm not a suspect. We've determined that."

"He means protect you from this ceaseless questioning Morgan seems to want to put you through," Zach explained.

She breathed in. "I can take it."

I squeezed her hand. "But you shouldn't have to. Not after what you've already been through. You shouldn't be punished for coming forward to tell your story. You shouldn't be punished for trying to help us."

"Okay," she said softly. "If you both think it's best."

"Good enough." Zach closed the file folder in front of him. "Let's head to the courthouse and get this done. The sooner the better."

I stood and smiled at Zee, still holding her hand. "I guess we're about to be married."

She rose, her pallor kind of yellow. "I guess so."

"You don't have to do this," I said. "Just say the word, and we won't go through with it."

She shook her head. "I want what's best for all of us. I've come this far to help you, and I won't stop now."

~

WITH A LITTLE HELP from Benjamin Franklin, I was able to get a license and an appearance in front of a judge by one p.m. Zach stood as witness, along with Judge Brady's court clerk.

"Do you wish to be married?" Judge Brady asked.

"Yes," I said.

"And you, miss?" The judge nodded to Zee.

"Sure. I guess."

"Good enough." He scrawled his signature. "Both of you sign here, and you'll be married."

Zee stiffened next to me.

"Wait," I said. "What about the vows?"

"That's just a formality," Judge Brady said. "It's not necessary, and I've got a full docket this afternoon."

Zee dropped her mouth into an O while my stomach did a somersault.

Without vows, it didn't feel like a real marriage.

Then again, it *wasn't* a real marriage. It was a marriage of convenience to keep us from having to testify against each other.

So why did a giant lump form in my throat?

The judge handed me the certificate. I signed my name and handed it and the pen to Zee.

Her hand shaking, she signed and handed it back to me.

"Now the witnesses," Judge Brady said.

Zach and the clerk each signed, and Brady handed the certificate back to me. "It's done. I assume you've already paid the requisite fees?"

His clerk nodded. "They have, your honor."

"Good enough. Have a lovely life, Mr. and Mrs. Wolfe." Judge Brady smiled.

Mr. and Mrs. Wolfe.

I didn't hate the sound of it.

In fact, I kind of liked it.

"Off you go," the judge said, still smiling.

Why shouldn't he smile? He was a thousand dollars richer for ten minutes' work.

Zee didn't look happy. She didn't look unhappy either.

She looked, simply, stunned.

No reason for me to be unhappy. I'd just married the woman I love.

But clearly she didn't feel the same way.

No matter. I could still woo her. Still make her fall in love with me.

We just had to settle my father's murder first.

My brother's wife had been arrested. Arraignment shouldn't be until tomorrow morning, but Rock was working on that.

Yeah, money talks.

Bail would be set, probably at a million dollars or more.

Which we'd pay, and Lacey would be free to go, awaiting trial.

We had to figure this out. Soon.

Tomorrow.

But tonight? I had a wife, and she deserved a wedding night.

51

ZEE

I'd felt more with Reid Wolfe—now my husband—than I'd ever felt before.

More than I'd ever wanted to feel.

Yes, I'd fallen hard. But I desperately wanted a husband who loved me as much as I loved him.

My flesh still numb, I walked with Reid back to the Wolfe building. It was several blocks, and we didn't talk.

We took the elevator up to his apartment. He gathered his staff in the dining room. "I have some news," he said. "This lovely lady and I were married this afternoon, so you now work for her as well as for me. Whatever she wants, please see to her needs."

Lydia and the others were clearly surprised, but they all simply nodded and then went about their tasks.

I followed Reid to his bedroom. "I'll have your apartment packed up and your things delivered as soon as possible.'

"My job…" I began.

"I'll see if you can get an extended leave of absence."

"Mo. The others. They can't afford the rent without me."

"That isn't anything for you to worry about. I'll cover it until they can get a new roommate."

"My job…" I said again.

"I promise I'll take care of all of it," Reid said. "But you'll never have to go back if you don't want to, Zee. I'll see that you're always taken care of, even after the marriage ends."

After the marriage ends…

So the marriage *would* end, in his eyes.

My heart broke in two.

I was in love—married to the object of my affection.

And it was only temporary.

THE STORY of the Wolfes concludes in *Reckoning*, coming soon!

Craving more Helen Hardt?

Read on for an excerpt from *Reunited!*

My flesh tingled, my tummy tightened, and my heart made a mad dash to leap from my chest. My fingers, seemingly of their own accord, pushed the button to replay the message I'd just heard.

"I'm calling for Mr. or Mrs. Abbott. My name is Brett Falcone, and it looks like Maya's going to be on my soccer team. Practice will start next Monday at six o'clock..."

I let the words fade.

Brett Falcone.

His voice had deepened just a little, but it was him—the man from my past I thought I'd never see again. Yet that glimmer of hope, that flicker of desire, had always burned within my heart.

I hadn't known he was still in town. Of course I'd only been back a few months. After my divorce from Danny, I'd moved back to my hometown of Columbus, Ohio. Danny still lived in Cleveland, close enough that Maya could see him on the weekends.

Twenty years ago, I'd left Columbus and vowed never to return. I met Danny in California ten years later. Five years after that, when he received a job offer in Cleveland, I'd agreed to return to Ohio. Cleveland was far enough away from Columbus that I didn't have to think about my former life of heartbreak and humiliation.

When my marriage had crumbled, though, Columbus had seemed like the place to pick up the pieces. *Sometimes*, I'd said to myself, *you just want to go home.*

Home.

Amazing how, even after twenty years of telling myself I'd never set foot in Columbus again, it still felt like home. The townhome I'd rented had grown on me, and I enjoyed my pediatric practice at a local clinic. I'd even made a few friends, though I hadn't contacted anyone from my high school days. I couldn't.

Brett Falcone.

For twenty years I'd tried to erase him from my memory.

For twenty years I'd been unsuccessful.

What could I do? Call the county sports association and ask that Maya be put on a different team? Maybe. I couldn't withdraw Maya from soccer. She was only four, and she was excited about her first chance to play a team sport. I couldn't take that away from my daughter.

I checked my watch quickly. Four thirty. My mother was picking Maya up at the sitter's and taking her for the night. Danny would pick her up tomorrow morning and take her for the rest of the weekend. I had nowhere to go. Though it was Friday, someone would likely still be at the sports registration office until five. I shuffled the papers on my desk until I found the copy of Maya's registration and keyed in the number.

"Tri-County sports."

"Yes, hello. This is Kathryn Abbott. My daughter is registered for Pee Wee soccer, and I was wondering if there was any chance we could change her to a different team."

"I'm sorry, ma'am. All the teams are full. We didn't have as many volunteers for coaching, so there aren't any open slots. Unless you'd like to coach a team?"

I arched my brows. Avoiding Brett Falcone might be worth learning soccer. Unfortunately, I had no athletic talent whatsoever. The sheer unfairness of all this! Brett Falcone would be a great coach. He was a natural athlete, great at soccer and football. But his first love had been baseball.

"Ma'am?"

I jolted back to reality. "I'm sorry. No, I can't coach, though I wish I could. I know nothing about soccer, about any sports. I really want my daughter to learn. To do what I never had the talent to do."

God, I was babbling. The teenybopper on the other end of the line didn't care about my lack of sports experience.

"Then I'm afraid I can't help you."

"I understand. Thank you for your time."

I set the phone back on the cradle.

Brett Falcone.

The Italian Stallion.

How he'd lived up to that name.

I poured myself a glass of iced tea and sat down in my recliner. I took a long sip of the crisp beverage, letting it float over my tongue and coat my throat. Then another. I needed to cool off. Just the name Brett Falcone had made my entire body blaze like an inferno.

I set the tea down on an end table, leaned back, and closed my eyes.

Brett Falcone.

Twenty freaking years. Well, in three days, I'd see him again.

What would happen?

I had no idea.

Twenty years earlier

"You wanted to see me, Mr. Phillips?"

"Yes, Kathryn." The guidance counselor motioned for me to enter his office. "Close the door and have a seat."

I complied. I'd never been in a counselor's office. I was a straight A student, editor of the school newspaper, member of the orchestra, president of National Honor Society. I'd received early admission to Stanford, my dream school. Spring was here, the school year was nearly over, and graduation was just around the corner. Why was the senior guidance counselor summoning me? What had I done wrong?

I sat, quiet, and waited for him to tell me.

He cleared his throat. "I suppose you're wondering why I called you in here."

"I haven't done anything wrong, have I?"

He smiled. "No, of course not. You're a model student."

I heaved a sigh of relief. "Thank goodness."

Mr. Phillips chuckled, shaking his head, and part of his comb-over fell over one ear. "You weren't really worried about that, were you?"

"No. Not really, but you never know."

He nodded. "I called you here because I need your help, Kathryn."

"Of course. What do you need?"

"We have a student who needs a tutor. I think you might be the best fit."

"Oh? Who is the student?"

"Brett Falcone."

"The Italian Stallion?" I clamped my hand on my mouth. Not the thing to say to the senior guidance counselor.

Mr. Phillips, however, let out a laugh. "Yes. The Italian Stallion. He's failing math, Kathryn. If he doesn't get his grades up, he can't play baseball. Our team needs him."

"You're kidding, right? I don't mean to be disrespectful, but you want me to tutor Brett Falcone so he can play baseball? Why are sports so important, Mr. Phillips? Why isn't it important that he learn math because it's math? Math is a lot more useful in life than batting a ball."

I was overreacting, but still I seethed. The emphasis schools put on athletics angered me. I'd never been good at sports, was always the last picked for any team in gym class, and I'd revered the day, sophomore year, when I finished the last required physical education class of my high school career. No doubt all the jocks and jockettes had revered that day too. No longer would they be saddled with the class nerd on any of their teams.

"Normally, I'd agree with that assessment," Mr. Phillips said, "but he's already been offered a scholarship to play baseball at OSU. If he doesn't get his math grade up, he won't keep the scholarship."

"A scholarship?" I shook my head.

Brett Falcone would never make it in college. Clearly, he was barely making it through high school.

"So you want me to tutor him and get his math grade up so he can play in college?"

Mr. Phillips cleared his throat again and his cheeks reddened. "Yes, that's correct."

"I think I might be too busy. I have my own grades to think of, you know. And the newspaper and—"

"We all know you've already been admitted to Stanford. Your grades at high school level no longer matter."

I opened my mouth, but Mr. Phillips held up his hand.

"You're an incredibly gifted young lady, Kathryn. Your grades won't suffer for helping another. You know that as well as I do."

"Be that as it may, Mr. Phillips, I cannot help Brett Falcone. He and I have a...history."

"A history?"

Mr. Phillips's bulgy eyes bulged out even farther. No doubt he was wondering what kind of history the Italian Stallion could possibly have with Kathryn Zurakowsky, nerd extraordinaire.

"Yes."

"May I ask what kind of history?"

"Not a good one, and nothing I care to talk about."

"How would you have a history? You don't run in the same crowds. Do you even know Brett?"

Did I know Brett Falcone? Know was such an innocuous word. It didn't describe my relationship with Brett Falcone.

Granted, once we'd gotten to high school, he'd left me alone. Middle school, though, had been hell on earth, courtesy of the Italian Stallion.

But Mr. Phillips didn't know that, and I had no desire to enlighten him.

"I'm afraid I have to decline," I said. "I'm sure you can find another tutor for Brett."

"Kathryn, there isn't anyone else who can tutor him."

"That's ridiculous. How about Leon Bates? He's as good in math as I am. Seth Connors might even be better. Or do you want a female tutor? How about Mary Beth Rogers? She's pretty good. Or Amy Eckard."

"All fine students," Mr. Phillips said, "however none of them are acceptable."

"Why not?"

"Because"—he sighed—"Brett refuses to work with anyone but you."

I widened my eyes. "Me? That's the silliest thing I've ever heard. Brett hasn't said a word to me in four years."

"Believe me, I'm as flabbergasted as you are." Mr. Phillips nodded. "But Coach Henderson said Brett would only agree to a tutor if it was you."

My jaw dropped open. What in the world was Brett Falcone thinking?

"Well, it just so happens that I don't give a hoot whether Brett Falcone gets to play baseball in college, so the answer is no."

"Kathryn"—Mr. Phillips rose and came around to face me —"there's more at stake than that."

"Oh?"

"His family has suffered a setback. His father was injured on the job a few weeks ago."

"I'm very sorry, but—"

"A scholarship would be a great help to Brett and his family. Otherwise, if Brett doesn't go to school, he'll probably have to get a job and help support his family."

"Maybe that's his lot in life."

"Maybe so. But he can have so much more. Brett Falcone is not stupid. I shouldn't be telling you this, but he scored in the 'superior' range in the state-administered tests. The boy just needs some guidance, some hope for a future. You can help him."

"And if I don't?"

"Then you'll have to live with that."

"Mr. Phillips, I'm quite capable of living with that." I stood and turned to walk out the door, but Mr. Phillips's voice stopped me cold.

"Kathryn. *Please.*"

A NOTE FROM HELEN

Dear Reader,

Thank you for reading *Rake!* If you want to find out about my current backlist and future releases, please visit my website, like my Facebook page, and join my mailing list. If you're a fan, please join my street team to help spread the word about my books. I regularly do awesome giveaways for my street team members.

If you enjoyed the story, please take the time to leave a review. I welcome all feedback.

I wish you all the best!

Helen

Facebook
Facebook.com/helenhardt

Newsletter
Helenhardt.com/signup

Street Team
Facebook.com/groups/hardtandsoul

ALSO BY HELEN HARDT

Steel Brothers Saga:

Trilogy One—Talon and Jade

Craving

Obsession

Possession

Trilogy Two—Jonah and Melanie

Melt

Burn

Surrender

Trilogy Three—Ryan and Ruby

Shattered

Twisted

Unraveled

Trilogy Four—Bryce and Marjorie

Breathless

Ravenous

Insatiable

Trilogy Five—Brad and Daphne

Fate

Legacy

Descent

Trilogy Six—Dale and Ashley

Awakened

Cherished (coming soon)

Freed (coming soon)

Follow Me Series:

Follow Me Darkly

Follow Me Under

Follow Me Always (coming soon)

Blood Bond Saga:

Unchained

Unhinged

Undaunted

Unmasked

Undefeated

Sex and the Season:

Lily and the Duke

Rose in Bloom

Lady Alexandra's Lover

Sophie's Voice

Temptation Saga:

Tempting Dusty

Teasing Annie

Taking Catie

Taming Angelina

Treasuring Amber

Trusting Sydney

Tantalizing Maria

Standalone Novels and Novellas

Reunited

Misadventures:

Misadventures of a Good Wife (with Meredith Wild)

Misadventures with a Rockstar

The Cougar Chronicles:

The Cowboy and the Cougar

Calendar Boy

Daughters of the Prairie:

The Outlaw's Angel

Lessons of the Heart

Song of the Raven

Collections:

Destination Desire

Her Two Lovers

Non-Fiction:

got style?

ACKNOWLEDGMENTS

Thank you so much to the following individuals who helped make *Rake* shine: Christie Hartman, Martha Frantz, Karen Aguilera, Angela Tyler, Linda Pantlin Dunn, Serena Drummond, Kim Killion, and Marci Clark.

ABOUT THE AUTHOR

#1 *New York Times*, #1 *USA Today*, and #1 *Wall Street Journal* best-selling author Helen Hardt's passion for the written word began with the books her mother read to her at bedtime. She wrote her first story at age six and hasn't stopped since. In addition to being an award-winning author of romantic fiction, she's a mother, an attorney, a black belt in Taekwondo, a grammar geek, an appreciator of fine red wine, and a lover of Ben and Jerry's ice cream. She writes from her home in Colorado, where she lives with her family. Helen loves to hear from readers.

http://www.helenhardt.com

Printed in Great Britain
by Amazon

65207939R00182